Queen
of the
Waves

Queen
of the
Waves

JANICE THOMPSON

summerside
PRESS™

Summerside Press™
Minneapolis 55378
www.summersidepress.com

Queen of the Waves
© 2012 by Janice Hanna Thompson

ISBN 978-1-60936-686-5

Scripture references are from The Holy ible, King James Version (KJV).

Though this story is based on actual events, it is a work of fiction.

Cover design by Lookout Design | www.lookoutdesign.com
Interior Design by Müllerhaus Publishing Group | www.mullerhaus.net

Summerside Press™ is an inspirational publisher offering fresh,
irresistible books to uplift the heart and engage the mind.

Printed in USA.

Dedication

To my fellow passengers in the "Queen of the Waves" Facebook group, particularly our "captain," Cathy Peeling, the great-niece of real *Titanic* captain Edward Smith. Cathy, I praise the Lord for bringing us together and praise Him even more for raising you up from your "near-drowning" experience to new life! What great plans He must have for you. To all of my "Queen of the Waves" friends, thank you! You made my virtual *Titanic* cruise enjoyable on every level. I will never forget the night we reenacted the sinking of the ship. Thanks for trusting me to see you safely to shore. I've loved every minute.

In Memory of

Manca Karun. While visiting the *Titanic* museum in Branson, Missouri, I was given a pretend boarding pass with the name *Manca Karun* on it. Turned out Manca was a real passenger aboard the *Titanic*. I wouldn't find out until the end whether she survived the journey. I did learn that she was four years old, from Slovenia, and traveled third class. At the end of my tour I breathed a sigh of relief when I discovered that Manca survived the trip by climbing down the side of the *Titanic* into a lifeboat. I wish I'd known you, Manca. This book is dedicated to your memory and to the memory of those who traveled aboard the Queen of the Ocean for her ill-fated voyage.

God is our refuge and strength, a very present help in trouble.

Therefore will not we fear, though the earth be removed,

and though the mountains be carried into the midst of the sea;

though the waters thereof roar and be troubled,

though the mountains shake with the swelling thereof.

PSALM 46:1–3

Chapter One

Friday, March 8, 1912
Gloucestershire County, England

Tessa Bowen's dingy gray skirt tangled around her legs as she reached to grab hold of the feisty sow. "Easy now, Countess." She held on tight to the noisy porker's ear, guiding her back into the pen and then slamming the gate shut. With the back of her hand, Tessa brushed the loose hairs from around her face as she scolded herself for not paying closer attention to the rambunctious animal.

She glanced about, heaviness gripping her heart as she noticed the upturned crate in the corner of the littered stall. The naughty Countess seemed determined to break free from her confines these days. Tessa could certainly understand that. Empathize, even. Still, how would the piglets ever get adequate nutrition if their mama continued to fuss her way out of the farrowing crates? And how could Tessa's family raise the pigs to their proper slaughtering weight with the stalls in such continual disarray? No doubt this would infuriate Papa. He would have her head when he saw the mess. Tessa's knees ached, just thinking of the penance she would have to do.

She busied herself by tending to the piglets and making sure none had been harmed in the old sow's tirade. With the exception of a bit of mud, they appeared to be in tolerable shape. Tessa reached for the runt and held it as one might cradle a babe, listening to his tiny grunts and squeals. His nearness brought her some degree of comfort, as always. Still, he did not appear to be in a cuddling mood this morning, as was evidenced by his squirming and kicking.

"I understand," she whispered as she ran a fingertip over the piglet's head and down his back. "It's not much of a life, is it?"

No, indeed, it was not, whether one lived in the stall or the broken-down house nearby. Tessa did her best not to sigh aloud as she rose and placed the little porker back among the others in the litter. He let out another grunt. She felt like doing the same.

Waggling her finger in his direction, she pretended to scold. "Now, settle down, all of you, else I'll have to tell the lord and master of the house. And we all know what *he* will do." Her nerves jumbled as the words were spoken. Yes, she knew exactly what Pa would do, though the piglets wouldn't be the ones to pay the price. She would.

From a distance Mum approached, a passel of chickens scurrying about her feet, squawking and seemingly making a nuisance of themselves as usual. Maggie, the family's unkempt sheepdog, followed close behind. Mum clucked her tongue as she entered the messy stall and glanced Tessa's way. "Look at you, girl. You've been rolling in the mud with Countess again, eh?"

"Not of my own choosing, Mum." Tessa did her best to brush the mud spots from her skirt and then examined a tear in the hem that caught her eye. "The slippery she-devil got away from me and headed straight for the farrowing crates. Before I knew it, she'd upturned them and made a mess. Guess she's tired of nursing the litter. She wants to escape from her life."

"A predicament we can all sympathize with, of course." Mum

reached for the rake and gripped it tightly. "But what can be done about it now, other than tidy up and pretend it never happened?"

A shrug followed on Tessa's end. She dare not respond with a fast quip for fear it would lead to a scolding from her mother. Right now she needed someone on her side.

"Your father will come undone when he sees the mess in here." Mum handed her the near-toothless rake. "Clean up as best you can so as not to alarm him. You know how he is."

Yes. She certainly knew what her father was like, not just on days like this, but most other days besides. Swished and soused from drink, as her mother would call it. Hung over from several hours at the pub, ready to grumble at anyone who crossed him… and worse still, zealous in his religiosity. What was it about strong drink that made her father fervent about spiritual matters? She could not say. The man seemed bent on preaching while intoxicated. Tessa shuddered, thinking about the sermon to come.

"He just got home from the pub and he's in a sour mood, so get to work mucking this stall, girl." Mum turned her attention back to the errant chickens, shooing them into the side yard where they belonged.

Tessa made quick work of tidying up the stall. With straw flying through the air, her thoughts were finally free to drift back to the novel she'd been reading. She had committed the story to memory, of course. Living it out in her imagination brought hours of comfort. Through the lives of the characters, she could escape her drab life and replace it with a far more luxurious one.

She envisioned the stall a fine room in a castle, one complete with electric lights and indoor plumbing. A well-stocked wardrobe held a fine collection of dresses—only the most expensive. From Paris, naturally. Or Italy. Tessa curtsied, imagining herself the object of a handsome beau, one intent on marrying her and offering her a grand life. Tossing her braids over her shoulders, she released a girlish giggle.

Behind her, the gate slammed. Tessa turned, her heart rising to her throat as Pa staggered her way with his shoulders slumped forward. He drew nearer still, stumbling over Countess in the process and releasing a string of curses. His gaze shifted from the sow to the broken pen, then up to Tessa's muddy face.

"You good-fer-nuthin' girl." Her father's words carried the usual slur. Tessa shrank into the corner, hoping to avoid the inevitable sting of the back of his hand as it swung near her cheek. "Dinna I tell ya to tend to that sow afore she tore the place to shreds? What 'er ya doin' lettin' 'er loose like this?"

"Pa, I—"

"She's bent up the farrowin' crate, 'n' now I'll hafta repair it. 'N' all a' this before Saturday. We've a big day comin'."

"Yes, of course." Bartering day in the nearby village. Mum would trade whatever she could so that the family could make it through the spring season.

"This stall needs to shine like Buckingham Palace, lazy miss, and put some elbow grease into it."

"Yes, Pa."

His gaze narrowed. "Yer not the Queen o' Sheba, ya know. Just a pig farmer's daughter. No lollygagging about. And when yer done with yer work, we'll have our rock prayers. Yer in need of humblin', fer sure."

She trembled as the words "rock prayers" were spoken. Pain shot through her legs as she braced herself for the moment ahead when she would be forced to kneel atop a pile of broken rocks to repent for sins she hadn't really committed—all to appease her drunken father. If only she could avoid these religious rituals of his. Her knees would be in far better shape. So would her heart.

Out of the corners of her eyes, Tessa watched as Mum eased her way across the yard and toward the house. Coward. Then again, neither of the Bowen women stood much of a chance around Pa, did they?

If only Peter were here. He would know what to do.

Pa's face tightened and the stench of his breath sickened her stomach as he drew near. As the back of his hand stung her cheek, Tessa squeezed her eyes shut. Images of her older brother rushed over her, bringing peace. Truly, she could endure anything with the image of Peter's face there to bring comfort.

* * * * *

Friday, March 8, 1912
Abingdon Manor, Richmond, England

Jacquie Abingdon gazed through the front window of her family's country estate, the expansive gardens capturing her attention as always. A grove of mulberry trees framed the gently rolling lawn. Perfectly manicured shrubberies, well-tended with bits of vibrant green peeking through, spoke of the promise of spring, as did the budding flowers in the planted beds below.

Her gaze shifted to the graveled walk, which led to a smallish stone bridge. It inclined over the narrow ribbon of water in the creek below. She found the scene picturesque. Idyllic. If only such perfection existed in her own life. Releasing a sigh, she fixed her sights on the bridge. How she longed to hike her skirts and run across it then disappear into the meadow on the other side, never to be seen again.

She could not, of course. Gone were the carefree days of doing as she pleased, of playing the child. As this realization set in, tears sprang up and covered her lashes, and Jacquie brushed them away with the swipe of a hand. As was the custom with all well-bred British girls, she would play the role of the dutiful daughter, though every fiber of her being argued against it. Until then, she would take a seat in the parlor and disappear into a good book. While keeping an eye on the door to her father's study, of course.

She closed the drapes and walked to the parlor. After settling into a chair, Jacquie reached for her novel of choice, her thoughts as gloomy as the dense fog that so often descended upon the manor. In spite of her passion for romantic tales, the story could not hold her interest today, not with her thoughts in such a whirl. How could she maintain any sense of control over her imaginings with her future in the hands of a father who insisted upon clinging to outdated traditions and narrow-minded notions? She had never been much for blind obedience to such things, particularly of late.

"Customs shape the lives of the British, Jacqueline. We hold fast to our habits and conventions because they have served us well." How often had she heard those words?

"Served us well?" She placed the book in her lap and folded her hands over it in a prayerful stance. "When you're the lord of the manor, *everyone* serves you well." Jacquie glanced up at the gilded frame that held her father's portrait. His austere expression caused her to shudder. Not that she found her father cruel, of course. *Determined* would be a better word. He seemed bent on controlling every aspect of her life, a fact that brought anxiety on multiple levels.

At three minutes past the hour, Father's business associate,

Roland Palmer, emerged from behind the office door. His stride exuded confidence, and his morning coat, which suited his tall, stately physique, spoke of money. Rarely did monetary fame and fine looks go together, but in the case of Mr. Palmer, neither could be argued. Not that this made him any more appealing to Jacquie.

The heels of his polished shoes clicked in steady rhythm as he walked across the spacious grand foyer of Abingdon Manor. Upon reaching the front door, he glanced her way and offered a cursory nod before tipping his silk top hat. Jacquie lifted the book and pretended to read, then shifted her gaze to see if he noticed. A half smile crossed Roland's lips as he reached for his umbrella. He swung wide the door, spoke a cheerful "Good day," and headed outdoors.

Several questions rolled through Jacquie's mind as she tossed the book onto the side table and rose from the chair, but none of them could be voiced aloud. She took tentative steps toward the window and watched as Roland climbed into his impressive Rolls-Royce, which roared to life then motored down the drive-way toward the lane. The automobile soon disappeared from view, but Jacquie's troubles did not. Perhaps they were just beginning.

Father's firm voice rang out from inside his study. "Jacqueline, I will see you now."

A shiver ran down her spine as she anticipated their upcoming conversation. She made her way into the study and found her father in his leather chair behind the intricately carved mahogany desk, as always, surrounded by shelves lined with musty-scented books by the hundreds. He looked very much as he did in his portrait in the hallway—authoritative. His shoulders squared beneath the tailored suit as he straightened his stance in the chair. "Ah, there you are."

"Yes, sir."

Her father ran his fingers over his graying mustache then reached for a pen. "Sit, Jacquie."

He might as well have been speaking to the family's beagle. Still, she knew better than to disregard his instructions. As she eased her way into the wingback chair opposite him, Jacquie felt the knots in her stomach tighten a notch. Settling her gaze on the spectacles he had placed on the desk, she tried to remain focused. Visions of the garden danced through her mind, and she saw herself running across that bridge, over the creek, and toward freedom. If only she could actually do so.

He lifted his pen and glanced her way. "We have something of great importance to discuss." A half smile followed. "Good news, indeed."

No doubt *his* idea of good news, not her own.

Father rose, his tall frame commanding attention. He reached for the gold pocket watch fastened to his waistcoat and gave it a glance then walked to the door and called for her mother to join them. All the while, Jacquie's heart twisted and turned, though she tried to remain calm on the exterior.

Mama arrived moments later, fussing with her hair. "Was that Roland Palmer I saw leaving just now?" After taking a few steps to the window, she reached to pull back the heavy brocade draperies for a peek outside. "I'm sorry I missed him. I do so enjoy his visits."

"Yes. Have a seat, Helen." Jacquie's father tucked the watch back into its pocket and gestured for her to sit. He opened his cigar box and fussed over its contents, finally pulling out a cigar. As he ran it under his nose and inhaled, a look of pure contentment settled over him. He returned to his spot behind the desk, and

QUEEN OF THE WAVES

hints of sunlight from the window caused the silver strands in his hair to shimmer, which cast a deceptively angelic glow over him.

"Rather odd for Roland to leave his business midday for a social call." Jacquie's mother eased her ample frame into the chair, her green satin skirt pooling around her. Her gaze shifted to the window and then back again.

"He came on pressing business." Jacquie's father cleared his throat and rolled the cigar around in his hand.

Mama fussed with the pearl buttons on the sleeve of her white linen blouse, her brow wrinkling. "Something to do with the steel mill?"

"In a roundabout way, I suppose his visit could be linked to the mill. But he came with a proposition, one that involves our daughter, so I felt the whole family should be aware of the particulars."

Jacquie's heart rate doubled and a queasy feeling gripped her stomach. She fought it while offering a forced smile. "O–oh?"

Her father cut the cap from his cigar and reached for a match. "Roland Palmer is a competitive man, and he knows a good thing when he sees it. The automobile industry is young, but there is a lot of money to be made on both sides of the pond, especially when men work together. We're both smart enough to see that."

Jacquie remained silent, unsure what this had to do with her. She didn't know which "good thing" her father happened to be referring to—his burgeoning steel mill or his daughter. "Father, I'm sorry, but I don't quite understand. Are you saying that Roland is looking to merge his business in New York with yours, here in London?"

"I have no doubt that we will merge forces sooner or later, if all goes as planned." With a snap of her father's wrist, the match lit into a flame. Positioning the cigar in his mouth, his fingers

19

wrapped around the band. He began to puff as he rotated the cigar, his cheeks moving in and out until it was fully lit. Within seconds, the familiar pungent aroma filled the room. Jacquie had just started to relax when her father looked her way. "Roland Palmer has asked for your hand in marriage, my dear."

The smile that followed did little to lift her spirits.

Chapter Two

Friday, March 8, 1912
Abingdon Manor, Richmond, England

A wave of fear washed over Jacquie afresh as she tried to absorb the news.

Father dangled the cigar between his fingers. "I'm delighted about Roland's offer, as you might imagine. I do hope you will be as well. This has been a thoughtful undertaking."

"B–but…" She couldn't seem to manage anything else. The lump in her throat wouldn't allow it.

"He's a good man, and a kind one. I can't deny that the arrangement is advantageous for us all, but I do believe you will settle happily. He will treat you well and give you a good life. And you will never want for anything. Of this, we can be quite sure." Another puff of the cigar followed on her father's end and then a nod. "Roland has a large home in New York and has just purchased the Willingham estate here in Richmond near the Thames."

"Well, that sounds lovely." Jacquie's mother folded her hands in her lap and sat up a bit straighter.

"Yes." Father grinned. "And what a stroke of luck, marrying a man in the automobile industry. Not only will you have an enviable home, but you will also own the best vehicles in the county."

Jacquie swallowed hard as she thought about how to respond.

Of course her father found this news to be delightful. He would. But she could not—would not—marry a man she had no feelings for, especially when her heart remained affixed to another. She forced a smile and fought to quiet her racing heart, fearing it might somehow give her away.

"Father, this is 1912," she managed at last. "I hardly think—"

"Yes, a great year for the automobile industry." Her father leaned forward and pulled the cigar from his mouth. "You must consider how this will affect our family for generations to come, Jacqueline. *Abingdon and Palmer* has a nice ring to it, don't you think? And I can envision a houseful of little Palmers running around, bringing cheer to us all."

"But—"

"And who knows? Maybe one day your son—should you be blessed to have one—will carry on in my stead. I can't live forever, you know." Her father chuckled then leaned back in his chair and returned to smoking his cigar, his eyes now closed.

Jacquie glanced her mother's way and noticed the widened eyes.

"What a blessed day for us all." Mama pushed herself up from the chair and pulled Jacquie into a warm embrace. "Don't you agree, darling?"

"Well, I…"

Her mother stepped back and extended a hand. "Come with me, sweet girl. It would appear we have plans to set in motion, and the sooner the better."

"But Mother, I…" Jacquie couldn't seem to complete her sentence. Pressing the words out past the knot in her throat proved impossible. How could she be expected to transition her thinking in such a way? Why, just yesterday she was attending parties with her friends and giggling over boys. Boys her own age, not men twelve years her senior.

Jacquie's mother made her way across the room, the heels of her shoes clicking across the floor. "Your father has work to do, and it would appear we do as well." Turning her attention to Jacquie's father, she gave him a little wink. "You know how we ladies are, Henry. You don't mind if we escape for a bit to talk through the particulars of the upcoming nuptials, do you? We've a trousseau to prepare, after all. And we must begin to put together the guest list as soon as possible. We don't want to leave anyone out."

"Heaven forbid." Her father waved a hand. "Go on, now. Make all the plans you like. Our daughter's wedding day will be a cause for celebration for us all." He gave Jacqueline a brusque nod. "And lest I forget to say it, cost is no issue. Appease yourself by planning the largest, most opulent wedding London has ever seen. When a man has but one daughter, such frivolity is expected. I daresay the town gossips will fuss if I withhold any good thing from my precious girl."

Like her happiness, for instance?

She didn't speak the words aloud, of course, managing only a weak "Thank you, Father." Then Jacquie turned and followed on her mother's heels.

Once they reached the front hall, Mama took her hand and gave it a squeeze. "Upstairs," she whispered, the tiny wrinkles around her eyes growing more pronounced. "Don't breathe a word until we get there." Mama brushed a loose hair off Jacquie's face then put a finger to her lips.

Jacquie's curiosity rose, but she did not voice her questions. Instead, she climbed the stairs, remaining in her mother's shadow until they reached the lavish French doors leading to the master bedroom suite.

Mama swung them wide and marched inside. Then she released an unladylike groan. "This place is as dark as a tomb."

She walked to the window and pulled back the deep blue velvet draperies, allowing sunlight to enter the large suite. The brass canopy bed glistened as rays of light hit it, and the golden threads in the coverlet shimmered as if to show off their value. If only Father saw Jacquie as valuable, then he wouldn't insist upon marrying her off to further his business.

Mama kept walking as if on a mission. "Come with me, child." She led the way beyond the silk-papered walls into the spacious closet with its vaulted ceiling. Easing her way past the ball gowns and party shoes, she finally came to a stop in front of a set of shelves full of boxes and whatnot. Mama reached for a large hatbox then turned to Jacquie. "I know this is difficult, but you must ask no questions."

Ask no questions? Right now, all she had were questions. Dozens of them. And no answers. How could she be expected to remain silent when everything around her cried out for some sort of heavenly intervention?

Her mother's voice lowered to a whisper as she opened the hatbox and pressed several newspaper clippings into Jacquie's hands. "A new ocean liner is leaving Southampton in five weeks, headed for New York. Arrangements can be made for you to be onboard when she sails, but we must hurry." She pressed the now-empty hatbox back onto the shelf.

"W–what? You're sending me to America?" Jacquie shook her head as she stared down at the newspaper clippings. A photograph of the RMS *Titanic* stared back at her. "What are you saying, Mother? Have you and Father planned this as some sort of honeymoon gift?"

Mama shook her head. "I've known for weeks that your father was, well…working on a plan with Mr. Palmer, but I'm not talking about sending the two of you off on a honeymoon. Not at all." She led the way to the large canopy bed and settled onto the edge then patted the empty spot beside her. "Come. Sit."

Jacquie trembled as she took the place next to her mother. She tossed the newspaper clippings onto the bed, her frustration growing. None of this made any sense.

"Listen to me." Mama reached to grip her hand. "I know the pain of a forced union firsthand. My own father, God rest his soul, made sure I was advantageously matched as well." Her expression hardened. "My daughter will not be painted into that same corner. I would sooner die than allow it, trust me."

Jacquie couldn't help but gasp at this news. If her parents' marriage had been anything but love-centered, she'd never known it. Either her mother was a terrific actress—one capable of a career upon the stage—or she'd settled into her life here at Abingdon Manor with a compliant spirit.

"Surely you can see how it is with Roland and your father. Each has something to offer the other, and you're to be the bargain in the middle. The enticement, as it were. And something else is behind this decision, as well," Mama said. "Your feelings have not escaped me, Jacquie, though you've tried valiantly to hide them over these past many weeks."

"O–oh?" Her heart quickened, and her cheeks grew warm.

"You are in love with Peter Bowen. Don't deny it, child."

Jacquie's hands trembled and she found herself at a loss for words. She'd worked so hard to hide her feelings from everyone in the house. How had Mother managed to discern them?

"I'm not blind, Jacquie. And neither is Iris."

Jacquie grimaced as the name of her lady's maid was spoken. "She had no right to tell you."

"She didn't have to. Iris simply confirmed what I already knew to be true. I'm your mother, and I know infatuation when I see it." Mama sighed. "I do pray it's just that—an infatuation. Regardless, you must know that your father would sooner see himself hanged than let his only daughter marry the groundskeeper. I daresay he would marry you off to Roland tomorrow if he got wind of this. So consider yourself fortunate that he does not know."

The trembling intensified. Jacquie drew a deep breath and tried to steady her nerves. What could she possibly say in response to all of this?

Her mother reached for the newspaper clippings. "There is only one thing to do to solve both of these problems at once. I plan to wire your grandmother in New York this afternoon. She will purchase your ticket to America, and no one will be the wiser. By the time the *Titanic* sails, you will be on your way and your father's hands will be tied."

"But Peter..." She shook her head, the lump rising to her throat again.

"You have no choice, Jacquie. You must put him out of your mind." Her mother paused. "It's for the best, at least until this situation with Roland dies down." She gave Jacquie a pensive look and gripped the newspaper clippings in her hand. "This is the only thing I can think to offer. I will understand if you decide not to go. But if you do, your grandmother will welcome you with open arms. She will make a very pleasant life for you in New York and introduce you to the best of society. We've spoken at length about sending you—for years, in fact."

This news caught Jacqueline off guard. "What about Father? When he finds out, he'll—" She couldn't complete the sentence. A cold chill rushed over her as she contemplated his possible actions.

Mother's expression softened. "He will forgive us. Eventually. And he and Roland will likely merge their companies whether you marry or not, so don't fret over that. Business is business, and they are men, after all. They're motivated by their pocketbooks."

"Are you sure?" Jacquie whispered. It would be one thing to let her father down by not marrying a man he'd chosen for her, but another completely to throw his business into disarray.

"You're only nineteen, Jacquie." Her mother reached over to smooth her long tresses. "Far too young to carry the weight of the world on your shoulders just yet. Trust me when I say that there will be plenty of time for that later. Right now, we just need to get you out of England. It's your well-being I'm concerned with."

"My well-being." Jacquie glanced down at the newspaper clippings, sighing as she saw the picture of the RMS *Titanic* in all her glory. Had it really come to this? Was traveling to America her only option? She looked again at the picture, and a faint smile tipped up the edges of her lips as she thought the situation through. Truly, there were worse fates to befall a girl. Who among her friends would be fortunate enough to make the maiden voyage on one of the ocean's most famed vessels?

At once an idea formulated, one she would never consider voicing. Jacquie did her best to maintain her composure as she looked her mother's way, though her thoughts now tumbled madly. "You've offered the best possible solution, Mama. I can see that now." She rose and brushed her skirts, her smile quite genuine. "So I will accept Grandmother's offering. I will go to America." *And I won't look back, no matter who—or what—I've left behind.*

* * * * *

Tessa rose from the rocky path, her knees a bloody mess. Even in his inebriated state Pa continued to preach, proclaiming her to be the most woeful of sinners. On and on he went, even tossing in Scripture verses to punctuate his message.

As they made their way up the incline toward the cottage, Tessa bit back the temptation to cry. Tears would do her no good. This she knew from years of allowing them to flow after such a tirade on Pa's part. No, only one thing made sense: she would square her shoulders, bide her time, and then, when life presented just the right opportunity, run as fast and as far from this place as she possibly could.

Chapter Three

Wednesday, March 13, 1912
Abingdon Manor, Richmond, England

The next several days at Abingdon Manor were spent in a whirlwind. Jacquie smiled and nodded every time her father mentioned Roland's name, as if nothing were out of the ordinary. On the inside, however, she quivered like the cook's chocolate mousse.

She kept a watchful eye on *The Times*, her heart rate skipping to double time as she read various articles on the excitement surrounding *Titanic*'s upcoming voyage. To think, she would be onboard. The very idea gave her a chill. And if all went as planned, she would not be alone.

A delicious satisfaction wrapped her as she thought about the plan she'd concocted. Of course, she still had to run it by Peter, but how could he resist? Surely by now he'd read the note she'd left under her favorite flowerpot in the greenhouse. He knew about her so-called engagement to Roland. With that very thing in mind, Peter would surely jump on her idea. Then the two of them could get to work at ironing out the particulars. She could hardly wait.

Just four weeks shy of the ship's sailing, Jacquie was summoned to the master suite. She found her mother seated at the dressing table, fussing with her hair. As she gazed at the reflection in the oval mirror, Jacquie couldn't help but notice the wrinkles around Mama's eyes. They seemed to grow deeper every day. Perhaps the stress of their secret project had her mother feeling more anxious than usual.

"Jacquie, you're here." Mama turned and extended a hand, her eyes glistening with tears. "A present has arrived with your name on it." She slid open one of the tiny drawers on the vanity and pulled out some unfamiliar papers.

Jacquie took a step forward, smiling as she saw the insignia for the *Titanic* on the top page. "Is this—I mean, is this it? My ticket?"

"And your itinerary." Her mother rose and pulled her close, her voice still low. "Your grandmother has been extremely generous, my dear. You will have to thank her properly when you arrive in New York. The cost of a first-class ticket was, well—" She giggled. "Let's just say even Roland Palmer himself would have chosen a more reasonably priced room." Her expression grew more serious. "But you're worth it, Jacquie. You deserve the very best, which is exactly why I feel more strongly each day that you must leave here."

"Thank you, Mama."

"Your grandmother has booked a suite with two rooms so that Iris can travel with you."

"I–Iris?"

"Well, of course, silly girl. You didn't think I would send you off across the Atlantic without her, did you?" Mother's expression tightened. "No respectable young woman would travel such a great distance alone. Besides, you will need your lady's maid to help with dressing and hair and such. She will be a treasure to you, I'm sure. And what a great sacrifice she is making, to leave her family here in England so that she might attend to your needs. We owe her a great deal of thanks."

"Of course, but…" The words drifted off as Jacquie's heart wriggled its way into her stomach. She hadn't planned on this. Having Iris along would complicate her plans on many levels, though she certainly couldn't say so.

Mama turned back to the mirror and continued running the brush through her hair in careful, even strokes. She finally paused then spoke to Jacquie's reflection. "I guess you've heard that Roland is coming for lunch today. There was nothing I could do to avoid it, but I feel sure we'll muddle through somehow. A duller man never drew breath."

"I'm not sure that's true, Mother," Jacquie said. "He's quite amiable."

"Still, all that talk of steel and such will likely wear on my nerves. Perhaps I should take a headache powder to calm myself before he arrives."

"I'll do my best to be polite." Jacquie leaned down and wrapped her arms around her mother's neck. "And in case I haven't said it, Mama, I'm so thankful. When I think of what you've done for me, the lengths you've gone to…" She fought back tears, determined not to let her emotions get the best of her once again. Still, she could hardly imagine the efforts her mother and grandmother had gone to. How could she ever repay them?

Her mother turned and patted her hand. "Don't give it another thought. Just live your life, honey. Be happy enough for the both of us."

"I will." A ripple of guilt washed over Jacquie, but she pushed it away. No time for that today. Mama would eventually forgive her. Hopefully Father would, too, though his forgiveness might be longer in coming.

"Now, we must busy ourselves with your trousseau," her

mother said. "Your father has instructed me to spare no expense. He will be suspicious if we don't order up new clothes for you for your honeymoon."

"New clothes?"

"Of course. Every new bride gets a trousseau. I've been thinking about how pretty you look in creams and pinks. Just perfect for spring. What do you think about charmeuse silk for your going-away dress?" Mama's eyes sparkled. "We're not being dishonest if we call it a going-away dress, after all. You are going away." She gave Jacquie a kiss on the cheek. "And I've always thought charmeuse silk to be the loveliest on the market. So shiny, and it drapes beautifully."

The next few minutes were spent in hushed conversation about various wardrobe pieces. Before long Mother had made a list of the silks, satins, and other fabrics she planned to purchase for Jacquie's trip to America.

"We will keep Mrs. O'Shea busy with our requests," she said. "But she's a fast worker and will deliver what we ask for, even if it means working through the night. I won't have my daughter boarding the world's finest luxury liner in her old dresses."

"What will I do with the ones I no longer require?" Jacquie asked.

Mama shrugged. "Don't fret about that. Perhaps we can give them to the poor."

A strange notion, to Jacquie's way of thinking. "Mother, I doubt the poor will know what to do with my coming-out dresses and such. They don't see a lot of need for panne velvet or crepe-back satin."

"Hmm. We can think about that another day, I suppose. For now, I want to keep my thoughts on your upcoming pretties. Oh, and we will need to order new corsets too, of course. Something befitting a bride." She gave Jacquie a little wink. "A bride without a groom."

This bride might have a groom hiding in the wings, Mother, so buy the prettiest corsets available. Pick an exquisite silk damask with the most delicate embroidery and lovely satin roses. Only the best for my husband.

Though she tried to keep her giggles at bay, she could not. Jacquie felt her cheeks warm as unladylike thoughts traveled through her mind. Determined to stay focused, she smiled at her mother. "Well, let's get to work, shall we?"

They spent the next hour listing a variety of wardrobe items for her trousseau, which would be sewn by Mrs. O'Shea, Mother's favorite seamstress. Surely the woman would be delighted at the influx of work. And no one else could be trusted with such an undertaking. Hadn't Mrs. O'Shea provided Jacquie's sumptuous party dresses over the past many years? Didn't she specialize in ball gowns that made the young men swoon with delight?

Jacquie envisioned a wide range of new dresses in whites, blues, and creams. Velvet ribbons would trim out the new gowns with their décolleté round necklines. At least one evening gown would be of an off-the-shoulder design, and others would have beautifully flounced sleeves made of lace. Tea gowns, walking gowns, suits, capes, and more. Mrs. O'Shea and her team of seamstresses would certainly have her hands full with this order.

At ten thirty that morning Jacquie finally retreated to her room to dress for the luncheon with Roland. She chose a simple white gown with a pinched waist and full skirt. Iris entered the room to help with her ties in the back, chattering nonstop about their upcoming voyage.

"I cannot believe my good fortune." Iris giggled. "Every time I think about it, I'm giddy, miss."

"Yes, I'm delighted as well." About the trip, of course, but not about having Iris along. This would surely kink up the plans. She and Peter would have a lot to talk about. Then again, they already had a lot to discuss even without factoring Iris into the mix.

Roland arrived at exactly five till eleven, looking more than a little anxious. The man was nothing if not prompt. He gushed over Jacquie's appearance and even insisted upon sitting next to her at the dining room table, making quite the show about pulling out her chair. She took her seat, groaning inwardly. Truly, the only thing that made the whole experience tolerable was the glimpse of Peter she managed to catch through the window as he worked in the garden. For a moment their eyes met, and all was right with the world again.

"I must say, you look radiant."

"Excuse me?" Jacquie turned back to Roland, not quite sure she'd heard him correctly.

"You're exquisite in this white dress. I can only imagine how lovely you will look on our wedding day."

His cheeks flushed red, and Jacquie felt a wave of guilt wriggle through her. She offered him a gentle nod, hoping he wouldn't notice the trembling in her hands. No one had ever accused the man of being an ogre. For the most part, she found him agreeable. Still, not the sort she would ever want to marry, not if she waited her whole life. For one thing, the difference in their ages seemed too wide a gap. For another, her heart belonged to someone else.

"If you think she looks lovely today, just wait until you see the dresses we've ordered. Your new bride is going to be the toast of the town in her new gowns." Mother shared with great zeal about the various fabrics they'd chosen for Jacquie's so-called honeymoon ensemble, and another niggling of guilt ribboned through Jacquie.

In spite of this, the lunch hour passed tolerably well. Jacquie tried not to yawn aloud as Father and Roland lit into a conversation about automobiles. Though she enjoyed a good ride about town in one, especially one as lovely as Roland's Rolls-Royce, she hardly found them entertaining dinner-table conversation. Roland, it would seem, could talk for hours—about the latest technology and how his business was perfectly suited to the blossoming trends in the market, whatever that meant.

Then again, his nonstop chatter meant that Jacquie was required to say relatively little, which suited her purposes just fine. Instead, she nibbled on a chicken-salad sandwich and sipped her tea, all the while fighting the temptation to look out the window. She hoped to catch Peter's eyes just once more. Knowing he was right outside gave her the strength to bear this nonsense.

When the clock in the front hall struck twelve, Roland glanced her way and sighed. "I can't believe the hour has passed so quickly. I'm sorry, ladies, but work beckons." He eased his chair back and shrugged. "Do forgive me for going on so? I promise to let you do most of the talking once we're married, Jacqueline." He gave her a wink, which she almost found sweet. From the sparkle in his eyes, she could tell that his feelings for her must be growing. For a moment, she found herself feeling a bit sorry for him...until she realized how he would benefit from their potential union. Then, just as quickly, she released her guilt and breathed a sigh of relief.

Jacquie forced a smile and attempted to pacify him with humor. "And what will I talk about?"

His eyes sparkled with merriment. "Oh, whatever you like," he said with the wave of a hand. "The latest fashions. Who's courting who. Or would that be *whom*? Plans for your latest soiree. Anything and everything to keep my bride happy."

"Except automobiles?" She gave him a mock serious look.

He chuckled. "I can't promise that, but I will do my best. I can assure you, however, that you will be riding about town in the nicest one money can afford to buy. I do hope you like that idea."

Had she been staying in London and actually marrying the man, she would have. The situation being what it was, she could only manage a meager response. "Sounds lovely."

"A lovely coach for a lovely lady." After a lingering smile, he rested his hand on the back of her chair then glanced at her mother. "I must thank you all for the pleasure of your company."

"Always happy to have you, son," Jacquie's father said. He nodded in her direction and gave a wink. "This girl of mine is a pistol. Hope you can handle her."

His words caught Jacquie off guard, but she tried not to react. Instead, she offered the wave of a hand followed by, "Oh, pooh."

"I will give it my best shot, sir." Roland turned her way. "Will you walk me to the door, Jacqueline?"

Her stomach lurched as he pulled her chair back. She'd avoided spending time alone with him for the most part but could do so no longer. Jacquie stood and took his proffered arm. She gave her mother a cursory glance then walked alongside Roland through the front hall. He paused at the door and brushed a loose hair from her face.

"It won't be long now. You will be Mrs. Jacqueline Palmer, one of society's finest ladies."

"Mrs. Palmer." She echoed the words, which seemed to please him.

He traced her cheek with his finger. Jacquie resisted the urge to cringe and, instead, offered him a convincing smile.

Roland took this as a sign and leaned in to whisper in her

ear. "I don't know what good thing I've possibly done to deserve an angel like you," he said, "but I will spend the rest of my life thanking God for the opportunity to make you happy. I promise you will not be sorry you've accepted my hand, Jacqueline. I will do my best to be a good husband to you and a kind father to our children. Of that, you can be sure."

His heartfelt words were not quite what she'd expected. Shame washed over Jacquie as she absorbed his tender dissertation. She blinked several times and tried to focus. Through the open window, she caught a glimpse of Peter working in the front garden. Jacquie eased her way to the right, hoping to catch a better look.

"Thank you for the lunch invitation." Roland gave her fingers a little squeeze. "Everything was wonderful."

Yes. Everything *was* wonderful. Only, the delicious feelings coursing through her right now had nothing in the world to do with Roland Palmer. In fact, she could scarcely wait to get him out the door so she could focus on the true object of her affections.

She followed Roland outside, her spirits coming alive as she caught a glimpse of Peter on the far side of the garden. He looked her way, his brow wrinkling as he watched Mr. Palmer offer one final kiss on the cheek.

No worries, Peter. You can put your jealousies to rest. Once this man is gone, I will sweep you into my arms and kiss away any concerns you might have.

Less than fifteen minutes after seeing Roland off, Jacquie headed to the family's greenhouse to meet with Peter. Making her way through the gabled entry, she found him hard at work in the lovely glass room beneath the pitched roof, transferring roses from one pot to another. He looked over at her with a smile so warm, she felt sure it would melt her into a puddle. Her heart quickened as she took a couple of steps his way, beyond the row of lush ferns and into the domain of the brightly colored flowering plants.

Peter's brown curls were disheveled, no doubt from the hard work, but she found them appealing, as always. And no other young man in town had green eyes so captivating that they transported her to heaven with just one glance.

Peter released his hold on the roses, slipped off his gloves, and pulled her into a familiar embrace. Jacquie felt a rush of excitement wash over her. No proper young woman would be caught in such a compromising position, of course. Still, how could she help herself? A stronger force pulled them together than could be denied, at least by one so smitten.

Jacquie leaned her head against his broad shoulders. His muscular physique offered a sense of protection from the troubles that had plagued her of late.

"I've missed you." He planted several kisses along her hairline, sending tingles down her spine. "Why does it always have to be like this?"

"It doesn't. Not for long, anyway. A lot has happened since we last spoke."

"So I can see. That Palmer fellow has been here more times than I can count." He balled his fists, and his eyes narrowed. "I'd take him down a notch or two, if..." Peter didn't finish the sentence. Instead, he just shook his head, his fists still as tight as before. Jacquie had seen him worked up before. Several times, in fact. But never like this.

She stroked his cheek with the back of her hand, hoping it would calm him down. "Roland isn't a bad man. In fact, I daresay his trusting and genteel nature will serve our purposes just fine."

"Serve our purposes?"

"Yes." She gestured to a wrought-iron bench near the ferns, and they both sat together. "My boarding pass for the *Titanic* has arrived. I'm to leave on the tenth out of Southampton."

The edges of his lips curled down and wrinkles appeared around those gorgeous green eyes. "That doesn't give us much time together."

She gripped his hand, a newfound excitement taking hold. "What would you say if I told you that we could have all the time in the world together, not just now, but forevermore?" A burst of sunlight shone through the glass roof as if to punctuate her words.

He offered a sudden, arresting grin. "I would say I am intrigued by that comment."

Jacquie giggled. "I'm convinced I've come up with the perfect solution to our dilemma, one sure to change our lives for the better. And at no cost." *Other than losing the respect of my family, but surely they will understand—in time.*

"Tell me." He lifted her hand and gave the back of it a tender kiss.

"My ticket is for first class. Mama says it was very expensive. My grandmother only wants the finest for me. But what if—" She gazed into his beautiful eyes. "What if I gave it to you and you traded it in for two tickets?"

"Two tickets?" He looked perplexed.

"Yes, don't you see? One for each of us. Less expensive tickets, of course. Second class, even. I don't really mind about that. I'm sure we could still travel in style. Why, we could tell our children and grandchildren about the day we boarded the most famous ship in the world to escape our lives back in Europe. It's going to make for a marvelous story."

"Back in Europe?" He echoed her words, his grip on her hands loosening. "I—I don't know, Jacquie." His gaze shifted upward to the glass cupola.

"What do you mean?" For a moment, she felt sick. Could it be she'd misunderstood his feelings? She had considered this possibility only in passing, in fleeting moments of doubt. "You don't want to go with me? I thought you would relish the idea of starting over in New York. No doubt you will find work there quickly, with your green thumb." She gestured to the rows and rows of lovely plants, which he had cultivated and cared for. "I feel sure you will settle nicely in the States."

"I—" He shrugged. "I just don't know how I feel about leaving England. My family is here. You know our situation. My mother and sister depend on me now more than ever. They count on the money I send each month and on my care whenever my father goes through one of his...spells."

She longed for him to explain further, but he did not. Still, the pained expression in his eyes spoke volumes. A lump rose to her throat and she forced back tears. Had he really just dismissed her idea? Could such a thing be possible? Perhaps her feelings for Peter had been in vain after all. Perhaps he didn't care for her in the same way that she cared for him.

"I—I see," she managed at last. She didn't, of course, but would never say so. Jacquie swallowed hard and strengthened her resolve. Very well. She would make him love her. She would use her womanly wiles to accomplish the deed. A fluttering of eyelashes followed, her first attempt at flirtatious behavior set to win him over.

He didn't seem to notice.

"Thank you for understanding." He raked his fingers through his hair. "Besides, I can't help but think this is for the best for you as well. What would your grandmother say if you arrived in New York with a stranger in tow—a man, no less? She would send us both packing. We would end up on the streets with no place to go and no source of income."

"I hadn't thought about that." Jacquie rose and began to pace, finally stopping directly in front of him. As he stood, she slipped her hands into his and gave them a squeeze, tears now stinging her eyes. "Oh, I don't know, Peter. I only know that I love you, and I want to be with you—at any cost." Perhaps her impassioned words gave away too much of her heart. Still, how could she hold back, with her heart in such a state?

He gave her a pensive look. "Honestly?"

"Yes." She threw herself into his arms and the tears began in earnest as the weight of her situation took hold. If she couldn't win him over with her charms, perhaps he would fall prey to her emotions.

"No crying, Jacquie. Not today." He handed her a handkerchief. "Because I've had a few days to come up with an idea of my own, one that involves no travel across the Atlantic for either of us. I'm convinced that it will put a sparkle in your eyes and a smile on your face once again. In fact, I'm sure of it."

"Oh?" She gazed at him, hope rushing over her.

Over the next several minutes he shared his plan—his delicious, heavenly plan—and she couldn't help but smile. In fact, she might just go on smiling for the rest of her life.

Chapter Four

Saturday, March 30, 1912
Hotel DeVille, Paris, France

Nathan Patterson spent the better part of the dreary Saturday morning drawn into the pages of a fascinating novel. Though he tried to close the book to rest his eyes, he could not. The story held him spellbound. After nearly three hours, the pages complete, he left his suite at Paris's famous Hotel DeVille and made his way to the door of his mother's room. It took two knocks before her lady's maid, Greta, answered.

Nathan walked into the room, beyond the fringed lamp on the intricately carved mahogany table, past the expensive landscape-themed paintings that hung in gilded frames on the far wall, and toward the woman in the soft yellow gown, who sat perched upon the edge of the canopy bed like a queen awaiting her subjects. Mother had never looked more regal. Or more perturbed.

"Nathan, there you are." Her brow furrowed as she glanced his way. "I've been worried about you."

"Oh?"

"Yes." She released an exaggerated sigh. "What a morning this has been. My nerves are in a fragile state."

An exaggeration, no doubt. Still, he would play along. Playing along was easier. "And why is that?"

"There's just so much to do." Mother extended her hand, and he took a few steps in her direction. "Are you all packed? We leave for London on the four thirty train."

"Yes, I finished packing hours ago. Spent the rest of the morning reading."

"The paper?" she asked. "I took a look at it myself. Did you read that marvelous article about Marie Curie? Quite the scandal, you know." Mother fussed over a blouse and then passed it off to Greta, who folded it and placed it in the trunk.

"What sort of scandal?"

His mother quirked a brow. "They say she's dishonored the name of her late husband by engaging in a relationship with another man, but she's withstood the pressure quite well. I'm not sure I could handle such a public outcry over my behavior." She reached across the bed for her hat—a multifeathered number in a deep shade of purple—and placed it into a hatbox. Then she handed that off to Greta, who couldn't seem to figure out what to do with it.

Nathan chuckled. "Mother, the moment you start behaving scandalously, I will go to the papers myself."

She paled at his joke and fanned herself with her hand. "Don't tease like that. I'm simply trying to say that the woman won her latest Nobel Prize in the midst of this scandal. She's managed to hold her head high in spite of what others are saying behind her back. I find that to be an admirable trait. Don't you?"

"I suppose." He shrugged. "But to answer your question, I haven't read the article on Madame Curie," he said. "I spent the morning reading—"

"Oh, you must have seen the piece on the *Titanic*. She's being fitted out as we speak and will soon face her sea trials. Can you believe we'll be boarding her in less than two weeks?" His mother's nose wrinkled. "Not that I'm in a hurry to get back to New York, mind you. But I am looking forward to the luxurious accommodations." She lit into a lengthy dissertation about the ship, focusing on the fine amenities. "And look at this…" She pressed a newspaper into his hands, and he fought to translate the French advertisement but could not.

"What is it, Mother?"

"Soap. Vinolia soap, to be precise. Offering a higher standard of luxury and comfort at sea." She laughed and put the paper down. "As if a bar of soap could make me feel luxurious."

"Begging your pardon, ma'am," Greta interjected, "but if the soap doesn't make you feel like a queen, the other niceties onboard the ship will. I hear they've got everything a soul could ever want and more."

"Yes, Greta." His mother's expression soured. "I'm well aware of the fact that the *Titanic* is the finest ocean liner sailing the seas today. That's why we're taking her back to New York."

Nathan paced the room, his thoughts returning to the novel. "Well, speaking of ships, I find myself a bit unnerved at the proposition of traveling the high seas now."

"Unnerved?" His mother gave him an inquisitive look then nodded at Greta, who attempted to close the trunk. "Why is that, son?"

"The novel I've spent all morning reading. It's called *Futility*." He rose and helped Greta fasten the hinges on the oversized trunk.

"Rather sobering title." His mother rose and moved toward the vanity. She glanced at her reflection then fussed with her hair. "Don't believe I've heard of it."

"It's a novel about a British passenger liner called the *Titan*, written nearly fifteen years ago by an American author named

Robertson. Don't you find that strange?" Nathan hefted the trunk off the bed and placed it onto the floor.

"Strange that an American would write a book about a British ship, you mean?" Mother gave her reflection another look then turned his way. "Nothing too unusual about that."

"No, strange that he would name the ship the *Titan*, when we'll be sailing on the *Titanic* in a couple of weeks. The ship in the novel sailed in April, just like ours will. Can't help but wonder about the similarities." His thoughts continued to reel as he eased the trunk to a better location near the door.

"Well, don't give away the ending of the book," his mother said with the wave of a hand. "I hate it when someone spoils the ending of a good story for me. Maybe I'll read it while we're at sea. If you think it's something I might enjoy, I mean. You do seem to know my preferences better than most, even my own husband." She offered up a dramatic sigh. "Your father never notices any of my likes or dislikes."

Not for lack of trying on his part.

"I somehow doubt you would enjoy the book, Mother. As I said, it's rather disconcerting."

"Not that I will have much time to read onboard, anyway." She shrugged. "Likely I'll be too busy socializing. You know that many of our neighbors and acquaintances will be traveling alongside us, don't you? Why, people of every status and station will board, and we'll be in the thick of them."

"True. Though I haven't thought about what I will do aboard the ship, other than fill my belly with good food." He rubbed his stomach and chuckled. "As if this trip to Europe hasn't put ten pounds on me already."

"You hide it well," she said. "On the other hand, Greta will have to tighten my corset or I will never fit in my dresses." She paused. "The meals will be fabulous, I'm sure, but the company even more so."

"Aren't you looking forward to getting back home to Father?" Nathan rose and walked in his mother's direction.

Her thinly plucked eyebrows quirked. "Well, I might have preferred more time in Paris. I do wish we could spend more time shopping before the boat sails. I had hoped to replace most of my old gowns while I was here. I've grown weary with wearing the same dresses to every social function. It would have been nice to purchase new things."

"The dress you wore to the theater last night was new."

"Well, yes, but it was one of the few purchases I've had time to make. Everything seems so rushed." She sighed. "I don't suppose I'll ever see Helena Rubinstein's salon. I had every intention of visiting it while in Paris."

As she carried on, he bit back the need to ask, *How will you manage without a day at the salon?*

"It's just so sad that we have to leave for London already." Her lips curled downward in a pout. "Your father knew that I wanted to spend two more weeks on this leg of the journey, but you know how he is."

Yes, Nathan knew how his father was, of course. Kindhearted. Loving. And far too sympathetic to Mother's spoiled nature and off-the-cuff comments.

"The man is pushing us off to London, likely under the mistaken impression that I will do less damage to his pocketbook there." She giggled. "Sometimes I wonder if he knows me at all."

Point well taken.

"I've missed Father," Nathan said. "And as much as I'm looking forward to boarding the *Titanic*, I must say I'm even more excited about going home again. It will be nice to settle into my new job at the insurance company."

His mother eased her way into a nearby chair and rolled her eyes. "Yes, that's all we need, the son and the husband both married to the business. And little old me, fiddling around for things to occupy my time because no one takes an interest in me."

Nathan fought the temptation to roll his eyes. As if anyone could ignore his mother when she so easily pressed herself upon all.

Mother waved her hand in his direction. "Well, go on with you, then, and join your father's firm. See if I care. I should have had a daughter. A daughter wouldn't have deserted me."

"Perhaps one day you will have a daughter-in-law. She can shop with you and throw fine parties. How would that be?"

"Hardly a good substitute for the son I would prefer to spend time with, but I suppose it will have to do. Have you someone in mind that I've not heard of? Has Bridgette Cannady finally convinced you to court her, perhaps?"

"Bridgette?" He laughed. "Hardly. She's the last girl I would consider marrying."

"Good." His mother turned to give him a stern look. "Just promise me one thing, son. Don't let anyone convince you to marry someone who doesn't truly deserve you. I don't think I could bear that."

Deserve me? "Mother, should I marry, my bride will be God's perfect choice for me. My complement and my equal."

"Then you will be among the rarer set, for few find such a thing in reality. In novels like the one you're reading, perhaps, but not in real life."

"Are you saying there's no such thing as true love?"

Her elongated pause gave him reason to wonder. Still, as the conversation shifted back to their upcoming trip, he breathed a sigh of relief. Before long he would be on the ship, sailing for home. His European adventures would be behind him once and for all, and he could get on with life as usual.

* * * * *

Saturday, March 30, 1912
Gloucestershire County, England

Tessa looked up from her labors as a shiny Mercedes limousine pulled into the lane in front of her family's meager cottage. Her heart raced to her throat. Why had such an impressive automobile found its way to their humble abode? Had someone died, perhaps? Her anxieties did not lessen as a liveried chauffeur stepped out. Tessa shuddered then dropped the rake and started toward the lane, scarcely able to breathe.

The chauffeur opened the rear passenger door and a beautiful young lady dressed in brilliant blue appeared. Even from a distance the girl reeked of money. That much one could observe from her stance, her coiffed hair, and the tailored gown. But why had she come? Perhaps her automobile had broken down.

Only when Tessa's older brother climbed out of the limousine did Tessa pause to catch her breath. "Peter!" She let out a squeal and ran across the yard toward the lane, her tangled hair flying in the breeze. She drew near and fought to catch her breath. "W–why didn't you t–tell us you were coming?"

He pulled her into a warm embrace and kissed her forehead. "No one knows I'm here. I've come on a mission." His brow creased, and he glanced toward the cottage. "Is Mum at home?"

"She will be soon. She's gone to the village to barter."

"I'd hoped as much but asked the driver to let us out here, just in case." Peter's lips pursed. "Pa?"

"Where do you think?" *At the tavern, of course.*

"Then the timing of our little visit couldn't be more ideal." Peter spoke a few words to the chauffeur, who got into the expensive car and drove away, leaving the three of them standing on the edge of the lane.

Peter smiled and extended his hand to the lovely young woman, who slipped easily into his arms. The stranger's china-doll cheeks were pinked with the slightest bit of rouge, and those lips— those full, perfect lips—were painted on, no doubt about it. Tessa tried not to stare at her gown, though she'd never seen anything like it. The majestic blue was a perfect match for the sparkling eyes of the unfamiliar girl standing before her. Still, what was such a creature doing curled into Peter's arms?

Peter looked at the girl with tenderness in his expression then glanced Tessa's way. "Tessa, this is Jacquie Abingdon. I work for her father."

She started to reach out to shake the stranger's gloved hand but then pulled back, concerned about the dirt on her own.

"It's fine." The young woman took a step in her direction and reached for her hand. "I'm not put off by hard work. I admire it, in fact." The afternoon breeze toyed with a tendril of her lovely chestnut hair as she gave Tessa's hand a firm shake. "Nice to meet you, Tessa. I've heard so much about you."

"You—you have?" She pulled back her calloused hand, shame washing over her at how she must appear to this pristine woman.

"I've only told her the good things." Peter slung his arm over Tessa's shoulder, pulling her into a familiar, comfortable hug, one that put her at ease right away. "She doesn't know what a rapscallion you were as a child."

"Rapscallion? Me?" Tessa laughed as she crossed her arms at her chest in defiant fashion. Just as quickly, her gaze shifted back to the beautifully attired stranger.

Jacquie's silk dress shimmered in the afternoon sunlight, as did the pearl combs that held her beautifully coiffed hair. Her pristine button-up shoes caught Tessa's eye, but nothing compared to the exquisite feather-plumed hat with its tiny silk bird. For a moment Tessa envisioned herself in that bird's place, perched and ready to fly off to the skies, away from this godforsaken place. Just as quickly, her thoughts shifted back to her brother, who pointed to the stalls as an annoying squeal rang out.

"Is that Countess I hear?" A hint of a smile graced his lips.

"Naturally." Tessa pressed back the desire to groan aloud. "She's made a mess of things again. I've repaired the crates three times this month alone. And you won't believe the holes she's dug, trying to escape. I've never met a more determined sow."

"Well, let's go visit with her. It will give us a chance to tell you why we've come." His near smile twisted into something more suspicious, and her heart fluttered. They'd come specifically to talk to her? Why?

"You want to talk—in the barn?" In the muddy recesses of the pig stall? With Countess in rare form and the piglets squalling at fever pitch? What would this lovely vision in blue think of such a meeting place? Tessa's cheeks heated in embarrassment.

Before she could voice the question aloud, Peter led the way across the yard toward the barn. As they drew near, the young woman on his arm pulled an embroidered handkerchief from her reticule and pressed it to her nose. No doubt the smell of the pigs and goats left something to be desired, though Tessa had grown used to it. One of the hens, likely stirred up by their approach, scurried around Jacquie's feet and pecked her on the leg.

"Oh!" Blue Eyes let out a squeal. "Well, that was a fine how-do-you-do!"

Peter waved his hand at the intrusive bird and sent it on its way. Then they arrived at the barn, and he headed straight for the farrowing crates, setting them aright and giving Countess a scolding as only he could.

Tessa looked on, confused. Peter glanced her way, and she could read the concern in his eyes. Her heart twisted within her as she anticipated his words. Clearly, he had come on a mission, one that involved her. With her pulse now pounding in her ears, Tessa settled onto a bale of hay to hear what her brother had come to say.

Chapter Five

Tessa brushed her calloused hands across her dirty skirt and gazed up at Peter and Jacquie. Her brother paced the stall, his gaze on the muddy floor. After a moment of awkward silence, Jacquie pulled down the hankie she'd held to her nose and cleared her throat.

"Tessa, we won't keep you waiting. I know you must be curious about why we've come."

"I am, yes." *To say the least.*

Jacquie took several steps in Tessa's direction, finally, stopping in front of her. "I know that you and I are total strangers, and you might find this odd, but I've come to encroach upon your kindness to ask a favor."

"A favor?" A thousand questions flittered through Tessa's mind at once. What could she possibly do for someone such as this?

"Yes. I know I have no right to ask or expect anything of you, but I feel sure once you've heard our story that your heart will be affected." Jacquie paused and glanced in the direction of the piglets then back at Tessa. "No doubt what I have to say will startle you, but if you will hear me out, I would be grateful."

"Well, of course I will hear you out." What could this china doll possibly have to say that might cause Tessa to be ill at ease?

"Please have a seat." Jacquie perched on a bale of hay, and Tessa glanced out the barn door, knowing Mum would arrive shortly. And heaven help them all if Pa arrived home from the tavern to find Tessa seated on the job.

The lovely scent of Jacquie's perfume wafted across the stall and countered the smell of the pigs. Almost, anyway. She gazed at Tessa, her eyes pooling. "This is going to come as a shock, I'm afraid, but your brother and I, well…" She looked up at Peter with a sheepish grin.

"What she means to say is, we are giving thought to marriage." His cheeks flushed deep red, and though his broad-shouldered stance spoke of confidence, the worry lines on his forehead gave him away. Something about this did not feel right.

Tessa looked back and forth between them, her mouth widening into an O. "How— I mean, how is this—?"

"Possible?" Jacquie rose and twisted her handkerchief in her hands. "Yes, well, I see your point there. My father would never approve." A roll of those big blue eyes followed her comment. "Not that I pay any mind to such things, but he is steeped in the customs and traditions of our family, customs that go back for generations." Jacquie paused and gazed at Peter with longing. "But that does not negate the fact that I am in love with your brother. He is my life. And we will marry, when the time is right. After a proper courtship, anyway."

The young woman took a few steps toward Peter and leaned her head on his shoulder. He offered what appeared to be a genuine smile. Still, Tessa couldn't help but wonder why Peter's expression did not match the look of sheer bliss on Jacquie's face.

"I—I see." Tessa rose and smoothed her dirty skirt. She didn't really see, of course. Not a lick of this made any sense to her. What business did Peter have, toying with his employer's daughter? Had city life confused him? Made him think more highly of himself than he ought? Did he plan to marry this girl to advance himself, somehow? The Peter she knew would never do such a thing.

Her gaze shifted once again to the little silk bird on Jacquie's hat. It bobbed up and down as the young woman spoke, as if ready to take to the skies.

"My father has arranged for me to marry a wealthy business-man, but I cannot abide the idea." Jacquie's nose wrinkled. "Roland Palmer is as dull as paint. Mama has concocted a plan so that I might escape this fate. But I have a plan of my own. I wish for her to think that I've actually boarded the ship."

"Boarded the ship?"

"So sorry. I'm getting ahead of myself." Tessa giggled. "I'm referring to the *Titanic*. She sails out of Southampton in two weeks. Mama will see me off, and I will supposedly sail for New York, where my grandmother awaits."

Behind them, the piglets tousled with one another, their impish squeals interrupting the conversation. Countess rooted through her brood, nudging the babes this way and that with her snout, which only served to get them more excited.

"But what has this to do with me?" Tessa ran her dirty palms over her skirt again, more confused than ever.

Jacquie's voice grew more passionate with each word, which she spoke above the noise coming from the animals. "I do not wish to go to New York. Not now, not ever. I want to stay here, with Peter."

"I see." Only, she didn't. Not really.

Jacquie took Tessa's hand and gave it a squeeze. "We've come up with a plan that should change all of our lives for the better.

I want to offer you the opportunity to escape from your life here, Tessa."

"To escape?"

"Yes." Peter drew near and slipped an arm over Tessa's shoulders. "I know how it is with Father. He's cruel and he—"

Tessa put her hand up as tears sprang to her eyes. "Say no more."

"He does not treat you well." Peter's arms tightened around her in protective measure. "But there is a solution, Tessa. One where you can leave his evil ways behind and move forward with your life."

"You're making no sense, Peter." Tessa plopped back down onto the bale of hay, her thoughts in a whirl. Truly, the yelps from the piglets made more sense than the peculiar conversation with these two lovebirds.

"I want you to take my place aboard the *Titanic*." Jacquie's words were whispered, but they might as well have been shouted in Tessa's ear, they took her by such force.

"W–what?" A wave of nausea passed over Tessa, followed by a dizzy spell.

"Yes, don't you see? As soon as Mama gets me settled in my room aboard the ship, we will trade places—trade lives, as it were—and you can sail to New York in my place. You will take my boarding pass, my clothing, my…life. All of that I will gladly trade for the pure joy of marrying your brother and spending my days as his wife, here in England." She batted her eyelashes in Peter's direction, and he responded with a smile, though it looked a bit strained.

Still, Tessa couldn't make sense of this. Was the girl daft? Had years of wearing tight corsets squeezed the common sense out of her?

"It's the perfect solution." Peter turned to Tessa, pleading with his eyes. "Don't you agree? Jacquie does not care to leave, and you...well, you need to leave. I will feel better knowing you're safely away from here." His gaze shifted to the house and then back to her.

"I do not agree." Tessa rose and marched across the barn. "You've both spent too much time consuming rich foods, I fear. It has affected your reasoning. Do you really think, for one moment, that I could possibly play the role of a—a—" She pointed to Jacquie, not wanting to be rude.

"A society girl?" Jacquie offered a confident smile. "Yes, I do believe it possible. You're the right size for my dresses, the perfect hair color, everything."

"Not everything." Tessa folded her hands over her chest and glared at her brother's beau, taking in the wealth of dark hair and perfectly arched brows. Her gaze traveled to the narrow, fitted waist on the beautifully trimmed-out dress and finally landed on the pristine shoes with their pointed toes. Her feet ached just thinking about them.

Jacquie cleared her throat, which brought Tessa back to her senses. Resolved to put an end to this ridiculous conversation, she looked her way and spoke with fervor. "I can wear the dress, but I cannot wear the life. I do not speak like you or walk like you or put on prissy airs like—" She stopped herself.

"I will teach you all of that." Jacquie gripped her hand with such force that Tessa felt it might break. "We have two weeks to accomplish it. I feel sure it can be done."

"And in two weeks, you think I can learn to be a proper English lady?" Tessa snorted and ran her rough palms across her dirty skirt. "If so, then you truly don't know me. I am far more at home here, in the stalls, with a swine who thinks she's a countess, than rubbing shoulders with the real thing."

Jacquie's eyes pooled. "You want to leave this place. That much I do know. From what Peter has shared, your life is very difficult. What you've had to endure is beyond comprehension."

Tessa trembled and glared at her brother. How dare he share her personal stories with this stranger?

"You, of all people, deserve a fresh start," Jacquie said. "And I hope to offer you that. Please consider this, Tessa. It will be my gift to you. And yours to me, of course."

"Consider it, Tessa." Peter's eyes brimmed with tears. "Please." Something about the tone of his voice gave her reason to actually do so.

The erratic thumping of Tessa's heart nearly knocked the breath out of her. She rose and paced the barn before turning toward her brother, doing her best to suppress the anger threatening to erupt.

"What will you tell Pa when I turn up missing? He will be furious. You know how he depends on me to work the farm. I'm the only one left, you know." Her comment was meant as an accusation, and from the pained expression on her brother's face, the words hit their intended mark. Just as quickly, his wrinkled brow softened.

"We've the perfect solution for that," Peter said. "We will tell him that you have been offered a lucrative position as a companion to Jacquie's grandmother in New York."

"A companion?" For a moment, the idea held some appeal. A kind, elderly woman with soft, wrinkled skin would make the perfect friend, one who wouldn't grind her knees against the stony pavement or curse at her when things didn't go as planned.

"Yes, don't you see?" Jacquie's smile seemed convincing enough. "And I have no doubt you *will* make a perfect companion to her. She will need you once all is revealed."

"You don't suppose she will send me packing the moment I arrive?" Tessa's ire rose. "Then I'll be living on the streets in New York. How is that any better than my situation here? At least here I have a bed to sleep in and a roof over my head."

"She will not turn you out." Jacquie's gaze narrowed. "I will send a letter with you, one meant to sway her. Grandmother is a good woman, prone to kindness. She will, I'm sure, take you in as her own granddaughter. But let's don't fret over that part just yet. One thing at a time."

"But…" Tessa started to say more but caught a glimpse of Mum headed up the lane toward the cottage with Pa—who was tripping over his own shadow but following closely behind.

The pair disappeared into the cottage and Peter glanced Tessa's way, his eyes pleading. "Will you do it, Tessa? I will understand if you say no, but if you agree to this, you will change all our lives for the better. You will not be sorry."

Oh, how she wished he could turn his words into a promise. If she could, she wouldn't think twice. She would board the *Titanic* as a well-to-do china doll and pray that nothing happened to cause that doll to break between England and America.

Tessa glanced once again at the little silk bird on Jacquie's elaborate hat and prayed for the courage to take flight.

* * * * *

Jacquie's breath caught in her throat as she walked with Peter and Tessa toward the broken-down cottage with its crumbling exterior and sagging porch railing. As they stepped inside, the stench of rotting food accosted her, coupled with the sight of dirty dishes in the sink.

A woman in a tattered gray dress approached, her eyes welling with tears as she saw Peter. "My boy." She opened her arms to him and he raced to give her a warm embrace.

"Mother." He pressed a tender kiss onto her wrinkled cheek.

"And who have you brought with you?" His mother's expression shifted to Jacquie then back to Peter as she mumbled, "You should warn a person when there's company comin'." Her fingers rose to rake her tangled gray hair, only making it messier still.

"Oh, there's no need to do anything special on my behalf." Jacquie extended her hand. "I'm Jacquie Abingdon, Mrs. Bowen, and I've come to ask a favor."

"A favor?"

Peter's eyes sparked with a hint of what she could only perceive as fear. "Where's Pa? This will involve him, as well, for it's about Tessa."

"What about Tessa?" A man in torn slacks with unfastened suspenders over a graying shirt entered the room. His bleary eyes told the tale of too much whiskey. Or gin. And the slurred speech confirmed it, as did the horrendous odor emanating from his every pore. Surely this couldn't be Peter's father. To imagine this man raising Peter—her beautiful, perfect Peter—seemed impossible.

At once the fellow lit into a rant about Tessa's laziness, and the young woman flinched as if expecting the back of his hand to come down on her.

"Pa, Mum..." Peter hesitated. "Jacquie here has come with a proposition."

"One that I hope will benefit us all." She broadened her smile and did her best to appear confident.

"Well, then, I will give a listen." Mr. Bowen dropped into a half-broken chair at the table and leaned back, folding his arms at his chest. "Spit it out, girl. I don't have all day."

He gestured for his wife to bring him a plate of food, which bought Jacquie a few seconds to think through her explanation. "My grandmother in New York isn't well, you see," she said at last. "She hasn't been for some time." That much was true. The last Jacquie had heard, Granny's rheumatism was giving her fits.

"What has this to do with us?" Mr. Bowen reached for his bowl of stew and slopped a spoonful into his mouth, speaking around it. "You want I should feed and tend to her as well as my own family?" A bit of mashed carrot fell out of his mouth and he brushed it away. "If so, you've come barkin' up the wrong tree."

"Oh, no, sir. Nothing of the sort. I have been seeking to hire a young woman capable of tending to my grandmother's needs."

"W–what 'r' you askin'?" Mrs. Bowen wrung the dishcloth in her hands.

"I've been telling her about Tessa, Mum," Peter said. "And we both agree that she would make a perfect candidate. Remember what a good job she did with caring for Grand, before she passed? And she was a valuable asset to old Mrs. Johnston, as well."

"But…New York?" Mrs. Bowen did not look pleased by this proposition.

"Can't run the farm without her." Mr. Bowen shoveled more food down.

"But, Pa." Tessa took a couple of steps in her father's direction. "I would really like to—"

"No, girl." He looked up from his stew, the sternness in his eyes setting every hair on edge. "Your laziness won't be rewarded with a trip across the ocean."

"That's a shame." Jacquie put on her most businesslike voice. "For the job pays quite well. My father is known for his generosity in such matters." She didn't have to lie about this. Most who knew Father considered him a philanthropist as well as an entrepreneur. Not that he planned to pay anyone to serve as companion, but Peter's father need not know where the money was coming from.

At this, Mr. Bowen set down his spoon and gazed at her with some intensity. "That so?"

"Oh, indeed." Jacquie swept a loose hair from her face and tried to appear unwavering. "Not that Tessa would require money to live on. My grandmother's estate in New York is lovely, and her every need would be met. She would want for nothing."

"The idea of Tessa livin' like a queen holds no appeal." Mr. Bowen grunted and turned back to his food. "She's done nothing to deserve such reward, and I won't see her livin' in the lap o' luxury while the rest of us sit in squalor."

"This isn't about Tessa, Pa." Peter took a seat across from him. "We've been thinking of you and Mum."

"Oh?" Mr. Bowen seemed to perk up at this news.

"Tessa could send most of the money back home for the running of the farm. You could hire out the help. Get someone strong and capable." Peter turned to face Tessa and grinned. "Not implying that you're not strong and capable, of course."

"No offense taken. Besides, you and I both know I can arm wrestle you to the ground." A smile turned up the edges of Tessa's lips, capturing Jacquie's curiosity. Perhaps she had already been won over.

"If that's a challenge, I'm up for it." Peter flexed his arm and showed off his muscles, which only served to bolster Jacquie's confidence further.

"I will have to think on this." Mr. Bowen spoke between bites. "Not sure how I feel about it."

"While you're thinking on it, please accept my father's first payment." Jacquie fished around in her purse, finally coming up with an envelope that contained enough money for the man to drink himself into a stupor, should he choose to do so. "He's quite anxious to find someone quickly because the ship sails in two weeks, so time is of the essence." Only a half lie, of course.

"Hmm." Mr. Bowen reached for the envelope and turned it in his hands. "Well, now. You've given me much to think on."

"While you're thinking, I'd like for Tessa and Jacquie to get to know one another better." Peter flashed a smile. "How would that be? Could we walk the property while you're mulling over Jacquie's request?"

"I won't stop you." Mr. Bowen grunted before slopping down another spoonful of stew.

As they made their way outside once again into the late afternoon sunlight, Jacquie breathed a sigh of relief. She glanced over at Peter, who gave her a woeful shrug then slipped his arm over Tessa's shoulders.

"How do you think that went?" Jacquie asked.

"He will go along with it. He needs the money too desperately to turn down such an offer."

"Even if it means losing a daughter." Tessa sighed and kicked the dirt with the toe of her shoe. Glancing up, Jacquie noticed the tears in her eyes. "Not that I consider him a real father, anyway. What sort of father would trade his daughter for money?"

What sort, indeed? Jacquie's thoughts shifted to her father's arrangement with Roland Palmer as she slipped her arm through Tessa's. "I think we have more in common than I realized. I do believe you're the perfect person to take on this challenge."

"Perfect, I'm not." A smirk followed on Tessa's end. "But you have piqued my curiosity and I will go along with your scheme, should Pa agree, though it will require tutoring in every area one might imagine."

After several profuse thank-yous from Jacquie, Tessa turned back toward the barn to quiet the rambunctious sow. Then she cradled the piglets, gushing over them like babes.

Peter turned to face Jacquie and reached for her hands. He gestured to the farm, his eyes narrowing. "Jacquie, I can only imagine what you must be thinking." A pause followed. "It's true, I'm a farmer's son, but this is not my life. I can—and will—give you more than this."

Though his words felt hesitant, she accepted them as an offering of love. "I don't need more," she whispered as she slipped her arm around his waist and rested her head against his. "All I need—is you."

The words weren't completely true, of course. She also needed the help of a certain young woman, one with a torn, muddy skirt who was currently struggling to hold onto a feisty, squealing piglet. Without Tessa's cooperation, the whole plan would fall apart before the *Titanic* left port.

Chapter Six

Saturday Evening, March 30, 1912
Abingdon Manor, Richmond, England

The evening skies over London hovered in varying shades of pink and gray as the sun slipped off to the west. Tessa looked through the limousine window, her thoughts in a whirl. In less than two hours, every aspect of her life had changed. Pa had really and truly done it. He'd traded her off for a fistful of bills. Well, good riddance. She wouldn't miss him or his rock prayers. Instead, she would step into a new life, one that had been handed to her on a costly—albeit unexpected—silver platter.

And to think, Mum and Pa only knew the half of it. Every time she thought about boarding the *Titanic* to take on the persona of a society girl, a quiver of excitement ran through her. And the destination—New York! Every girl her age dreamed of such a trip, to a home across the seas. Just as quickly, her thoughts transitioned and she felt terrified. Could she really board the ship alone, without the hand of a mother or brother to guide her?

To her right, Jacquie and Peter stole secret glances and even the squeeze of a hand. Clearly, these two had feelings for one another, though somewhat lopsided, if her instincts were correct. She could not imagine how they planned to marry. No doubt Jacquie's father would come after Peter with a gun. Fear coursed through Tessa as this idea took root. What if Jacquie's father came after her with a gun, as well?

She continued to look out the window as the lush English countryside gave way to London's more polished suburbia. Only when the limousine pulled up in front of a home the size of Buckingham Palace did her breath catch in her throat.

"Welcome to Abingdon Manor." Jacquie looped her arm through Tessa's after the limousine driver helped them out of the car. "I do hope you enjoy your stay. It will be brief but highly educational." A tiny wink followed.

"No doubt." Tessa looked around at the expansive estate with its lush gardens and shook her head. "How did I get here?"

"In a Mercedes limousine, of course." Jacquie giggled. "And the driver was kind enough to drop us off at the gate so as not to alert the servants. Follow me, if you will." Under the shadowy haze of the twilight, she led the way beyond the front gates to the garden. Off to the west side of the beautiful rolling lawn, Tessa noticed a creek with a lovely bridge.

"This is beautiful," she said. "Peter, you are the grounds-keeper here?"

"Yes." His face beamed. "Tell me what you think of the way I've shaped the bushes to look like animals. I learned to do that just last spring. Clever, don't you think?"

"Very. They seem very lifelike." So lifelike, in fact, that she felt sure the lion to her right let out a roar. Or was that just her heart responding to the nervous flutter in her stomach?

"Follow me, Tessa." Jacquie led the way down a cobblestone path far away from the main house. Tessa traipsed along, a silent partner in this crime of passion, as the path narrowed under a canopy of vines overhead. Several minutes of walking the pathway finally led to a stream and, beyond that, a vine-covered cottage, looking like something from the cover of a storybook as the setting sun cast its shadows overhead.

Jacquie led the way to the front door and opened it. She stepped inside, brushed away a couple of thin cobwebs from the doorway, then glanced Tessa's way. "Welcome to your new home. For the next two weeks, anyway."

Tessa's nerves jumbled madly as she glanced around the tiny cabin. "Are you sure I will be safe here?"

"Quite. No one comes here unless we've guests, so you are more than safe, I assure you. Besides, Papa is out of town on business for the next week and Mama is at a society function this evening. We've the whole place to ourselves."

From the back bedroom, a young woman in a simple black dress with a white collar and a ruffled apron approached. She took one look at Tessa and rolled her eyes. *Nothing like making a person feel welcome.* A cold chill came over Tessa, and she fought the temptation to bolt toward the door as the stranger took to fussing with her white cap.

Jacquie smiled and gestured to the woman. "Tessa, this is Iris. She is my—your—lady's maid."

Tessa felt her breath catch in her throat as she took in the blond. "My what?"

Iris muttered something under her breath, finally speaking aloud. "Your lady's maid, miss."

"But, I…" No words would come. Tessa shook her head, unsure how to respond. To be served by another? This seemed a foreign concept to one who had only ever served.

"Iris has become my confidant." Jacquie flitted across the room and gave the maid a warm embrace. "And she is fully onboard with our plan." A giggle followed. "Fully onboard. What an ironic slip of the tongue." She patted Iris on the back and then laughed.

The petite blond didn't smile. Instead, she offered a hesitant nod. "Against my better judgment, I daresay. But I will not break confidence, Miss Jacquie. I've given you my word and I will not go back on it." The pained expression that followed made Tessa wonder about that.

Iris went about the business of lighting the lanterns overhead, one after the other, and soon the room was filled with the glow of flickering light.

"You're sure no one will find us here?" Tessa trembled as the very idea took hold. "Won't the lights give us away?"

Jacquie shook her head. "We are a great distance from the main house, so please don't fret. Besides, I don't recall Mama setting foot in this cottage for years. She has an aversion to spiders."

Tessa laughed. "If I had such an aversion, I would have to rid myself of it in a hurry. Working with the countess has taught me to overcome my fear of the creepy-crawlies."

"You work with a countess?" Iris looked up from the lanterns, her brow wrinkled.

This got a snicker from Peter, who had entered the room behind them carrying Tessa's bags.

"Probably not the sort you're accustomed to." Tessa giggled but did not say more. Instead, a yawn worked its way to the surface. She tried to stifle it but could not.

Jacquie gave her a sympathetic look. "Poor girl. I know you must be exhausted from the trip, but we've got so much to do, and with Mama gone tonight, this is the perfect time to get started. Do you mind?"

"No. Whatever you think is best, miss." She put a hand to

her mouth at the obvious blunder then pushed back another yawn and smiled.

"First of all, let's get rid of this 'miss' business, shall we? You will call me Jacquie."

"Whatever you think is best, miss…er, Jacquie."

"Good. Now, I've asked Iris to set out some food so that we can have a little lesson in table etiquette. And I do hope you've enough energy left to try on a few of my new dresses after the fact, in case they need to be fitted."

"Try on your new dresses?" Her heart did a funny little flip-flop as she thought about it.

"Of course." Jacquie giggled. "I still can't believe my good fortune. My father just paid for a host of new gowns for my trousseau, which means I have two wardrobes at my disposal."

"Your father purchased gowns for your marriage to my brother?" Tessa could hardly imagine such a thing possible. This story grew stranger and stranger.

"No." Jacquie's nose wrinkled. "My father believes me to be engaged to another man, remember? Mr. Roland Palmer."

"Ah, yes. I recall hearing that name mentioned." Of course, she had heard a great many things over the past few hours, had she not? How could she ever keep up with this playacting with no script to follow?

Jacquie's nose wrinkled. "I must admit, it gave me a moment's pause to think that you would end up with the new wardrobe, but I have no choice in that matter. Mama will help pack my trunk for the ship, and she will place my finest things inside. She will never know that they've been tweaked to fit you, of course."

"Wait." Tessa put her hand up, still confused. "You're saying that the new wardrobe pieces are to be mine?" She could hardly believe such a thing.

"Yes." Jacquie shrugged. "It's a small sacrifice on my part, really." A pause lingered in the air between them. "Besides, I won't really have need for such fine things once I'm a married woman. I daresay my new life will be—simpler."

Peter glanced up, and his eyes clouded over with something that could only be described as discomfort. He gave a little shrug followed by a muttered "Yes. Simpler." He hesitated and then added, "When the time comes, I mean."

Jacquie's expression shifted to one of concern before she turned her attention to Tessa once again. "Anyway, I have much to teach you, but we will begin with dinner-party basics. I will talk you through the various plates and silverware pieces and then move on to proper body positioning and the woman's role at the table. I can share suggestions for conversation starters and even advise you on the foods you should order once you board the ship. Are you up for it?"

"I suppose." The food part sounded good, anyway. Tessa's mouth watered just thinking about the possibilities.

"This would be a fine time for me to scoot." Peter pulled Jacquie into his arms and gave her a kiss on the forehead. He gazed at Jacquie. "Can you do without me?"

"Yes, but don't stay away long."

"Never."

Peter turned his attention to Tessa. He doubled his fist and gave her a playful punch. "Not sure how I can ever thank you, Tess."

Her heart flew to her throat and she fought the sting of tears with a shrug. "I'm sure I'll think of something."

He chuckled as he made his way out of the cottage, turning back only long enough to give the ladies a playful wink.

"Now then. Let's get to work." Jacquie's lovely blue skirt

swished this way and that as she made her way to the table. Playing the role of servant, she pulled out a chair and gestured for Tessa to sit, which Tessa did, but not without tripping over the chair leg.

"S–sorry."

A winsome smile graced Jacquie's lips as she pointed her index finger upward. "Rule number one—a lady rarely acknowledges her own faux pas. She pretends it never existed."

"What's a *faux pas*?" Tessa asked, her gaze shifting to the rows of silverware surrounding the plate in front of her.

"A mistake. A woman rarely acknowledges her mistakes, at least not publicly. She simply moves forward as if the incident did not take place. That way, you leave the other people wondering if, perhaps, they might have imagined things." A light giggle followed from Jacquie, along with fluttering eyelashes. How did one go about getting their lashes to flutter like that? Tessa would have to try it. Later, of course, when no one was looking.

They spent the next half hour going over the rules of the table—everything from silverware to goblets to the way one held one's pinkie finger while sipping tea. Before long Tessa's belly was full of crumpets and tea, but her head was even fuller. How could she possibly remember all of Jacquie's instructions? Worn out, Tessa slumped back in her chair and let out an exaggerated groan.

"I know, I know." Jacquie chuckled. "It's a lot to take in." The lovely young woman paused, and her gaze shifted to Tessa's hands. "Next we're headed to the bedroom to try on dresses, but before we leave the table, would it offend you terribly if I asked to see your hands?"

"My...hands?" Tessa pressed them behind her back, embarrassment taking hold.

"Yes, if you don't mind." Jacquie's eyebrows arched as she

extended slender, beautifully manicured fingers Tessa's way. "You will wear gloves much of the time, of course, but a lady's hands give her away, so one can never be too careful."

Tessa held out her calloused hands, palms down.

The look on Jacquie's face spoke all as she took hold of them and leaned down for a closer examination. "Well, I can see we have much work to do. When we're done with our lesson, I'll have Iris help you soak these nails and give them a good scrubbing. Cleaning beneath the nails is so important. A clean palette is a good start. But we must do more." She turned Tessa's hand over then ran her delicate fingertip along the rough, blistered palms. "I will have Iris bring around some petroleum jelly as well. You must apply it at night before bed, then sleep with gloves on."

"Sleep—with gloves on?" Tessa bit back a chuckle. "Truly?"

"Yes. It's a trick I learned from Mother. Within weeks you will have the hands of a lady." Jacquie blushed and shook her head. "I do hope you will forgive me for that."

"For what?"

"For implying that you are anything but a lady already. I didn't mean to suggest such a thing with my comment. Will you forgive me?"

"Me? A lady?" Tessa snorted. "Miss, there's no need to pretend I'm something I'm not."

"It's Jacquie. And what do you mean, pretend?" Jacquie used her napkin to brush crumbs from her lip.

Tessa's dander rose. "Don't coddle me. We both know I'm not a proper lady, and there's certainly no reason to think I'll take to the role with ease. This will be a stretch, at best. Impossible, at worst."

"Oh, posh. I'm sure you'll do fine. You're lovely, Tessa, and I know the manners will come with time."

"Me? Lovely?" Tessa felt her cheeks grow warm. "Oh no. I'm not naturally good-looking, as many young ladies are. My appearance is tolerable. I've come to terms with this, so there's no point in stretching the truth to make me feel better."

"Tolerable?" Jacquie's eyes widened as she rose from the table. "You really don't have any idea, do you? You're a beauty, Tessa. Your hair is the prettiest shade of brown, and your eyes are beautiful. You've got a lovely figure too, one that will show off nicely in my dresses."

"Hmm." Tessa couldn't think of much to add, so she kept her thoughts to herself.

"Now, come with me. We're going to get you dolled up in the three new gowns Mrs. O'Shea has completed. Several others are expected before the ship sails, but we will manage those once they arrive. One thing at a time, I say."

Tessa tagged along on Jacquie's heels to the bedroom. The damask coverlet on the bed caught her eye at once, but she was more taken with what she found atop the covers. Tessa's gaze landed on the exquisite pink satin gown, and she gasped. "I—I—" Truly, in all of her days, she'd never seen the like.

Jacquie reached down to lift the dress. "If you think it's hard to breathe just looking at it, wait till I lace you up in the corset."

Tessa ran her fingers along the sleeve, mesmerized by the sheer fabric. Never had she worn anything so delicate, so fine. "What are these?" She pointed to several bead-like bits embellishing the front and the sleeves.

"Pieces of glass. Aren't they marvelous?" Jacquie held the dress close and cradled it like a baby. "And the silk is imported from India. Father travels there frequently, you see."

"India?"

"Yes, and look at the threading running through it. It's metallic. Have you ever seen anything like it?"

"I can truly say I never have."

"We need to get you into this dress, Tessa, so that Iris can take it up in the shoulders. It's clear you're smaller than I am."

"Smaller than—you?" Tessa shook her head. Was the china doll teasing? Such a tiny waist had never been seen. "If anything, you will need to let them out."

"Oh no. Just wait until you get the corset on. Then you will see how small your waist truly is."

She ran her fingers—her poor, rough fingers—along the delicate silk corset, eyeing the intricate embroidered rosettes and white laces. Sheer perfection.

Moments later, laced in so tightly she could scarcely catch her breath, she saw, all right. "I—I can't breathe. And I certainly can't sit down." Tessa gasped for air but gazed at her reflection in the oval mirror, astonished by how tiny her midsection looked.

Jacquie laughed. "You will get used to it, I assure you. And you can sit. You will simply have a straighter spine."

"Straighter than Cupid's arrow and twice as painful." Tessa ran her rough palms along the luxurious silk-and-lace undergarment and winced as the pain in her ribs grew worse when Iris tied off the laces. Was it her imagination, or did the young woman seem to pull them tighter still?

"I will certainly not be able to eat while wearing this." Tessa fought to catch her breath. "No doubt I'll trim down in a hurry."

"Perhaps Iris can release the pressure a bit. Let's try the dress on over it. Then we will know if the laces can be loosened." Jacquie reached for the gown and, with Iris's help, pulled it over Tessa's head.

Iris worked with diligence to fasten the hooks in the back of the dress, not saying a word all the while. She stepped back when finished and pursed her lips. Tessa could scarcely breathe but did not complain.

"Wonderful!" Jacquie clapped, clearly delighted. "It's lovely. And plenty big enough in the waist, which means Iris won't have to pull so tight next time."

From the smirk on the maid's face, Tessa had no doubt she would pull even tighter, if it meant inflicting pain. Not that she blamed the poor girl for being angry. A lady's maid, having to cater to the whims of a lowly farmer's daughter? No doubt the idea met with a sting.

Jacquie clasped her hands together. "Iris, please fetch Peter. He will be delighted."

When Iris left the room, Tessa gazed at her reflection in the mirror, mesmerized by what she saw there. She focused on the gown with its full skirts and colorful beads and counted herself fortunate to wear such a thing of beauty.

Minutes later, Peter entered the room. He took one look at her and gasped. "You shine up like a new penny, Tess. Hardly recognized you."

She pressed her fists onto her hips and stuck out her tongue.

"Ah, *now* I recognize you." He gave her a brotherly squeeze. "A pig farmer's daughter, all done up with bells and whistles, putting on airs."

"I beg to differ." Jacquie fussed with Tessa's hair, twisting it up into a chignon. "Before that ship sails, no one will see Tessa as anything other than a lady."

"Yes, I'm a real lady, I am. But at least my 'airs,' as you call them, don't stink like Countess's stall." Tessa plopped into the wingback chair in a whoosh of pink satin and crinkling petti-coats, the pain around her midsection catching her off guard. Not at all what she was accustomed to. In fact, she had to wonder if she would ever get used to such frippery. She sat up straight, the corset offering no other option.

Peter chuckled. "I daresay, when you enter the ship with so many trunks and hatboxes, you will be perceived as quite the lady."

"So I am to be defined by my possessions, then?" Tessa jutted her chin. "Is that it?"

Jacquie sighed and gave a little shrug. "I'm afraid you must play the role of one who would find that notion to be quite accept-able. Can you do so?"

Tessa paused to think it through. If she could pretend to be a fine lady, she could surely pretend to enjoy fine things.

"Can she do it?" Peter doubled over with laughter. "She's a devil of an actress. You should see the performances she's put on through the years. Always pretending, this one."

"Quite the little Sarah Bernhardt, eh?" Jacquie slipped her arm around Tessa's shoulder. "Well, she has made a career of it. Perhaps you can too. Once you land in New York, I mean. I under-stand they have wonderful theaters there."

Tessa didn't have a clue who Sarah Bernhardt was but didn't say so. Instead, as Peter had a good laugh at her expense, she and Jacquie went into the other room to change into a simpler every-day dress, one made of the prettiest blue-and-white cotton. It felt like heaven against her skin. As she lifted the dress to adjust the petticoat, she noticed Jacquie glancing over at her scabbed knees. Tessa quickly pulled the dress down and sat on the edge of the bed.

"Do you mind if I ask—?" Jacquie paused then bit her lip, her gaze shifting once again to Tessa's legs. "Have you been injured?"

On the outside? No.

"I..." Tessa shook her head, unable to speak. She tugged at her skirt, making sure her knees were properly covered. A girl like Jacquie would never understand. Still, from the look of concern on her face, she wasn't likely to let the conversation fizzle out, so Tessa released a lingering breath and tried her best to explain. "When Pa's angry..."

Jacquie shook her head. "He what?"

"It only happens when he's been drinking." Tessa's words grew more passionate. "He makes me repent for my wickedness."

"Your wickedness?"

"That's what he calls it, anyway." She forged ahead with the story. "When my work on the farm is shoddy, or when he's upset, he makes me repent."

"And what has this to do with your knees?"

Tessa bit her lip, unsure if she should continue. Still, the barrel had been opened, had it not? She might as well pour from it. "Off to the side of the pig stall, there's a rocky path. Sharp. Deep." She shuddered. "When Pa is soused, when he's good and worked up about something I've done wrong, he makes me kneel on the broken bits until I've prayed through my sins and offered full repentance. He calls 'em my rock prayers. There are times when he weighs me down with bags of feed on each shoulder to add to the burden. I've carried more than my share of burdens over the years, and my knees have taken the brunt of it, I'm afraid."

Vivid memories of Pa's hand pressed against her back arose. She pinched her eyes shut to close out the many times he had shoved her down until she had fully repented for being such a disappointment to him. Bile rose in her throat as she relived the latest prayer session.

Jacquie gripped her hand. "Oh, Tessa. I am so sorry. You have endured so much."

A lump rose in Tessa's throat, but she managed to speak over it. "Peter has saved me more than once from Pa's wrath. But now that Peter is gone…" Her lashes grew damp, and she swiped at them with the back of her calloused hand. Just as quickly, she hid her hands behind her back. Would she always feel such shame? With Pa, and now with this girl?

"You poor thing. Say no more." Jacquie's eyes brimmed with tears. "I can promise you one thing. You will never again offer up rock prayers. The only prayers you'll need to pray are the ones for a safe voyage to a new life, one where men like your father don't exist and prayers are answered with happily-ever-afters."

Jacquie slipped her arms around Tessa and pulled her into a sisterly hug. For the first time in her life, Tessa released the tears. She wept—not just for the pain Pa had inflicted, but for the pain she felt every time she thought about boarding that ship and leaving her brother behind.

Still, she would do it. Out of love, she would do it.

Chapter Seven

Saturday, April 6, 1912
Savoy Hotel, London, England

On the Saturday before the *Titanic* sailed, Nathan Patterson found himself eager to head back to New York. Once he boarded the ship, his thoughts could transition fully to the work awaiting him back home at his father's insurance company. In the meantime, Nathan sat across the dining table from his mother at the Savoy in Westminster, listening to her ramble on about the various stores she had visited during their stay in London. He gave an occasional nod but couldn't keep up. Not that any of it held his interest anyway.

Mother chattered on about the many people she hoped to meet once they boarded the *Titanic*. He pretended to listen, but his thoughts shifted back to his upcoming job with his father. The insurance business captivated his thoughts more often than not lately. Perhaps it had something to do with his desire to care for those less fortunate and tend to folks in their time of need. Wasn't that the biblical mandate, after all—to defend the defenseless? And working with his father held great appeal. Never had he known a kinder man or one who so exemplified Christlikeness in all he did.

"Nathan, what do you think of that?" Mother's voice hinted of displeasure.

"Hmm?" He glanced up from his cup of lukewarm tea into her narrowed eyes. "Think of what?"

"I had a feeling you weren't paying attention." She almost lost her hold on the slice of beef dangling from the prongs of her fork but managed to catch it just in time and pop it into her mouth. Then she placed her fork on the table and dabbed at her lips with a lace-trimmed napkin. "I asked what you thought about going to the opera tonight. With only four days until we sail, I want to take advantage of every opportunity to get out among people. Once we arrive back in New York, I'll be shut up in that musty old house without a chance to socialize. It vexes me to think about it."

"You will hardly be shut up away from society." He chuckled. "You'll have Margaret Hinkle over for tea the day we get back, and the two of you will schedule a canasta game with the other ladies within the week. From there, you will plan a tea party, and after that you will throw some sort of soiree to welcome one dignitary or another into the fold."

"True." She sighed. "But back home I'm surrounded on every side by friends I don't really care for. Spending time with them isn't the same as going to the opera in London. And when will we ever get back to England? Besides, it will be a family affair tonight. James has asked us to accompany him. He paid a pretty penny for the tickets, too, snagging us seats on the third row. Can you believe it?"

Nathan put his cup down on its matching saucer and released a slow breath. "Really, Mother? Isn't it enough that we have to see James Carson so often at home? Must we really visit with him in London too?"

"I thought you would be thrilled at this news." Mother's smile faded and her cheeks flamed pink. "James is the best sort of family friend. And he's been so kind to us over the years."

"Too kind." How could Nathan speak his mind without hurting Mother's feelings? James Carson was a thoughtful, caring man, but presumptuous at best. Why he felt the need to turn up at every social function, Nathan could not be sure. If Mother didn't watch her step, the gossips would have their way with her story, making far too much of her relationship with the man.

Mother's brow wrinkled and she pouted. "Well, I, for one, want to see the London Opera House's production of *La Bohème* this evening. The paper gave it rave reviews. Won't you consider coming with us?"

Us? Nathan shook his head. "Are you saying that you will go with James even if I choose not to?" Surely not. Even Mother had enough common sense to know better than that. He hoped.

She dabbed at her lips with a napkin. "The man is like an uncle to you, for heaven's sake. And he's your father's dearest friend. Surely no one will question the fact that we're spending a civil evening together—in a public setting, no less." Her cheeks flushed. "Honestly, I can't believe you're making such a fuss. I just want one last night on the town before our ship sails. Now please tuck your stubbornness into your pocket and come with us. Let's celebrate our time together."

"Fine." He spoke the word, but it sounded false in light of how he felt. Something about this situation with his mother soured his thoughts and gave him cause to wonder. Still, he said nothing, only responding with a forced smile and nod. Though he cared little about what happened on the stage, he would go to the opera house, if for no other reason than to keep an eye on things in the third row.

* * * * *

Tessa paced the front room of the tiny cottage where she'd spent the past week. Except for the occasional visit from Jacquie or Iris, she'd felt like a prisoner in the castle tower. In her quiet times she found herself aching for the farm, for the familiar routine of chasing Countess around the stall or cradling the baby piglets against her cheek. Strange, that she would swap the opportunity of a lifetime for a feisty porker and her babes, but at times the idea held appeal—and never more so than during etiquette lessons.

"Try it again, Tessa." Jacquie pointed to the delicate china place setting in front of her.

Tessa shook off her ponderings and took a seat at the table. She stared at the plate and the various pieces of silverware surrounding it, finding herself more confused than ever as she looked at the spoon and knives on the right and the forks in their varying sizes on the left. She examined the butter-pat server with its delicate knife, and then her gaze shifted to the fruit fork. Ready to give up, she glanced over at Jacquie and sighed. "I just don't think I can do this. I can never get it right."

"Now, please don't fret, Tessa," Jacquie said. "Chances are quite good that the other guests will be distracted with their chatter and won't even notice that you're confused. Just watch the ladies and do what they do."

"If I spend the whole meal watching them, I won't eat a bite." Tessa reached down and grabbed the roll from the table then yanked off a piece. Stuffing it into her mouth, she attempted to speak around it. "I'll starve."

"No, you won't. You'll do just fine, trust me." Jacquie spoke the words with sureness, but the worry lines on her forehead told a different story. "Now, if you've been invited to afternoon tea, offer to serve the others. It will put you in their good graces and show that you are comfortable as hostess."

"But I'm not comfortable as hostess," Tessa huffed. She struggled with the desire to pick up all the forks and hurl them across the room. Instead, she silently counted to three then turned her gaze to her mentor. "I'm not comfortable with any of this. And no matter how many times we go over it, I'm not sure I ever will be. Don't you see? This is all so pointless."

"Don't be silly. You have come leaps and bounds over the past ten days. I'm very proud of you. And your diction is coming along nicely too." Jacquie beamed, clearly proud of herself for being such a great tutor. "But if you're truly uncomfortable with serving, just choose to take your tea in your room while onboard the ship. Feign a headache. That's what Mama does when she's uncomfortable in a social setting. It works every time."

"I wouldn't have to pretend to have a headache." Tessa rolled her eyes.

This got a laugh out of Jacquie, who returned to the lesson on table manners. As soon as they finished their tea, she turned her attention to discussing the latest fashions. Tessa took notes as Jacquie spoke but couldn't make sense out of much of it. Who cared if charmeuse silk was in fashion? What did it matter, in the grand scheme of things? And why would she consider entering into a conversation about plumed hats, of all things?

"Feathers should be kept on peacocks, where they belong," she muttered.

This got another laugh out of Jacquie, who lit into a conversation about the need for beautifully designed chapeaus. When she shifted the chatter from hats to politics, Tessa groaned and dropped her head into her hands in dramatic fashion. "I truly do have a headache," she said. "This is wearing me out."

The clock chimed four times and Jacquie gasped as she glanced at it. "Is it really four o'clock?"

"Yes." *And we've been sitting here since two o'clock, going over and over the same things we've discussed for ten days.*

Jacquie pushed the chair back and stood. "I have to go. Mother will be worried."

Fear coursed through Tessa. "You don't think she'll come looking for you, do you?"

"No." Jacquie shook her head. "She thinks I'm with my best friend, having tea." She offered a smile and reached out to take Tessa by the hand. "Then again, I am having tea with a dear friend. You've become like a sister to me, Tessa. I'm truly going to miss you when you're gone. I really mean that."

"And I you." A lump rose in Tessa's throat. She would miss Jacquie. A little. But she would miss Peter even more. And Countess, of course.

Jacquie scurried toward the door. "I wish we had more time together, but I have to get back now. We're going out tonight— to the opera."

Tessa tried to imagine what that would be like. Perhaps it would be a bit like the novels she read in secret, a fanciful world where problems did not exist.

"I'll tell you all about it tomorrow." Jacquie's nose wrinkled. "I hope I'm not bored to tears sitting next to Roland. At least he got good seats. We're up front near the orchestra, so close that I can see the performers without binoculars." A sigh followed. "I love *La Bohème*. It's a heart-wrenching love story, one filled with delights of every kind." Her smile faded as quickly as it had arisen. "But

QUEEN OF THE WAVES

such a tragic ending. Poor Mimi dies before she experiences all that love has to offer." Jacquie released a little sigh then waved her good-byes and disappeared out the door.

Left alone in the little cottage, Tessa thought about the opera house and wondered what it might be like to go to such a grand place. To hear the orchestra play, their majestic harmonies filling the air. To see the costumes in all their glorious, vibrant colors. To hear the tremor of the singers' voices as they shared their woeful tales.

Oh well. Right now she had a greater drama to play out. This one involved a very real heroine setting out on an adventure across the seas. Tessa only prayed the ending of her story was not as tragic as the one in *La Bohème*. Dying before one had a chance to experience love was highly overrated, after all.

* * * * *

As Jacquie ran along the cobblestone path toward the manor, her thoughts tumbled madly. She spent a moment or two fretting over Tessa and whispered up a prayer that all would go well once the young woman boarded the ship.

Not that the Almighty was in the business of helping people deceive others, but perhaps He would make an exception in this case. Surely the Lord cared deeply that she and Peter were so desperately in love. Wasn't he the Author of love, after all? Of course. The reverend had said as much in his sermon just last Sunday. If the Lord instigated love, surely He would approve of going to such lengths to make it possible. She hoped.

Jacquie ran across the little bridge, over the creek, and through the maze of beautifully sculpted bushes. When she arrived at the house, she paused to catch her breath. No point in making Mother worry about what she had been up to.

Finally convinced that she had control of herself, Jacquie fussed with her hair and then entered the house. Iris met her in the foyer and pursed her lips then whispered, "She's looking for you."

"I guessed as much. I will tell her that I got held up at Melinda's house."

"You'd better go up now."

Jacquie climbed the stairs, holding tightly to the polished railing as she tried to steady her breathing. Along the way, she contemplated the letter she still needed to write to Grandmother, the one Tessa would carry with her aboard *Titanic*. Coming up with just the right words would be critical. Surely Gran would not put Tessa out on the street—would she? Jacquie pushed aside her concerns as she crafted the letter in her head. Tonight she would pen it, her words carefully chosen. Until then, she must remain focused.

Seconds later she rapped on the door of the master suite, and her mother's "Come in" rang out. Forcing a smile, Jacquie entered the room with shoulders squared and smile in place.

"There you are." Her mother took several quick steps in her direction. "It's after four. We have to leave at five thirty."

"Yes, I'm sorry. Melinda and I were caught up in a lovely chat. I'm going to miss her so much when I leave."

The look in her mother's eyes spoke of suspicion. "I have a feeling you were not with Melinda at all."

"O–oh?"

"You've been slipping away to spend time with Peter, haven't you?"

A wave of relief washed over Jacquie. "Mother, I can assure you, I was not with Peter." *Not this time, anyway.*

"Well, good." A smile turned up the edges of Mother's lips. "I was afraid you were still pining for him, and that troubled me. I would hate to see you hurt in any way." She gave Jacquie's hand a squeeze. "Let me remind you that you are young. There are many wonderful young men out there."

"That's true." *And most are horrible bores.*

Mama winked. "Who knows? You might meet one on the ship. More likely, in New York, once you settle in with your grandmother." Her eyes sparkled with obvious delight. "Perhaps this whole lovely journey is part of some larger adventure to bring about your happiness."

Jacquie couldn't have put it any better herself. Still, she knew better than to say so. "I will keep my eyes open for the ideal candidate," she managed and then smiled, knowing that none fit the bill any better than the young man who kissed away her concerns every day when no one else was looking. He alone held the answers to any problems life might bring, and she would spend her life making him happy.

Mama's lashes grew damp. "Keep your eyes open for someone who can give you the world, sweet girl. You deserve it."

A rush of guilt swept over Jacquie at her mother's proclamation. She did not deserve it, and yet she longed for it above all else.

"And in the meantime, I suppose we will have to be agreeable with Mr. Palmer tonight. But look on the bright side, dear. This could very well be the last time you have to put up with him."

A strange twinge caught Jacquie off guard. "I don't find him disagreeable, only dull. But this evening will give me ample opportunity to appear publicly with him before I leave."

"I can hardly believe our plan is all going so smoothly."

Jacquie's mother chuckled. "I feel as if we've pulled off a bank heist. Such a covert operation, this. And to think, you even got a new wardrobe out of it." Her smile faded. "But it's the strangest thing. I'd hoped you could wear the new pink satin this evening, and it's turned up missing."

"Oh." Jacquie fought to come up with a reason. "I asked Iris to take it back to Mrs. O'Shea to be taken in at the waist. With all that's going on, I've dropped a few pounds."

"Lovely dilemma." Her mother smiled. "One's waist can never be too small."

"Yes." Jacquie found herself in need of a change in the conversation. "Speaking of my wardrobe, did you manage to convince Father about going to Paris on the morning of the tenth?"

"Yes, he doesn't suspect a thing, thank goodness. He even advanced me a delightful amount of money to purchase specialty items for your trousseau while we're there. For all of his flaws, your father is a very generous man."

Jacquie hated to comment, in part because she had never really focused on her father's flaws and didn't care to do so now. A wave of guilt passed over her as she thought about how she had deceived her father to get those new gowns, gowns she would never get to wear. Her guilt was magnified as she pondered the fact that Mama would eventually catch her in her game, as well. What would happen once her parents realized she had run off to marry Peter? Nausea gripped her suddenly, and she wondered if, perhaps, she could actually go through with this. The whole thing seemed strangely impossible at the moment. How complicated and twisted this had all become.

"Are you unwell, Jacquie? You look a bit pale."

She glanced into her mother's concerned eyes and swallowed hard. "Oh. Yes, I, um…"

"You're going to miss me, aren't you, baby girl?" Mama swept her into her arms and gave her a kiss on the forehead. "It's breaking my heart too. You're not even gone yet and I miss you already."

"Miss her already?" Father's voice rang out from behind them and Jacquie flinched. How long had he been standing there?

Mama's grasp loosened and they both turned to face him.

"Jacquie, don't fret. The Willingham estate is just a few miles away. You can come back to visit your mother any time you like after you and Roland are married."

Pain shot through her chest as she pondered the fact that she could not come to visit Mama whenever she liked. Once she and Peter ran off to get married, there would be no coming and going from Abingdon Manor. No, once the deed was done, the parents she'd known and loved would embrace her no more.

Oh, how she hoped it would all be worth it.

* * * * *

Nathan settled into his seat at the theater, his gaze shifting from the stage to the balconies and then to the people alongside them. His breath caught in his throat when he noticed a beautiful young woman about his same age just a few seats down. Her exquisite blue dress brought out the color in her sapphire eyes, which held him spellbound. She caught his gaze and offered a nod then turned her attentions to the gentleman next to her. Nathan felt his cheeks grow warm as he turned to face the closed curtains at the front of the stage.

As the orchestra tuned their instruments, the house lights flickered, signaling audience members to take their seats. Clearly oblivious, his mother lit into a conversation with James, who, to Nathan's way of thinking, paid her far too much attention.

Mother rambled about the beautiful theater, speaking at length above the din of the instruments. "This is the loveliest opera house I've ever seen." A giggle followed. "But I'm sure the ship will be equally as nice. I hear the first-class quarters are beyond all sense of expectation. I can hardly wait to see them firsthand."

To their right, a fellow in a formal black tailcoat jacket turned to face them with a smile as he took his seat. "Are you, perchance, speaking of the *Titanic*, madam?"

"I am." Mother clasped her hands together. "We're traveling out of Southampton on the tenth. Will you be boarding, as well?"

"No, I'm afraid not." The fellow shook his head. "I hail from New York, but my business, at least for now, is here. In England." A smile followed as he gestured to the beautiful woman with the mesmerizing eyes. "This lovely lady has agreed to be my bride. I'm the luckiest man in all of London. Our impending marriage offers me all the enticement I need to stay on awhile in England."

The young woman offered a faint smile, and her eyelashes fluttered.

"Well then! Congratulations are in order." Mama's voice rang out a bit too loud as the tuning of the instruments winded down.

The gentleman's smile spoke of true happiness. "I am a blessed man, to be sure. She has won my heart. So, where she stays, I will stay. And for now, that's in London."

Mama didn't seem content with this answer. She sat on the edge of her chair, now speaking with her hands. "Oh, you should really consider marrying right away and honeymooning onboard the *Titanic*. Now wouldn't that be the best way to start off your life together?" She began a lengthy conversation about the possibilities, offering advice far too intrusive to be considered helpful. Nathan cringed and wished she would stop.

"Perhaps." The man turned to give his bride-to-be a smile when Mother finally paused for breath. "But I daresay, even my beautiful bride-to-be could never manage a wedding that fast."

"True." Mother fussed with her gloves, finally pulling them off and handing them to James, who seemed at a loss to know what to do with them. "These things take time, I suppose." Off she went on another tangent, sharing about how much time and effort went into the planning of her own wedding.

Nathan couldn't help but smile as he watched the man slip his arms over his fiancée's shoulders. Clearly, the fellow was smitten. The sparkle in his eyes spoke as much. The same could not be said about the young woman seated beside him, perhaps. Her expression could only be described as pained. And was it Nathan's imagination, or had she flinched when Mother mentioned the *Titanic*? Very odd. She must have some sort of aversion to sea travel. Or maybe all of that chatter about marrying quickly had given her cause to fret. Regardless, she looked a bit unsettled.

Not that he had time to ponder the issue much longer. The orchestra bellowed out the first notes of the prelude, and Nathan settled back in his chair, anxious to get this performance behind him so that he could focus on what really mattered—his trip home.

Chapter Eight

On the morning of April 10, Tessa rose from the bed after a near-sleepless night. She'd spent several hours with her stomach tied up in knots. Now, with the budding of a new day, she found herself questioning her decision to leave. Should she board the ship or turn back to her former life? Neither made sense right now, but the moment had come to take a step in one direction or the other. If she stayed in England, Peter's life would change forever. If she took Jacquie's place on the *Titanic*, hers would.

She threw herself onto the bed once again, ushering fitful prayers heavenward. If what Pa said was true, God punished reprobates by returning evil for evil. The very act of boarding the ship in Jacquie's place qualified Tessa as a reprobate, a sinner of the highest degree. The Lord would surely smite her. He would bring catastrophe upon her life, no doubt. But if she chose not to go, her brother's chances for happiness would be dashed forever. Surely the Lord understood that, didn't He? She spent several minutes pleading with Him, hoping to find the peace she needed to board the ship.

Or not to board the ship.

Lord, show me what to do. Please.

Peter arrived at the cottage a few minutes after seven, looking pale and drawn. He found her in a puddle of tears. In true brotherly fashion he pulled her into a warm embrace, and she let the tears flow. "Tessa, listen to me." The tremor in his voice gave away his emotion. "You don't have to go through with this for my sake." With the tip of his finger he lifted her chin. "I want you to know that."

"W–what?" She gazed up at him, surprised. Was this the answer she had prayed for, perhaps?

"I mean it." He reached to grip her hand. "I want you to know—I need you to know—that I would never have suggested all this in the first place if I didn't think it was the best possible opportunity for you. Do you understand what I'm saying?"

"I—I think so."

"This isn't about me. It's about you." He paused, and she noticed the trembling in his hands. "I've been thinking of you all along. All of this has been for you. Every decision. Every plan. All of it."

His pensive gaze left her more than a little confused. "Peter, what are you saying? What about Jacquie?"

He rose and raked his fingers through his hair. "I care a great deal about her, of course. And I wouldn't do anything to deliberately hurt her. It's not in my heart to do so."

"I—I see."

"But Tessa, you must know this—since I left home last year I've thought of little else but you," he said. "Every day I've prayed for your safety. When I think about Pa and how he treats you..." Peter shook his head, his jaw growing tense. "I had to find a way to get you out from under his thumb and into a better life. This is my attempt to do that."

She tried to absorb the true meaning behind his words, to

make sense out of what he *wasn't* saying. "What will you do when I'm gone? Will you go through with the marriage as you've planned?"

He paced the room, finally coming to a stop in front of her. "I am a man of my word. And I feel sure we can make this work for all of us. I do have feelings for her. She will make a wonderful wife. Truly, one I don't deserve. I will earn her respect, I promise, and I have no doubt my feelings will grow with time. So, go to New York, Tessa. If you're brave enough to start over, I mean. But don't do it because of me. Do it in spite of me. Do it for yourself. If anyone deserves a fresh start, it's you."

"Oh, Peter." Her heart flooded with love for him like she'd never known. She flung her arms around his neck, overwhelmed with gratitude.

"Give yourself the life you deserve," he said. "The one free from ogres like Pa. Go and find happiness like you've never known before. Do it for me."

She nodded, resolve now building. She would board the *Titanic*. Not so that her brother could have a better life...but so that she could.

* * * * *

Jacquie folded the note to her grandmother and slipped it into an envelope. She pressed it into her coat pocket then looked around her bedroom, overwhelmed with childhood memories. Today she would walk away from those memories, away from the safety and comfort of home. She would trade all of that for love. And though it pained her to think of leaving her parents behind, the life ahead of her would be worth every loss.

She prayed.

Or, rather, she didn't pray. In fact, she hadn't truly asked the Lord's opinion on any of this, for fear He might actually give it. No, in cases such as these, one simply followed after one's heart and hoped for the best possible outcome. Surely Father would forgive her in time. And Mother too, once she realized that Jacquie had betrayed her by not staying onboard the *Titanic*.

Betrayed her. Those words hung heavy in her heart.

"Jacquie, are you ready?" Mama's voice sounded behind her.

Jacquie glanced her way and forced a smile. "Yes, Mother. I'm ready."

"Your father is waiting downstairs in the foyer with Iris. Her bags are already loaded into the automobile." Mother reached for her gloves. "Your father wanted to come with us to the train station. I had a doozy of a time convincing him to let us go alone. Made up a story about how it would be easier to say our good-byes privately rather than publicly." She shook her head. "But I couldn't very well let him tag along, especially since we're not really going anywhere near the train station. At least, not this morning."

"I'm so glad you managed to talk him out of it."

"It took some doing." Mother sat on the edge of the bed. "I don't know about you, but I'm feeling a bit queasy."

"Deception will do that to you, I suppose." Jacquie shrugged, feeling a bit nauseous as well. "But in the end, all will be well."

"I do hope so." Mother pulled on her gloves and adjusted the fingers. "To be honest, I do feel a little bad about the fact that your father actually purchased train tickets for us, but what else could we do?"

"Well, look on the bright side, Mother. You and Cousin Minerva will have a fine time in Paris."

"True. She will make a wonderful shopping partner."

"True. Minerva has always been one for shopping. And the four days you spend in Paris will buy us both the necessary time we need to make this work. You're going to need time to work up the courage to tell Father where I've really gone." *Or, rather, where you think I've gone.*

"I've always loved April in Paris." Her mother's expression brightened. "And Minerva always brings me such comfort."

"That's what you need right now, Mother. Someone to bring you comfort."

"Indeed, I do." Mama's eyes brimmed with tears. "You're so right."

From downstairs, Father's voice rang out. "Ladies, are you coming? I need to leave for the office soon."

Jacquie looked at her mother and sighed as she realized the moment had come at last. "I do hope my acting skills are up to par."

"Mine as well."

Jacquie walked down the stairs on Mama's heels. The moment she laid eyes on her father, a lump rose in her throat, one she could scarcely speak above. In that moment she doubted everything— her plan to run away with Peter, her scheme to betray Mama's confidence—all of it. And as her father wrapped her in his arms and whispered words of love over her, she wondered if she would ever experience his fatherly embrace again. Not likely, after he discovered that she had betrayed him.

"I—I love you, Father."

"Well, I love you too, sweet girl." Father touched the end of her nose with his index finger and grinned. "I've always got your best interests at heart. So go on to Paris and buy whatever you need.

But come back to see me soon. This big old house won't be the same without the two of you in it." He extended a hand to Jacquie's mother and she took it, her cheeks flushed. Then he turned his attention to Iris, who stood near the door. "You will be missed as well, Iris. I hope you have a wonderful time. Jacquie tells me you are interested in fashion, so you should find Paris fascinating."

"Yes, sir. And, thank you." Her lashes grew damp and she swiped them away with the back of her hand.

"No need to get emotional, ladies." Father chuckled. "It's just a matter of days until we are together again."

"True." Mother looked his way and smiled. "I've no doubt you have plenty to keep you busy while we are away."

"Yes, and Roland will be here often as we discuss the merger." Father ran his fingers over his graying mustache and then smiled. "I've found him to be such an agreeable man. This new merger will serve us all well, I believe."

Jacquie's heart sailed to her throat as she thought about Roland. Over the past few weeks she had given plenty of thought to Mother's reaction. And Father's, of course. But she'd scarcely pondered Roland's loss at all. Hopefully the man wouldn't be too devastated.

They made their way outside and the chauffeur loaded Jacquie's trunk, the one filled with her fine, new things. He also loaded Mother's smaller bag, which she would carry on to Paris after leaving Southampton tomorrow morning.

Father shook his head as he offered the chauffer a hand. "It never ceases to amaze me how much luggage a woman carries with her. You would think you three ladies were going to be in Paris for months, not a few measly days." His chuckle shared his thoughts on the matter.

"Oh, Father." Jacquie tried to dismiss his concerns with a wave of a hand, but the trembling nearly gave away her nerves. "You know how we are."

"Indeed I do." He offered her a fatherly wink.

The chauffer opened the back door of the car, and Iris climbed inside as Mother clucked her tongue.

"Henry, shame on you. A lady has to look her best, especially in Paris. You know that. You wouldn't want us to turn up looking like social outcasts. Of course not. We will not bring shame to the Abingdon name."

"As if either of you could possibly bring shame to my name." He pulled Jacquie into his arms and gave her a tender kiss on the cheek. "I will miss you while you're gone. Bring me one of those silly little Eiffel tower statuettes, will you?"

Jacquie forced a laugh, but the sting of tears nearly stopped her. "I—I will." Not that she was going anywhere near Paris, but perhaps Mother would buy one for him. Hopefully.

Surely one day Father would forgive her for all this. Mother would too. And Grandmother. She hoped. In the meantime, forging ahead was the only answer. Jacquie's gaze darted to the gardens and beyond. She wondered what was happening in the cottage. Were Tessa and Peter already on their way to the dock as planned? Had the driver kept his word to remain silent? Would Tessa meet her at the gate at precisely 11:45 to trade places?"

With so many things rolling through her brain, she almost didn't notice the familiar Rolls-Royce until it came to a stop behind them.

Roland emerged from the vehicle dressed in a dark gray business suit and looking quite dapper. He took several quick steps her way, and her heart fluttered into her throat.

"Roland? What are you doing here?"

"I'm sorry, my dear." He grinned as he reached for her hand, which he gripped with fervor. "I know you're only going to be gone a few days, but I had to stop by to say good-bye. I'm going to miss you." He pressed a tiny kiss onto her cheek.

"Oh?" Heat rushed over her face. "I—I will miss you too."

"Well, here's a little something to remember me by." He reached into his pocket and came out with a tiny box, which he opened.

"Oh, Roland!" The brilliant opal ring simply took her breath away. Exquisite diamonds framed the lovely stone. They caught the morning sunlight, radiating sparkle and shine.

Roland's deep brown eyes shimmered with equal brightness as he held tight to the beautiful ring. "I should have given you this weeks ago when you agreed to be my bride. Will you forgive me for the delay? I ordered it from the jewelers ages ago, but it had to be shipped all the way from Australia."

"Australia? Oh my."

He slipped it onto her finger and then held up her hand to have a closer look. "Now every time you look at this, you can think of me and look forward to our union."

"I—I will." A lump rose in her throat as she fingered the exquisite ring. How he had managed such a perfect fit, she could not say. Still, the ring felt as comfortable on her hand as if it had always been there. And to think, he had ordered it ages ago.

"Could I have something of yours to keep while you're in Paris?" Roland asked.

"Something of mine?" She opened her reticule and searched inside, finally coming out with an embroidered handkerchief. "Will this do?"

"Yes." He drew it to his face, a contented look in his eyes. "It smells of your perfume, so I will feel like you're still with me even though we're apart."

"Well, she won't be gone long, you know." Mother took her seat in the cab and gestured for Jacquie to join her. "But we really must be on our way, gentlemen. The train to Paris awaits."

"Don't let me keep you, then." Roland kissed the back of Jacquie's hand then gazed into her eyes. "There's nothing I would deny you, sweet girl. If you ask me for the world, I will do my best to give it to you."

"Th–thank you, Roland." She climbed into the cab, took the seat next to Iris, and leaned her throbbing head back as the driver closed the door. For a moment she thought she might be ill. Closing her eyes, she fought the feeling with every fiber of her being.

By the time her eyes opened, the cab was moving down the lane, away from Abingdon Manor—and away from everything she had ever held dear.

* * * * *

Nathan did his best to help the bellman with his mother's trunks, but they were ridiculously heavy after her latest shopping spree. Hopefully her many purchases wouldn't weigh down the ship. If so, they were all in trouble. He chuckled just thinking about the potential for disaster.

Mother scurried around the lobby of the Savoy, fussing at Nathan the whole way. "We need to hurry, my dear. First-class passengers will start boarding in two hours, and it takes nearly that long to get to Southampton from here."

From around the corner of the hotel lobby, James Carson

appeared with his luggage. Nathan looked back and forth between Mother and the pesky fellow.

"Are you leaving today too, James?" Nathan asked.

"Well, of course. Thanks to the coal strike, my ticket to board the *Lusitania* was switched to the *Titanic*." He offered a smile. "So it looks as if we will all be traveling together. A happy problem, at least from my perspective. I do hope you both agree."

"Well, isn't that wonderful." Mother clasped her gloved hands together in apparent glee. "A lady always feels more at ease when traveling with a gentleman she trusts."

Nathan bit his tongue as he looked away from the unlikely pair. Two things bothered him about his mother's statement. One, she had acknowledged both her desire and her need for James Carson to travel alongside them. Two, she clearly didn't see her own son as a grown man. If she did, she would surely realize that she was already traveling with a gentleman and did not require an additional one at her side.

Strange. The only person who appeared to be ill at ease this morning was Nathan. He prayed the feeling would pass before he boarded the ship for home.

Chapter Nine

Wednesday Morning, April 10, 1912
Southampton, England, near the White Star Line Dock

At exactly ten o'clock in the morning, Jacquie peered through the limousine window at the crowd in Southampton. Hundreds of people swarmed around them, much like mosquitoes coming in for the kill. Many moved at a frenzied pace; still others milled about, curious onlookers.

"I never expected such a frenzy." Mother's eyes widened as she glanced about.

"Nor I. Have you ever seen so many people clustered into one space?" Jacquie gazed at the scene with wonder. Truly, one could scarcely imagine so many people converging upon a town in such numbers as had gathered in Southampton to see the illustrious ship cast off to sea. And what a vast array of people, at that! They came on bicycles and in cars. In carriages and on foot. Folks in every sort of garb—traveling clothes, uniforms, and more. She pressed her nose against the window to have a closer look.

To her right, Jacquie saw a woman in a fur stole and a feather-plumed hat. Next to her, a younger woman in a high-collared green dress. Many of the others wore black or gray traveling coats, but several turned up in their spring finest in spite of an undeniable nip in the air. Likely they cared more about impressing onlookers than the weather.

To Jacquie's left, Iris laughed. "Oh my!" She pointed down the street. "See that double-decker horse-drawn carriage? I've never seen such a thing."

Jacquie caught a glimpse of it through the crowd, her gaze landing on the COL. MUSTARD advertisement on the side. Several of the people aboard the top of the vehicle dangled over the sides, waving at the people below. A couple of the bawdy fellows danced about atop the moving vehicle as if they hadn't a care in the world. Ladies in everyday dress watched and clapped their approval.

Jacquie watched as a young woman not much older than herself tumbled and fell into a laughing fellow's open arms. "Gracious." She shook her head. "I do hope those people riding on top are safe up there."

"They have a better view of the ship, to be sure." Mother fussed with her handkerchief, twisting it in her hands. "And they appear to be having a glorious time."

"Oh, no doubt." Iris laughed again. "What a day this is. It will go down in the record books, I daresay." She cracked her window and leaned out. "Oh, do you hear that? Music. Reminds me of home."

Off in the distance a drum corps played as flags waved in the early morning breeze. People in traveling clothes milled about, all headed to the White Star Line Dock still several blocks away.

As their automobile rounded a turn in the road, Jacquie gasped. She had tried to imagine what the *Titanic* would look like, but nothing in her imagination had come close to the sight of the majestic vessel that rested upon the water. Indeed, *majestic* didn't seem an effective word. The gigantic ship loomed in splendor, a true marvel to shipbuilding and proof positive that the British knew how to outshine their competitors. Standing several decks tall, *Titanic*'s four smokestacks stretched to the clouds above, beacons to all who would gaze upon her.

"Oh, Mother." Jacquie released a slow breath and tried to take it in. To her right, Iris's eyes widened. The view had apparently rendered her speechless. Her lips moved, but nothing came out.

"Oh my goodness!" Iris said at last as she pressed her nose against the window. "Look at her! Was there ever a ship more worthy of the sea?"

"Absolutely not." Jacquie could scarcely catch her breath as she took it in.

"Have you ever seen anything of such proportion?" Mother's eyes widened. "Why, she dwarfs everything else in sight."

The limousine eased its way toward the White Star Line Dock and the throng of people increasing every inch of the way. Wellwishers waved their good-byes to those boarding, many with tears but most with shouts of exuberance. Some of the gentlemen—if one could call them that—waved their hats at those on deck. The passengers, a happy lot, waved back and shouted a few cheers of their own.

"Well, there you have it, ladies," the driver said, his words laced with pride. "The RMS *Titanic*, a symbol of the British Empire at her finest."

"Indeed." Jacquie shook her head, trying to take it all in.

"The biggest, fastest, and most reliable vessel on the Atlantic, sure to put our German competitors out of business in a hurry." He chuckled. "Who wants to travel aboard the *Lusitania* when you can board a ship such as this?"

"Not me." Iris giggled. "Oh, I can hardly wait to climb aboard."

The chauffer brought the vehicle to a stop at the corner near a sign pointing toward the White Star Line Dock. "Not sure how close I can get, ma'am."

At that moment, a fellow who looked to be a bum leaned over and pressed his face against the glass window, startling them all. Mother let out a gasp. "The nerve."

"Don't mind him, ma'am," the driver said. "Just excited, I imagine."

"Still…" Mother fanned herself.

As she took another look at the monstrous ship, Jacquie's heart quickened. The next hour or so would change her life forever. If things went as planned.

Her thoughts gravitated to Peter and Tessa. She whispered up a frantic—albeit silent—prayer that they would arrive in time. The cab could very well be here already, hidden away amongst the thousands. Hopefully Tessa and Peter would arrive at the appropriate time. Now, to board the ship and somehow talk Mama into shooing quickly.

Another wave of guilt washed over her afresh as she turned and saw the tears in her mother's eyes.

"Oh, don't mind me." Mama waved her hand and smiled. "I'm just a silly old fool. I'm going to miss you, Jacquie. I feel as if a piece of my heart is boarding that ship." She leaned forward to whisper the rest, so that even Iris couldn't hear. "Promise me you will live your life, daughter. Have the joys and the adventures that I only dreamed of having."

Oh, I will, Mother. Trust me, I will.

She managed a lame nod as the chauffer opened their door. Then she climbed out of the vehicle.

The sound of a thousand voices raised in conversation and songs rang out along the dock. A woman passed by wearing a fox stole over an exquisite purple dress, an expensive silk number with a shiny overlay. Her hat—many times larger than fashion dictated—made a fine nesting place for a trio of silk swallows. They seemed quite at home.

The woman carried a fuzzy dog in her arms, and she tended to him as a mother would a small child. As she passed by, she bumped into Jacquie, and the little canine let out a growl. The woman attempted to comfort him in baby talk, which only resulted in a yappy barking spree. After glaring at Jacquie, she headed off in the opposite direction, muttering something under her breath.

"You don't suppose they're taking dogs aboard the ship, do you?" Iris wrinkled her nose. "Nasty creatures."

A couple of intoxicated fellows ambled by, their voices raised in inebriated song as they headed ship-ward.

"I daresay the ship will be filled with all sorts of animals." Mama pinched her eyes shut and then back open again. "You girls must promise me that you will be on the lookout at all times for your safety. No lollygagging about, and no talking to strange men."

Jacquie nodded. "I assure you, Mother, I will not speak to strangers on the ship." Easy enough to promise, since she didn't plan on staying aboard.

"I know a surefire way to keep the fellows away." Iris giggled. "Wear your hair down, Miss Jacquie."

"Wear my hair down?"

"Yes." Iris nodded. "I read the fashion magazines. British young ladies put up their hair to signify that they have reached maturity. A woman with her hair up is offering herself on the marriage market." Iris giggled then clamped a hand over her mouth, her cheeks turning pink.

"Well, for pity's sake." Jacquie's mother glanced at Jacquie's upswept hair and feather-plumed hat. "Wear it down, then. Not right now, of course, but from now on."

"On the other hand, I also read that a young lady who wears her hair down is sometimes seen as promiscuous," Iris added. "So that might be problematic."

"Oh my." Mother wrinkled her nose then glanced Jacquie's way. "Well, you really can't win for losing, can you? I would say keep the hat on and pull the hair loosely up."

The chauffer led the way to the gangplank and stopped to check with the steward. Then he turned back to Jacquie to share what he'd learned. "You will board via the first-class main entrance, miss. That's on B Deck. After that, you're to go to the purser's office."

"We won't be subject to the medical inspection, will we?" Jacquie asked.

"No, miss. Medical inspection is only necessary for the third-class passengers."

"I can join my daughter until the ship sails, can't I?" Mother asked. "To get her settled?"

"Yes, you may stay aboard until the 'all ashore' is called." He turned to signal a porter. "I will make sure the trunks are loaded onboard while you ladies get situated and then will be waiting for you when you return." He turned his attention to the trunks, and Jacquie forged ahead through the crowd, Mother's arm now tightly linked with hers.

"Which way?" Iris asked from behind them.

A fellow in a White Star Line uniform pointed through the crowd, and Jacquie took tentative steps in that direction. Minutes later, they were met at the first-class entrance by a fellow who introduced himself as Chief Steward Andrew Latimer. The fellow looked pressed and dressed for the task at hand and was surrounded on both sides by his staff. He greeted them with a smile, and a young steward led the way to the purser's office. They wound their way through the mob inside, pausing only to allow a fellow with a camera to snap their photo.

Jacquie handed the purser her boarding pass, and he met her gaze with a welcoming smile. "Welcome about the RMS *Titanic*, miss."

"Thank you." *I won't be staying long.*

"Our British passengers are among the first to board," the purser said. "Most of those traveling from other countries will arrive by boat train."

"Well, I'm relieved to come aboard early then," Jacquie said. "It will give me time to see the ship in all her glory." *For the first and last time.* Her heart grew heavy for a moment, but she pushed those feelings aside and kept going.

The purser looked over her boarding pass and marked several notes in his book. "Everything looks to be in order. You'll be in B-54. Billings, here, will show you to your room. As you go by the Grand Staircase, be sure you take a look at the glass dome overhead. There's a wondrous display of light streaming down through the glass. I think you will enjoy it."

"Sounds lovely." Jacquie did her best not to sigh aloud.

"It is. And while you're there, be on the lookout for Honour and Glory."

"Honour and glory?" She repeated the words, unsure of his meaning.

"Yes." He quirked a brow. "They sit to the right and the left of the hour."

The fellow's words made no sense, and the line about honor

and glory stirred her guilt even more. How could she be called honorable after running off with a young man her parents didn't approve of? Shame flooded over her.

"Follow that up to B Deck," he continued. "Your room will be down the hallway to the left. Miss? Are you all right?"

"Oh, yes." In truth, she felt a bit queasy, as she thought through her plan to jump ship before it sailed.

Concern filled his eyes as he gave her a closer look. "If you get to feeling seasick, you might consider an afternoon stroll around the Boat Deck once we set sail. The fresh air will do you good."

"Ah, yes. I'll do that."

Jacquie left the purser's office and, with Mother on her arm, followed behind the steward as they wove their way through the crowd.

Mother beamed with delight as she observed the elevators in the distance. "The *Titanic* is the first ship with lifts. I read all about it in the paper."

"Yes, that's right, ma'am," the steward said. "Though you might prefer to take the Grand Staircase up to your room."

"Yes, let's do," she said.

The steward led them to the lobby, and Jacquie froze in place, gasping as she caught a glimpse of the stairway. "Oh my goodness." She gestured to the glorious scene before them. "Have you ever seen anything like this?"

Her gaze traveled up the magnificent stairs, and her breath caught in her throat as she took in the splendor of it all. Just as the purser has said, the glass-domed ceiling had a heavenly appearance. The polished oak wall paneling glistened, a happy candidate for the streams of sunlight pouring in from above. Truly, the whole thing felt like some sort of heavenly gift, a pinch from a falling star, equal in brightness and beauty.

"Oh, Jacquie, look." Mother ran her hand along the railing and across one of the balustrades then pointed upward at a large carved panel. It held an ornate clock, surely like one she had never seen before, flanked on both sides by intricately carved classical figures. The detailing took her breath away.

"Ooh, this must be Honour and Glory." Jacquie pointed to the carved figures. "Remember what the purser said?"

"Honour and Glory." Mother repeated the words and nodded. "They are something to behold."

Iris let out a lingering sigh and placed her hand on the banister railing. "Oh, Miss Jacquie, this is too much. It's Buckingham Palace floating atop the Atlantic, a wonder for the eyes and the soul. I don't know how I will ever repay you for including me." Off she went on a tangent, talking about the adventures she planned to have over the next several days. An older woman in a purple hat passed by, smiling as she took in Iris's enthusiastic speech, which was now being delivered from the top step of the Grand Staircase in full view of the watching crowd below.

"Don't be silly, Iris." Mother took hold of the railing and took a couple of steps up, offering a nod to a chambermaid coming down the opposite direction. "I've been to Buckingham Palace several times, and Kensington, as well. And I daresay I know a fine palace when I see one. Most have stood the test of time."

"In other words, they're old." Jacquie chuckled. "Everything onboard *Titanic* is brand-spanking-new. We will dine off of new plates and drink from new crystal." *At least, Tessa will.*

"Still, she's the closest thing I've ever seen to the inside of a real palace." Iris sighed and ran her hand across the wood-carved figures next to the clock. "So beautiful."

"I must say, you're right about that."

Minutes later they arrived at B Deck. The steward used his key to open the door then held it ajar for Jacquie to step inside. She took tentative steps inside the room—that glorious, unimaginable room—and gasped. "Oh, Mother!"

The gilded wall sconces took her breath away, as did the detailed mirror on the wall and the wallpaper, a rich shade of red velvet. What really captivated her attention, however, was the exquisite four-poster bed with its canopy top. She would never know what it felt like to sleep on that bed, but she could imagine it would be quite lovely.

A chambermaid in a crisp black dress with a white apron and cap arrived at the door and stood to attention. "I'm Nancy, miss. If there's anything you need, just ask for me. I will be at your beck and call."

Jacquie nodded. Hopefully once she left the ship and Tessa took her place, the chambermaid would forget she'd ever seen her in the first place. Maybe she wouldn't ask why one young woman took possession of the room and another slipped into her place.

"I do hope your things arrive before I have to leave." Mother took a few steps toward the bed and sat down. She ran her hands across the brocade coverlet and sighed. "I want to see your pretty dresses and fine things one last time. It is a pity that I won't be able to see them on you, my dear."

Neither will I.

Minutes later, after looking over the second bedroom and finding the suite to their liking, Jacquie's trunk arrived. Mama put Iris to work at unpacking Jacquie's new dresses—the ones only Tessa would wear—and hanging them in the wardrobe.

"Let's take a walk about the deck." Mama reached for Jacquie's arm.

"Of course." Jacquie's heart grew heavy as she pondered the fact that this could very well be the last conversation she would have with her mother for quite some time. They made their way outside to the Boat Deck, and Mama slipped her arm through Jacquie's as they strolled through the ever-growing crowd of passengers.

"It seems as if the whole world is represented on this one ship," Mother said as she looked about. "I've never seen such a collection of people."

"I daresay it will be quite the adventure," Jacquie agreed.

"You deserve the best sort of adventure, my dear." Mother's eyes misted over, and she pulled Jacquie into her arms. "Oh, how I'm going to miss you, sweet girl. I dread parting ways with you."

A lump rose in Jacquie's throat. "As do I."

"I didn't want to say our good-byes in front of Iris," Mother whispered in Jacquie's ear. "I feel bad enough for involving her in all this. That's why I suggested we come outside."

"Mother, Iris is thrilled to be off on such an adventure. And I also believe she's hoping to learn more about women's fashion while onboard." Jacquie chuckled. "I've seen her sketching gowns on paper for weeks now. So don't feel too badly for her. This is the ideal setting for her to capture more of them on the page."

"Still..." Mother shook her head. "She is doing us the best of favors, is she not?"

"Yes. She is." *More than you know.*

"You're worth it all, darling girl." Mother dabbed at her eyes. "I'd made up my mind not to cry, so a fast good-bye is in order. Besides, the sooner I leave, the sooner I can meet Minerva at the hotel."

"You're staying at the Grand Harbour tonight before leaving for Paris in the morning?" Jacquie asked.

"Yes. We will be on the first train out of London tomorrow morning." Mama stifled a yawn. "Which means we will have to rise before the sun. I'm afraid I haven't slept much. All this deception and intrigue has me awake at night. And I daresay tonight won't be much better. I'll probably toss and turn for hours, worrying about how this will end."

"Don't worry, Mother. I'm sure it will all end well." Jacquie paused. "Though, I will miss you terribly."

"And I, you." Mother paused and slipped her arm around Jacquie's waist, drawing her close. "What will I do without my darling girl to keep me company?" Tears now coursed down her cheeks. "There will be no one to pacify this lonely old heart of mine."

"It's not as if I'm going away forever." Jacquie spoke the words, hoping they were true. When Mother realized she hadn't sailed aboard the *Titanic* for New York, she might very well see to it that Jacquie never set foot in Abingdon Manor again.

Jacquie felt the sting of tears as her mother swept her into her arms for a final hug. "Oh, my precious girl. Do be happy."

"I—I will."

"Find love. Find joy. Settle well, but not necessarily for money." She wrinkled her nose. "Well, a bit of money wouldn't hurt, of course." Mother giggled. "No doubt your grandmother already has three or four potential beaux lined up for you. Her latest telegraph implied as much."

"I will follow my heart, Mother." Jacquie's thoughts filled with images of Peter. He might not have much in the way of worldly things, but he offered her something Roland Palmer, with all of his wealth, could not—a heart filled with the kind of love that could sustain them for years to come. Who needed fancy automobiles and fine clothes? What would be the point of having all those things but no one to love you—to really, truly love you as Peter loved her? No, she would gladly trade it all.

A renewed confidence filled Jacquie as she wrapped her arms around Mama's neck and gave her a kiss on the cheek. As soon as her mother left the ship, Jacquie's plans would move forward. She would meet Tessa at the gate and trade places. Until then, she would have a stroll about the ship so that she would always have a memory of the time she almost sailed aboard the *Titanic* to America.

* * * * *

Nathan boarded the massive ship amid a horde of other first-class passengers. With Mother on one side and James Carson on the other, they pressed their way through the crowd, encompassed about on every side by strangers speaking a multiplicity of languages.

James elbowed him and pointed up at the looming ship with its expansive smokestacks and multiple decks. "Those arrogant British are at it again. Always out to prove they can show up every other dog in the hunt."

"Well, you must admit, they've done an admirable job this time." Nathan took in his surroundings and let out a whistle. "She's something else, isn't she?" He had traveled aboard fine liners before, of course, but nothing like this. *Titanic* loomed above everything else nearby, making both the people and the buildings seem microscopic in comparison.

As he glanced about, Nathan's gaze fell on a familiar young woman in a blue dress with a plumed hat. The girl from the opera house. The shy fiancée of the amiable fellow from New York. She stood next to her teary-eyed mother, who appeared to be distraught, for some reason. The girl looked Nathan's way but didn't seem to notice him. At first. Soon enough, their eyes met. Hers widened and she slipped out of her mother's arms and ducked through the crowd, disappearing from view.

Poor thing. She must really be shy. Yes, she'd responded the same way at the opera, as well, hadn't she? Still, there was something about those pensive blue eyes—the color of the sea—that drew him in. If only he'd gotten her name. He could have called out to her. Maybe she would have stopped for a conversation. However, he couldn't imagine why she would board the ship. Her fiancé had made it clear he would not be traveling aboard the *Titanic*. Had they ended their engagement, perhaps? The very idea aroused his curiosity.

Stop it, Nathan. She's another man's fiancée.

He shook off his ponderings, the phantom girl now long gone.

"Yes, she's really something." James's voice rang out from behind him, and Nathan winced. If only he didn't have to put up with the intrusive fellow for the next five days. "I can see why you're smitten, Nathan. But remember, buddy boy, she's already got a ring on her finger."

Actually, he hadn't noticed a ring the night of the opera. But that didn't change the fact that she was another man's intended. Nathan needed to shake off the spell cast by those blue eyes and move on. Maybe he would see her in the dining saloon. They could talk about the opera. Or maybe he would keep his distance so that his heart wouldn't become entangled. Yes, keeping his distance would be best. After all, he had other things to think about—not the least of which was his new position at Father's insurance firm.

Suddenly, Nathan could hardly wait to get home.

Chapter Ten

Tessa felt as if she might very well suffocate in the cab as they inched their way toward the White Star Line Dock. She could hardly catch her breath. Every few moments she felt as if she might faint. Then again, the corset threatened to squeeze the goodness out of her. Not that she had been able to fasten the laces as tightly as she ought without Iris's help, but the irritating thing still vexed her.

"Are you all right?" Peter glanced her way, and she reached for his hand.

"I am, for now."

His boyish smile caught her off guard. "Tessa, in case I haven't said it already, you look lovely."

"Th–thank you." Warmth and appreciation flooded over her.

Peter gave her a penetrating gaze. "Mum would be beside herself if she saw you looking like this, though I'm not altogether sure she would recognize you."

Tessa's heart twisted as she thought about her mother living in that broken-down cottage and dealing with Pa alone. For a moment, she thought about asking the cab driver to turn back. Just as quickly, she forced her thoughts ahead to her new life.

"Have I really changed that much?" she asked.

"Yes, but it suits you," Peter said, gesturing to her dress. "And I believe the lifestyle will too."

A quick glance down at the blue-and-cream gown lifted her spirits at once. This must surely be what the royals felt like, gilded and pranced about for show. To wear such finery seemed a bit silly, and yet she could not deny the way the embellished gown made her feel. Truly, it elevated her spirits and bolstered her courage. For a moment, she almost saw herself as a fine lady ready to board the *Titanic*, happy to cruise to lands yet unknown. An adventure of the highest magnitude.

Indeed, one could call her current situation an adventure, in and of itself. Outside the window, a multitude of people surrounded the vehicle, all walking the same direction, toward the White Star Line Dock. They bustled about in costumes of all sorts—many in typical British garb, but many in unusual attire coupled with decorative colors and styles. She found the whole scene rather intriguing.

"What a remarkable day we live in." Peter pointed to an electric trolley. "Look at that, will you?" He let out a whistle. "Ever seen anything like it?"

She fought the temptation to roll her eyes. "Peter, I'd never even been out of Gloucestershire County until two weeks ago. You know that. This is all foreign and strange to me." *And yet wildly exciting. In a terrifying sort of way.* Whether or not she could plant herself in the midst of such people and grow as a flower in a garden, she could not say. Still, she would give it all that she had.

Peter's eyes sparkled as he looked her way. "Think of this as a production upon the stage. You are the starring player. You just have to stick to the script." He jabbed her with his elbow. "You've always been quite good at playacting, if I recall." A tiny wink followed.

"True." She released a slow breath, determined to stay calm. "I will do my best."

Her gaze shifted out of the window of the cab as it wound its way through the mob near the dock. She'd never seen such an mix of people before—young, old, rich, poor. She even caught a glimpse of a boy, maybe ten or so, picking the pocket of an older fellow in a fancy suit. A better person would have put down her window and called for the police, but right now the last thing Tessa wanted was to draw attention to herself. If she could just get through the next five days at sea, maybe the churning in her stomach would cease. She hoped so, anyway.

Still the madness in the streets caused the strangest sensation to rise up inside of her. She focused on a woman in a tattered dress not unlike the one Tessa wore on the day she tousled with Countess in the stall. The pained expression on the young woman's face was evident as she said her good-byes to a young man in a White Star Line uniform. A lump rose in Tessa's throat as she thought about leaving Peter—possibly for good.

Her gaze shifted back to the pickpocket, his victim now chasing him through the crowd to fetch his missing wallet. Something about all of this seemed strangely exciting, like a grand theatrical, playing out on a stage far more real than any a theater could boast.

Off in the distance, a group of women not much older than herself marched along in militant fashion, holding signs. Tessa strained to read the words: VOTES FOR WOMEN. Truly? They wanted to vote? Why? Didn't life offer enough complications without involving politics? If she could vote for anything right now, it would be for the right to live a pleasant, comfortable life, one with Peter in it. Her eyes stung with tears, which she brushed away.

"Blasted suffragettes." The cab driver hurled an insult through his open window as the women passed by in front of the cab. One of them turned and narrowed her gaze.

"Frightening, that one." The cab driver chuckled as he pointed to the lady with the sour expression. "Looks as if she wants to do me harm."

"She might start swinging her sign and take us all down." Peter laughed and teased the woman with a boyish wave. "But who can blame these rowdy gals? They know enough to take advantage of a crowd. This is a fine platform for their demonstration, what with so many ladies about."

"And men too." The hairs on Tessa's arms stood up as she saw a group of intoxicated fellows bumbling their way down the street in a pack, their merry voices raised in off-key song. Hopefully they would move on, away from the ship. Still, the idea of traveling alone, without her brother to protect her, brought a wave of fear.

Peter's eyes filled with concern. "Yes, well, let's not focus on the men. In fact, I would prefer you keep your distance from them on this trip, if you please."

"Oh, I will, I promise." No doubt she would stay as far away as possible, likely hiding out in her suite until they arrived in New York. Oh, but when she saw the people, when she heard the strains of music rising up from the drum corps in the distance, she almost imagined it possible to merge into this world, to play her role with finesse and ease. Almost.

"Look around you, Peter," Tessa said after a moment's pause. "What do you see?"

He turned toward the window and shrugged. "I see motor-buses. Trolleys. Delivery wagons. Bicycles. And people as thick as thieves. I hope the crowd will thin so we can make it to the dock."

"I will get you there, sir," the cab driver said, a lilt in his voice. "Sooner or later."

"What *else* do you see?" Tessa pressed him to envision it all through her eyes.

Her brother shrugged. "Horses? Mounted policemen? Automobiles? Carriages?" He leaned a bit closer to the window. "I see a double-decker horse-drawn carriage with a scrolling stairway bearing a sign about Nestlé's chocolate. Makes me wish I had some." He smacked his lips.

"Would you like to know what I see?" Tessa asked, her thoughts on something far different.

"No doubt you will tell me even if I do not respond, so go ahead."

"Fine." She swallowed the lump in her throat to share. "I see people dwelling in poverty. I see families not unlike our own living in unsanitary conditions. I see immigrants and tradesmen, beggars and entrepreneurs. I see people of a variety of ethnicities. I see industries, large and small, vying for the pocketbooks of those walking by. I see pickpockets and suffragettes, ladies in traveling suits, and gentlemen smoking cigars. I see their valets and chambermaids, trimmed out and ready for service. I see spectators by the hundreds, standing along the shoreline, ready to wave their good-byes. But do you know what I see beyond it all?"

"No. But I'm intrigued."

Tessa found herself energized by the sudden burst of confidence that swept over her as she spoke her thoughts aloud. "I see hope—on every face. It's etched into the brow of the young women boarding the ship. It's evident in the square-shouldered stance of the young man who's worked all year to afford his third-class passage. It's bolstering the courage of the elderly widow who is setting off to live with her daughter in a strange, new land."

Indeed, she saw beyond the high lace collars and corseted waists. She looked deeper than the traveling clothes and the frilly hats. What mattered was the person, not the attire. And every person in view had his or her own story to tell, just as she did.

Peter's brows elevated, and he glanced out the window. "You can see all of their faces from here?"

"A few. They are hopeful that life in America will change their situation for the better." A hesitant sigh followed. "And I am among them. I'm so grateful, Peter. Truly, I am. You've offered me a new life. How can I begin to thank you for that?"

"You don't have to." Peter gripped her hand and gazed with such intensity into her eyes that she felt the sting of tears. "I can't begin to tell you how relieved I am to hear you say this. I'm overjoyed, in fact. For the first time, you truly sound hopeful about your trip, and that brings me a sense of peace. I could not live with myself if I knew that you were unhappy, Tessa. I see this as the best possible way to get you away from Father." His gaze penetrated her heart, nearly ripping it to shreds. "You do see now why I would go to such lengths, don't you? I want to protect you."

"And I'm very grateful." A pain in her ribs reminded her of the corset, and she squirmed, trying to get comfortable. "Some things will take more getting used to than others, but I want you to know that I'm ready for a change."

"I'm so glad," he said. "No doubt life in America will be everything we've read about in books and newspapers, filled with opportunities for new beginnings."

"Yes." Her imagination almost ran away with her as she tried to evision it all. Just as quickly, she thought about Jacquie's grandmother—the one who would be waiting in New York— and a shiver ran down her spine. How would she get beyond the initial how-do-you-do to begin her new life? Even with Jacquie's letter in hand, the situation would be difficult.

A rush of fear ran over her. "I do hope Jacquie remembers to leave the letter in my cabin."

"She will. Don't worry, Tessa. All will be well." Peter's words spoke of confidence, but the wrinkles between his brows said otherwise. After a moment of silence, he looked her way with a smile. "You must promise to write the minute you arrive in New York. Send your correspondence to Jacquie at the Willingham Hotel in Southampton. She will stay there for the time being."

"I will. And you promise me that somehow, someway, we will see each other again."

"We will." He slipped his arm over her shoulders and pressed a kiss into her hair, which only caused her to tear up all over again. "I will come in time, if only for a visit. Or I will bring you back when you've had your fill of your new life." He chuckled and withdrew his arm. "Though I daresay you will probably settle in nicely and forget all about us."

"Impossible."

A lone tear trickled down her cheek and he reached to brush it away with a fingertip then shrugged. The crowd thinned, and off in the distance, along the edge of the White Star Line Dock, the RMS *Titanic* loomed, in glorious splendor.

Tessa's breath caught in her throat as she took in the magnificent ship. Regal and grand, it stood taller than she had imagined—with far more decks. She lost count of them as her gaze swept upward. The smokestacks seemed to reach to the sky, all four of them. And dotting the decks of the ship as they strolled about, passengers as tiny as ants. From this distance, anyway. Soon, she would join them. A shiver ran down her spine at the very thought of it. Tessa continued to stare at the massive vessel, overcome by its sheer beauty and size.

"The Queen of the Ocean." Peter's words rang out as he pointed to the ship. "The most sumptuous liner afloat, awaiting her finest passenger." He elbowed Tessa once again and laughed.

"Oh, Peter." Could she really board an ocean liner the size of a city and float across the waters to some place she'd only imagined in her dreams? Before she could think it through, a fancy touring car came to a stop in front of them, just beyond the White Star Line sign.

"Who do you suppose that is?" She squinted to get a better look. "I've never seen such a large vehicle."

"That's a Daimler landaulet." Peter let out a whistle. "Must be someone important."

They watched as the chauffer climbed out of the car, opened the back door, and stood to attention. A trio of youngsters emerged, followed by a young woman. A fellow in a fine traveling suit got out next, followed by a woman who was dressed to the nines. They fussed over their trunks then ushered the children aboard the ship.

Tessa's nerves felt jumbled. To be surrounded by such people, folks accustomed to money, unnerved her. Could she really keep up her role as a socialite with ease, or would she spend this entire trip holed up in her suite? Not that traveling in a grand suite would be problematic, of course. She could very well enjoy the cruise just as nicely from inside.

Oh, but the water! And the waves. They called out to her, beckoning her to gaze down at them. And those lovely decks, teeming with people. Did they not call her name? Could she not spend many a fine hour strolling in the afternoon sunlight with the salty breeze whipping through her hair?

A policeman in full regalia gestured for the vehicle to stop, and she was granted only seconds to say her good-byes to Peter. She clutched his arm and forced herself to remain calm. "Promise you won't leave me here until you're sure I've boarded?" Her words came out sounding as frantic as they felt. "Just in case something goes wrong?"

"It won't." He wrapped her in his arms and planted a kiss in her hair. "At eleven forty-five Jacquie will be waiting at the starboard gate. Meet her there."

Tessa's heart quickened. "I will."

Peter's eyes filled with tears and he leaned in to give her a hug. "I pray your new life is everything you hope it will be. You, of all people, deserve the best."

"Oh, Peter." She flung her arms around his neck and cried until her heart was relieved of its pain.

Off in the distance a tower clock bonged the hour. Peter pulled away. "We're out of time. Do you know what to do?"

"I've rehearsed it so many times in my mind, I think I can manage." She gave him an extended hug and then, with her heart in her throat, opened the door and sprinted toward the ship, determined to push aside her emotions until she was safely settled onboard. She eased her way through the throng of people, her gaze traveling ever upward to the ship.

* * * * *

Jacquie paced the cabin as she fussed with her gloves. With her nerves in such a frazzled state, she couldn't seem to get them on properly. Iris stepped up beside her and offered assistance. Afterward, Jacquie looked up at her and sighed. "Thank you."

"You're welcome, Miss Jacquie." Iris's eyes brimmed with tears, and she looked away.

Jacquie patted her arm. "I know this situation displeases you, Iris. I hear it in the words you're not speaking and see it every time I look into your eyes. You're unhappy with my decision."

"I am grateful for the passage to New York and excited about my prospects there." Iris turned back and opened her mouth as if to say more but spoke nothing. Instead, tears dribbled over her lower lashes.

"And I am happy to provide the opportunity, but I'm going to miss you terribly." Jacquie reached to offer her a warm embrace. "We've been more like sisters, have we not?"

"We have." Iris swiped at her eyes with the back of her hand.

Jacquie squared her shoulders and tried to appear confident as she offered her farewell speech. "I've always valued your advice, Iris. So I do hope you will trust me in this. I know what I'm doing."

The lady's maid did not appear to be convinced. Instead, she turned to help Jacquie with her reticule, not saying a word.

"You are making the ultimate sacrifice for me," Jacquie added, her words laced with genuine compassion. "And for that I'm extremely grateful." She reached inside her reticule and withdrew the letter for her grandmother.

"Yes, well…" Iris's words lingered in the air.

"I hope you will treat Tessa kindly." Jacquie lowered her voice and gave Iris a sheepish look. "Do it…for me? And for Tessa too. She is making sacrifices as well."

"Tessa? Making sacrifices?" Iris rolled her eyes.

"Oh, but she is. She's leaving hearth and home, mother and father, for a world yet known. People unknown. And traveling in uncomfortable circumstances." Jacquie fingered the letter, her thoughts shifting.

"Uncomfortable?" Iris gestured to the grand suite.

Jacquie placed the letter on the desk and turned to face her. "Well, not uncomfortable in the physical sense, of course, but in other ways. So you must do all you can to help her. Advise, of course, but more than that, befriend. Treat her as you've treated me all of these years."

"But Miss Jacquie, I can't possibly—"

"You can. And I pray you will. She will lean on you for strength." Jacquie wrapped Iris in another embrace. "And remember, my dear friend, whatever you do to or for her, you're actually doing for me. So any sacrifice you might make on her behalf is one I will feel the benefit of as I journey into my new life."

"Y–yes, Miss Jacquie."

She offered Iris a tight hug. "Oh, I will miss you, my friend. More than anyone, I have come to lean on you. Please promise me you will enjoy your new life in America. I've asked my grandmother to watch over you as well as Tessa. You will be in safe keeping, I promise, so relish all that life has to offer in New York."

"I—I will do my best, miss."

"No more *miss*. I'm just Jacquie to you now."

"Jacquie." Iris swiped the tears from her cheeks and smiled. "I do hope your life is all you dreamed it would be."

"I know it will be, because Peter is in it." She smiled, her heart near to overflowing with joy as she thought about the man she loved. Just as quickly, fear wriggled its way down her spine. If things between them didn't work out…

No. She wouldn't think like that. They would marry and live happily ever after, just like the couples in the fairy tales she so enjoyed.

Jacquie rested her hands on her hips, deep in thought. "Now, a bit of last-minute business. If you need to reach me, I will be here, in Southampton, at the Willingham."

"For how long?" Iris asked.

"Indefinitely. Peter will come and go until we can marry. I advised him to keep his job at the manor. That way my parents won't suspect anything amiss. By the time my grandmother sends word that Tessa has arrived in my stead, perhaps Peter and I will be married. Or betrothed. At any rate, we won't make a move until you and Tessa are safely in America." Her thoughts contorted as she pondered how long she could afford to stay at the Willingham Hotel. Hopefully her finances would hold out.

"I wish you the best, Miss Jacquie. And I pray you find true love."

"Oh, I have." Jacquie's heart flooded with warmth once again as she thought about Peter, of their life together. "All this is for him." Indeed, all this was for him. If he asked her to sail the seven seas for him, she would do it. Anything for love. All for love.

Chapter Eleven

Tessa found herself swallowed up by the horde of people as she pressed her way toward the starboard gate. Up the gangway she inched her way along, her heart in her throat. Finding herself at the back of a long line of passengers, she continued to stare at the ship, unable to think clearly. Should she board it...or run back to the family's farm as fast as her feet would carry her? Before she could come to a decision, someone bumped into her from behind, sending her purse flying and nearly knocking her down in the process. She let out a little gasp, realizing that every penny she owned, all the cash Jacquie had passed her way, was in that purse.

"Pardon me, miss."

Tessa turned as she heard the voice. Her gaze fell on a stately looking man with dark hair and twinkling eyes. "Oh, I—" She reached for her bag, but he snatched it first. Only then did she notice that he wore a reverend's collar. To his right stood a young woman and a little girl maybe six or seven. The child gazed up at the ship, wide-eyed.

"Here you go. Sorry about that." The minister pressed the bag into Tessa's hands, and his eyes lingered on hers for a moment, as if he could see into her very soul. "God bless you, miss." He gave her a nod and disappeared into the crowd. Still, there was something about his penetrating gaze that made her vulnerable.

As she clutched her bag, Tessa whispered up a prayer. "Father, forgive me. If what I'm about to do is wrong…"

She didn't have a chance to finish. Tessa couldn't continue. In spite of the opportunity that sailing on this ship provided, what she was doing *was* wrong. She felt it in the pit of her stomach. Still, Peter wished this for her. Sacrificed to make this possible, no less. Turning back now wouldn't be a very fine thank-you, would it? No, certainly not. And so, onto the *Titanic* she would go.

Tessa fought to get her bearings. Clutching her little purse tighter than ever, she thought through the plan once more, the one she had reluctantly agreed to.

Meet Jacquie at the gate. Take her ticket, her passport…her life.

It all sounded so simple.

A wave of nausea swept over Tessa as she contemplated it for the hundredth time. There would be no going back once she boarded the ship under Jacquie's name. From that moment on, she would *be* Jacquie Abingdon, London socialite, bound for New York. After all the coaching she had received over the past two weeks, she would play the role with vigor. She would even dress the part in Jacquie's beautiful gowns.

Lord, help me.

On the other hand, did she really have the right to ask for her heavenly Father's assistance with a plan that seemed deceptive, at best?

Oh, but when she thought about her older brother, thought about how much he had sacrificed to make all of this possible, she found herself relishing the opportunity for a second chance at life—free from the pain of the past. Yes, surely even the Lord

Himself knew what it felt like to offer second chances. He would certainly understand and even help her.

Of course, Pa would drive her knees into the gravel, should he find out. Tessa trembled as she thought about the rocky path behind Countess's stall where she'd served her time, her bloody knees crying out for mercy. No more. Pa would never know of her deception. He would no longer control her actions, her thoughts, or her prayers.

She drew in a deep breath and made her way through the crowd toward the gate. Off in the distance, she finally caught a glimpse of Jacquie, who glanced her way wide-eyed. Tessa paced her breathing.

Take your time. You've rehearsed this part.

She watched as Jacquie eased her way off the ship. At just the right moment Tessa made her move, easing through the crowd. She stepped alongside Jacquie, who slipped the boarding pass and passport into her reticule. No hug. No embrace. Just a tight squeeze of the hand and a rushed "Bless you" from Jacquie.

Then, life as Tessa Bowen once knew it changed forever. She took a calculated step onto the *Titanic*, ready for the charade to begin.

* * * * *

Nathan did his best to put the blue-eyed beauty out of his mind as he followed on his mother's heels to their suite. As the steward opened the door and ushered them inside, Mama let out a gasp.

"Oh, Nathan!" She gestured to the luxurious drawing room space and spun about like a mesmerized child. "This is lovely."

"Very nice." Much nicer than the *Lusitania*, in fact, though he decided not to state as much.

Mother gestured to the steward, who stood at attention at

the door. "When our trunk arrives, expect a call from me. I will require your help."

"Of course, ma'am." The older fellow paused and stayed at attention, as if awaiting his marching orders. "Will there be anything else?"

"No."

After he disappeared through the door, Mother walked to the window and gazed outside. "My goodness, what a mess. People everywhere."

He stepped alongside her, his gaze on the sea. "Yes, but look beyond it at the water. Before long, we will be sailing atop it." Nathan smiled and pondered the only words that came to mind: *"The earth was without form, and void; and darkness was upon the face of the deep. And the Spirit of God moved upon the face of the waters."*

He paused to think through the verse, his imagination running free. "It never ceases to amaze me how God shows Himself in nature…in the trees, the mountains, the ocean…. And doesn't it astound you to think of His Spirit hovering over the face of the waters? Such a concept is nearly beyond comprehension."

"It is that." She rolled her eyes and then eased her way onto the settee. "You are so like your father—ever the philosopher."

Nathan turned to face her, guarding his words. "Not a philosopher, Mother. I enjoy studying the Scriptures. The Bible is filled with sage advice for happy living. I take comfort in it."

She tilted her head to the side and offered a little shrug. "Of course, of course. It's a fine book. But I've rarely known anyone to quote it as you do. Didn't they teach you anything else in that fancy school of yours?"

"Certainly." He bit his tongue to keep from speaking his next thought aloud. Still, he couldn't keep it from rolling through his head. *They taught me to honor my father and mother, though you make it a challenge at times.*

She fussed with her ornate hat, finally unpinning it. "I don't know about you, but I'm happy to be away from the chaos on the gangway. Felt like those ghastly people were pressing the air out of me." She glanced around the room. "I would love to take a stroll around the ship, but my head aches. I think it might be best if I rest before attempting it. Do you mind?"

"No. Though I would love to take a look around while you're napping. I promise to come back with all sorts of seaworthy tales about the people I meet along the way."

"Sounds lovely." Mama disappeared into her room, still muttering something about her headache as she closed the door with a click.

Happy to be alone, Nathan gazed out the window and took in the view. Off in the distance, the dock swarmed with people. It would appear all of Britain had converged in this one place to bear witness to the miracle that was *Titanic*. The Ocean's Queen was a fine ship, to be sure. Still, grand or not, she didn't deserve the credit. *Titanic* was, after all, just a man-made object. Neither did the builders deserve the credit. They were mere men made in God's image.

These fine folks, exuberant in celebration, reminded him of a mighty chorus as they sang their praises of a ship and the Empire who'd built her. What would it be like, he wondered, to hear as many voices raised in grateful chorus to the One capable of spinning a world into existence with nothing but a spoken word?

Suddenly he could hardly wait for a stroll around the Boat Deck. Nathan left the suite, headed to the Grand Staircase. As he made his way down it, he paused to look up at the domed ceiling and the gleaming wrought-iron trim. His gaze shifted to the clock, and he couldn't help but draw near for a closer look. The carved figures to the right and left caught his eye. Such intricacy captivated him. Still, with the crowd pressing in around him, he couldn't stand in one place for long before they pressed him ever upward toward the Boat Deck.

After winding his way through the mass of passengers headed to their cabins, Nathan found himself strolling in the late morning sunlight. He tipped his hat at several of the others and then made his way to the railing. Leaning against it, his gaze shifted to the sea below. Of course Mother would call him philosophical, but another Scripture came to mind. "You will cast all our sins into the depths of the sea." He didn't mean to speak the words aloud, but there they were, for all to hear.

"Begging your pardon, sir?" A young man came up beside him and glanced down at the water several stories below.

"Oh, nothing." Embarrassment washed over Nathan. "Just thinking out loud."

"Well, don't be casting anything into the sea just yet," the fellow said with a cockeyed grin. " 'Less it's one of those yappy dogs I've been seeing about. But even then I would think twice. I've never been one for swimming in the Atlantic. Gets mighty cold this time of year."

"I don't plan to go for a swim, that's a fact." Nathan gestured over the railing. "In the Atlantic, I mean. I hear there's a fine swimming pool onboard. Heated. I might give that a gander."

"Doubt I'll have much time to swim," the man said. "Likely I'll be up to me eyeballs in smoke and steam down below. Not complainin' though."

This certainly piqued Nathan's interest. "Are you working onboard, then?"

"Only just." The fellow chuckled. "It's the luck o' the Irish to blame."

"Oh?"

"Yes. I planted myself dockside early this morning all in the hopes that a stoker position would open up."

"And it did?"

"Yes, and quite the tale, from what I hear. A handful of slouches overstayed their welcome at a local pub. Had one pint too many and let the time get away from them." The fellow slapped his knee, and a raucous laugh followed. They arrived portside just as that gangway was pulled up. Missed boarding by a quarter inch, they did."

"You're saying they were turned away?"

"Indeed." He chuckled. "And not a mite happy about it, from what I hear. Almost started a fight with the petty officers when they held their ground on the matter."

Nathan shook his head as he tried to imagine the disappointment those men must be feeling right now. "All that for a few pints?" The fellow nodded and crossed his arms at his chest. "Their loss is me gain." He squared his shoulders and puffed out his chest. "The position has now been filled." When he offered a broad smile, it revealed a missing tooth. Not that the fellow seemed to notice or care. He continued to grin, his eyes wide with excitement. "Six days aboard the finest ship ever built. I don't mind crawling below to stoke the fires if it means I can take me meals like a gentleman. Even the crew will eat like kings aboard *Titanic*, I hear tell."

"Yes, I understand the food is marvelous."

"Marvelous." The young man offered another near-toothless grin. "That's the word for it, yer right about that. Still a marvel to me that she's sailing at all, what with the coal strike. You know they've stripped the coal from other ships to make sure *Titanic* has what she needs for the journey?"

"So I read in the paper."

"I doubt you will see much of me, but that's not a complaint on my end. Happy to be onboard, I am."

Off in the distance a whistle sounded and the man started to attention. "That's my signal. I'd best be gettin' on my way. Nice to meet you, sir."

"And you as well," Nathan said. "I hope the trip is everything you've hoped for."

"No doubt it will be. And more." The fellow took off sprinting toward the stairwell, his voice fading away among the multitude of people.

As Nathan turned his attention back to the churning waters of the Atlantic, he couldn't help but think the fellow was right. This trip would turn out to be all they had dreamed. All, and much, much more.

* * * * *

Wednesday, April 10, 1912, 11:59 a.m.
The White Star Line Dock

Jacquie stopped to catch her breath, now safely ashore. Knowing that Tessa had made it onboard relieved her on several levels, but tendrils of fear still wrapped themselves around Jacquie's heart as she contemplated the fact that Mother was somewhere in this crowd, looking on. Hopefully they wouldn't stumble across one another.

A long, low whistle blast sounded from the ship one minute before noon. From the crowd came a roar of approval. From the top deck, flags flew and the band played with merriment. Within minutes, *Titanic* would begin her voyage toward America—with Tessa and Iris safely tucked away in Cabin B-54.

Chapter Twelve

Wednesday, April 10, 1912, Noon
Aboard the Titanic

Tessa gripped the Boat Deck railing and gulped for air. She fought to get control of her emotions. Her gaze shifted away from the large vessel, which now held her captive to her new life, and onto the rolling hills in the distance. For a moment—a few brief seconds, really—she longed for home. Just as quickly, the feeling passed. After the noon whistle blast, she realized there would be no turning back.

Off in the distance, the sound of the drum corps battled against several male voices singing "When Irish Eyes Are Smiling." Something about the mix made her a bit dizzy. Of course, this whole thing had her feeling dizzy. As the singing grew louder, she glanced up to see several fellows, with arms linked, making their way through the crowd in front of her. From the way they stumbled about, they'd had a few too many. She recognized the familiar stumble-bumble routine from years of watching Pa in such a state.

Pa.

Tessa pinched her eyes shut to avoid thinking about him. Still, as the inebriated fellows staggered by, their voices raised in ill-harmonized singing, her knees began to ache. When the men disappeared into the crowd, she drew a steady breath. "I'm onboard."

She had expected a confrontation. A challenge. And yet here

she stood, a lady dressed in an expensive gown with a very tight corset, holding a boarding pass in her hand. She glanced up as a group of women passed by. One was rather odd in appearance, dressed in a man's vest and smoking a cigar. Tessa waved her hand in front of her nose as the obnoxious odor permeated the air.

A spruced-up lady followed behind the group, practically dripping with diamonds and a variety of other colorful jewels. Her tall, feathered hat bobbed this way and that as she attempted to walk on shoes that were clearly too tight. As if she hadn't drawn enough attention to herself with her eccentric attire, the woman carried a smallish yappy dog in her arms, one that clearly didn't care for his surroundings. Interesting, how much the dog and the woman resembled one another, each wearing a diamond-studded collar.

The woman spoke to the fussy pup as one would coddle a child. A dapper fellow with a cane stepped into the spot behind her and the feisty canine bared his teeth. Just as quickly, the man tipped his derby, offered a wide berth, and disappeared into the crowd. The woman clung tightly to the little dog, still speaking in baby talk, as she headed off on her way.

Tessa closed her eyes and attempted to breath in the salty sea air but caught a whiff of overpowering perfume. Her eyes flew open as she heard youthful voices. Her heart soared to her throat as a group of young ladies about her age passed by. One of them wore an emerald-encrusted tiara, which sparkled under the ribbons of sunlight streaming down from above. Was she an heiress, perhaps? Or royalty of some sort?

Tessa pinched her eyes shut again, as if to hide herself away from the girls. Realizing how silly that must look, she opened them again. Hopefully they wouldn't stop to talk. No, thank goodness, they barely gave her a second glance before moving on.

Finally convinced she could manage the trip to her room, Tessa set off to find it. Inside the lobby, she approached the most impressive staircase she had ever seen. Her breath caught in her throat as she watched well-to-do passengers ascending and descending this magnificent flight of stairs, which seemed to lead to heaven itself. If she climbed it, would she find herself on a cloud, perhaps? Having dinner with an angel? Or would she step off into the unknown, never to be heard from again?

Tessa glanced up at the domed ceiling and gasped. Beams of sunlight rippled through, casting a rainbow of colors below. The whole thing felt like a scene from a fairy story, one set in palatial splendor. How could she, a pig farmer's daughter, have landed in such a place? Had she fallen asleep and dreamed it? Would she awaken to find she'd been booted overboard?

"I feel like Alice gone through the looking-glass," she whispered. "Is this really to be my home for the next six days?" She could hardly imagine such a thing possible, and yet here she stood, in the most opulent of surroundings, dressed in a gentlewoman's finery and feeling like a queen.

She gave her boarding pass another look. It was much larger than she had imagined, and more colorful. She ran her finger over the words: OCEANIC STEAM NAVIGATION CO LIMITED, WHITE STAR LINE, MESS: I's ISMAY, IMRIE & CO., 30 JAMES ST. LIVERPOOL.

It felt so…official. So real.

This is real, isn't it? I'm not dreaming?

No, from the sights, sounds, and smells enveloping her, *Titanic* was, indeed, real. Her opportunity to leave the past behind suddenly held appeal. Bright blue skies shone through the glass domed ceiling overhead as if to say, "Better things lay ahead, Tessa." For a moment, she felt invigorated, courageous. Just as quickly, she thought about Peter and wondered how she could possibly live without him.

From behind, someone bumped into her and she had no choice but to begin the ascent. One careful step after another she made the journey, pausing only to gaze at the exquisite clock in the middle. Another whistle blast sounded, deep, sobering. Then another followed. The ground beneath her feet began to tremble. Or was that *her* trembling?

A steward at the edge of the stairway gave her a little nod. "Do you need help finding your room, miss?"

"Oh, I…yes." She nodded and did her best to look calm and assured. "That would be very helpful. I'm searching for B Deck, but I'm afraid I'm a bit turned around."

The fellow offered a comforting smile. "Easy to get that way on the *Titanic*. She's larger than most and designed like a maze." He gave her detailed instructions for reaching B Deck, but she found it difficult to focus with so many people rushing by.

After she took just a couple of steps upward, the ship jarred, and she grabbed hold of the railing. She glanced back at the steward, who offered an assuring smile. "The engines have started now, miss. The hawsers are being dropped, and tugboats will pull us out to the River Test. You might want to put off finding your room until we've pulled away from shore. You don't want to miss this."

"Oh?"

"Yes. Why don't you head up to the Boat Deck at the top of the ship to watch as we pull away from Southampton? You may never get an opportunity to see something like this again. I daresay none of us will."

"All right, then." The idea of delaying the inevitable held some appeal, particularly when she thought about having to face Iris in Cabin B-54.

She ascended the stairway and, minutes later, found herself in the midday sunlight on the Boat Deck. Tessa managed to press herself into a spot along the harbor-side railing. Glancing out at the scene before her, she took in the crowd along the shore.

To her right several women decked out in furs and jewels stood at the railing, waving their lace handkerchiefs and smiling. From somewhere off in the distance the band continued to play its merry tune. Then, as the song ended, everything fell eerily silent. She could sense the breathlessness in the people at the railing as they waited for *Titanic* to press her way toward the mighty Atlantic.

Like a bird taking flight, the splendid ship began to ease away from her berth. Reverent silence was replaced with cheers and shouts as the people offshore waved their farewells. Passengers returned with waves and cheerful good-byes. Tessa's heart swelled within her as she took it all in. Truly, the majesty of such a moment could not be expressed in mere words. She silently thanked the steward who had suggested she witness firsthand such a grand occasion as this.

A passel of rowdy fellows standing near her whooped and hollered. One even played a mouth organ while waving his cap. All around her, people celebrated. Tessa felt a surge of excitement rush through her, coupled with the usual feelings of terror. Oh, how she longed to see her brother one last time. If only she could make out his face in the crowd. With so many pressed in together, she could not. Still, she imagined him standing among them, waving and wishing her well.

Tessa felt a gentle movement beneath her feet as the ship stirred. She peered over the edge at the rollicking waters below. As the

Titanic moved along, the massive vessel stirred the waters with such force that another smaller boat appeared to be in harm's way. A loud noise, much like a gunshot, rang out as the moorings broke. A collective gasp went up from all onboard the *Titanic* as they watch the little vessel steer frighteningly near. Would they crash before ever setting out to sea?

Titanic ground to a halt, and the smaller vessel quieted. With a bit of maneuvering, she got on her way again, avoiding catastrophe. Still, the near miss caused Tessa's heart to rise to her throat. Only when *Titanic* glided ever forward toward the River Test did she begin to relax.

Onlookers on the dock followed the ship's movements, running alongside at a steady pace, as if they could run all the way from Southampton across the waters to New York. Many hollered out their Godspeeds. Tessa felt their energy as it laced the air around them. Then, with the haughtiness of a queen approaching her throne, *Titanic* headed out to sea—bold, courageous, and just a bit too big for her britches.

* * * * *

Iris peered out of the cabin window at the small ship off in the distance. Unless her eyes deceived her, the smaller ship, the *New York,* bobbed up and down like a cork flung from its bottle. Clearly, the vessel was no match for the massive *Titanic.*

Iris certainly understood how that felt. Cowering under the rocky movement of Jacquie Abingdon's charade, she too felt like a ship pulled from its moorings. Why, oh why, had she allowed herself to be pulled into such a poorly conceived plan? Ah yes, to begin a new life in New York, one where rich debutants didn't rule the day, and where girls such as herself actually stood a chance at making something of their lives.

The rumble of the engines from deep within the bowels of the mighty ship convinced Iris that there was no turning back now. She looked away from the window and drew a deep breath as she reclined on the settee. Whether or not Tessa Bowen had made it onto the ship, Iris could not be sure. She half wished the irritating pig farmer's daughter remained ashore. Then Iris could travel to America in peace.

Yes, wouldn't that be lovely? She could spend her days in this room, eating fine foods and dreaming of a better life in America. And hopefully, like the little vessel outside her window, she would weather any storms life might bring her way and come out stronger in the end.

* * * * *

Wednesday, April 10, 1912, 12:15 p.m.
The White Star Line Dock

Jacquie wove her way through the crowd on the dock, avoiding anyone who even remotely looked like her mother. The next couple of days would be tricky. With Mama staying overnight at the Harbour Hotel and Jacquie at the nearby Willingham, she would have to guard her every step. Having her meals brought to her room would be the only solution. After Mama left for Paris on tomorrow morning's train, Jacquie could finally relax.

A niggling of fear ran through her as she thought about her plan. It would not include fancy rooms onboard a luxury liner, nor would it include fine foods or new dresses. But with Peter's hand in hers, it would be a life worth living.

Peter.

Just the mention of his name brought a rush of courage and joy. He would meet her at the Willingham tomorrow to discuss a plan. If they played their roles with ease, Father would be none the wiser. For now, anyway.

Six days. Jacquie had six days until the *Titanic* arrived in New York. Then her parents would know all. Until then, she could focus on planning the rest of her life with the man she loved.

Chapter Thirteen

Wednesday, April 10, 1912, Midafternoon
Aboard the Titanic, *on the Boat Deck*

The encounter with the smaller ship set Nathan's nerves on edge, but he breathed a sigh of relief when *Titanic* found her legs. "That was a close call." He gave a nod toward the vessel that still bobbed about on the rocky waters.

"I've been aboard the *New York*." An older man at his side pointed down at the smaller vessel. "She seemed large at the time, but no more."

Nathan chuckled. "Glad I'm not her skipper. That was a little too close for comfort. My congratulations to the captain for managing the maneuver with such detail."

"I have it on good authority that our captain is the finest in the industry. We're in good hands with Edward Smith at the stern."

"So I've heard. An admirable fellow. About ready to retire, I believe."

"Who could retire with a ship such as this? I think I'd stay in my position as long as possible, just to ride the pond aboard the *Titanic*." The man gestured to the smokestacks off in the distance. "Was there ever anything more impressive?"

"She's a beauty, that's for sure."

The man introduced himself as George A. Brayton just as four whistle blasts sounded. "Looks like we're passing the Royal Yacht Squadron," he called out.

Nathan's excitement heightened. "Perfect. We're on our way."

Mr. Brayton nodded. "Yes, it's just a twenty-four-mile journey down the River Test to the English Channel. After that, it will be smooth sailing to the coast of France."

"Smooth sailing." Nathan nodded, happy to be heading home. "Sounds mighty good."

"An hour and a half until we arrive in Cherbourg. Just enough time to win a pocket full of money with a hand of cards. Might I entice you to join me?"

"No, thank you." Nathan couldn't abide the idea of gambling while on land, let alone at sea. Still, he wouldn't insult the fellow by saying so aloud. "I think I'll have a look about the ship. There's much to see."

"All I care to see is a handful of aces, my friend." Mr. Brayton tipped his bowler, elevated a bushy brow, and headed off toward the stairs.

Convinced that everything was under control, Nathan strolled the Boat Deck, taking in the sights, the sounds, and the people. A little girl with dark curls skipped along, a jovial dance in her step. If one could judge from external appearances, the child had not a care in the world. She turned to call out to a man in an unfamiliar language, and he scooped her into his arms and twirled her around until she laughed with glee.

Well behind them, a woman of means tried to walk in her hobble skirt, her stance putting forth the image of one who was austere, proud. She drew attention to herself not just with her unusual attire, but in her inability to take more than a few steps without stumbling. Nathan did his best not to laugh at her obvious self-inflicted misfortune.

A fellow in a plain brown suit carried a large camera and paused several times to take pictures. Nathan watched his fellow passengers, completely mesmerized. What an eclectic mix of people.

Through the crowd he took note of a girl about his age standing at the rail. Even from such a distance, her beautiful face caused him to give her a second look.

Nathan took in the picture of perfection standing before him. The young woman held tightly to the railing, looking out over the crowd below. The flowing blue-and-cream-colored dress showed off her figure, curving and regal, and emphasized a tiny waistline. Did she have any idea just how beautiful she was? She seemed content to stare out at the water. Her expression was calm, peaceful… until she turned to look at the swarm of people surrounding her. Then the anxiety in her eyes became evident.

In spite of her beautiful gown and fine jewels, this girl did not have the same ostentatious manner so many of the girls back home possessed. No, unlike those in his circle, this one had a wide-eyed innocence that seemed genuine and captivating.

Her sweet, curved lips tilted up in a smile as she glanced back out over the water, and a rosy hue swept over her cheeks. Her face—really, as lovely as a painting—conveyed both strength and delicacy. She had a wealth of dark hair swept up in a loose fashion, with tendrils playing about her neckline. Soft wisps framed her face, the wind blowing them about at will. She bent her head forward and studied her hands.

In that moment, high-pitched chatter drew his attention away from her. Nathan turned to see three young ladies sashaying his direction, all flirtatious giggles and smiles as they drew near. Their gaudy gowns pinched so tightly in the middle that he wondered how they breathed. And those skirts! They were full and ridiculous.

The girl in the middle wore an equally ridiculous hat with feathers so tall they rivaled the ship's smokestacks, at least from this angle. Two of the girls carried in their hands parasols in bright colors—one yellow and the other a brilliant blue. As they passed by, one of them dropped her handkerchief. Nathan bent down to retrieve it and held it up to her. She took it with a flourish and the group disappeared into the crowd.

The young woman at the railing looked on, seemingly amused by this turn of events. She glanced Nathan's way and then looked back at the water as she spoke. "She did that on purpose, of course."

"Beg your pardon?"

The young woman glanced his way again, her brows arched. "That girl. The one with the awful hat. She dropped her handkerchief on purpose. If I were you, I would have left it on the ground. In fact, I would have paid money to watch her try to bend down to pick it up. Chances are pretty good she would've injured herself in the process."

"You would've paid to see that, eh?"

"Certainly. Might've been entertaining." Tilting her head back, she peered at his face, clearly unaware of the captivating picture she made when she smiled.

From the opposite direction an older lady strolled toward them, a duo of leashed dogs pulling her along. Nathan watched as the beautiful young woman in the blue-and-cream dress dropped to her knees in an unladylike fashion, her silk skirts pouncing in a flourish around her. She scooped one of the pups into her arms and nuzzled his long face against her cheek. The owner looked a bit startled but didn't appear to mind.

"What sort of dogs are these?" the young woman asked as she turned her attention to the other pup.

"They are King Charles spaniels. Show dogs." The older woman patted the first pooch on the head.

"Oh, they're beautiful. What lovely, shiny coats. And the coloring! Makes me miss Maggie so much." Her beautiful eyes glistened as she petted the rambunctious dogs. They responded by licking her on the cheek.

"Maggie?" Nathan knelt down and boxed the dogs' ears, his gaze on the girl, not the pups. "You have a dog named Maggie?"

"Yes, a sheepdog." The girl sighed, a long, lingering, unlady-like sigh, her eyes welling with tears above beautiful, rosy cheeks. "She's not as well-groomed and certainly isn't a show dog, but she's been a part of my life since I was little. I didn't realize how much I missed her until this very moment. If only I'd known I could've brought her with me...that would have changed everything. I've always found animals to be such a comfort."

"Yes, well..." The dog's owner reached down to adjust the larger pup's collar then nodded her good-byes and marched along the deck, garnering stares from many of the passengers.

When the older woman was well out of earshot, Nathan took a closer look at the young woman now standing before him. She might not be the elusive girl from the opera, but the dress suited her as nicely. No, her eyes weren't the same shade of blue, and she had a less polished look about her. Still, her outward beauty reminded him of a porcelain doll, one that appeared fragile on the surface but had an inner strength and fortitude.

As the dogs disappeared from view, Nathan gave the girl another glance. "You'll pardon me for saying so, but you don't strike me as the sheepdog sort. I find it hard to imagine you rounding up the sheep with a dog in tow."

"Well, appearances can be deceiving." The woman's cheeks

turned pink. "And for your information, Maggie drinks from a silver bowl and takes her kibble in a crystal dish." She clamped a hand over her mouth and then laughed as she pulled it away. "I have no idea why I just said that. None of it's true. Just being silly, I suppose."

As they stood talking, the ocean breeze lifted the woman's hat and sent it sailing through the air. She gasped and ran after it, but Nathan managed to grab the plumed wonder before it tipped over the railing and into the sea below. He offered a gentlemanly bow with hat in hand and then passed it her way. "Your hat, miss."

"Thank you." Her cheeks turned red as she slipped it back on. "I have such a time getting hats pinned into place."

"Oh, I understand. I have the same problem myself."

She looked at him as if to ask, "Are you quite serious?" and he felt his lips curl up in a grin. This one would be easy to tease. Not that he was usually the teasing sort. But something about her amiable way made teasing come naturally.

Slow down, Nathan. You don't even know this girl.

As she attempted to pin her hat back into place, Nathan did his best to look aside. Only when she gave up and looked as if she might toss the ornery headpiece overboard did he chuckle. "I'm Nathan Patterson, by the way." He extended his hand, and she flinched. Seconds later, she offered her gloved hand as well, and he lightly took hold of her fingers for a shake.

"I'm…Jacquie."

She hesitated to such a degree that he wanted to ask, "Are you sure?" but did not. In spite of her vivacious approach to canines, she appeared to be shy around humans.

The young woman's gaze shifted to an approaching couple. After the duo passed by, Jacquie drew in a deep breath and plopped onto a deck chair, a delighted look on her face. "Do you smell that?"

"Smell what? The ocean?"

"No." She giggled and waved her hand in front of her nose, as if trying to drink in the aroma. "That woman. The one who just walked by with that well-heeled fellow. She smelled—"

"Like fish soup?" Nathan tried.

"No." Jacquie closed her eyes and released a lingering breath. "She smelled like heaven."

"You know what heaven smells like?" he asked.

Jacquie's eyes popped open. "I do now. It smells of honey-suckle and roses. If I close my eyes, I can almost picture them growing on the trellis in the garden. My brother's a gardener, you know. He does the most glorious things with bushes. Shapes them into animals." She immediately clapped a hand over her mouth and her cheeks pinked. "Oh."

"No shame in gardening." Nathan stifled a chuckle. "Though I'm not sure I would agree that heaven smells of honeysuckle and roses. I would like to think it smells a bit like my grandmother's apple pie."

"Oh, Mum bakes the best apple pie you've ever tasted." Jacquie's eyes sparkled with youthful merriment. "With fresh-picked apples too. Well, whenever my brother could swipe them from our neighbor's tree, anyway. He was quite the rapscallion as a boy." She put a hand to her mouth. "Oh, sorry. I don't believe I was supposed to say that either."

"I've never met a boy yet who didn't steal apples from a tree, so your secret is safe with me." He did his best not to laugh at the childlike expression on her face. "I do find it fascinating that your version of heaven smells of perfume while mine smells of food. I suppose that says something about us."

"Maybe you're just hungry."

"I am, at that. It's been a long day. Quite the adventure getting here, and then that crowd at the dock. I can't wait for dinner tonight. You will be there, won't you?"

"Well, I..." She rose and walked to the railing, her gaze shifting out to the water below. "I'm not sure if I'm up to it. My stomach has been a bit unsettled." She turned back to him with her nose wrinkled. "In fact, I believe I should go back to my room and rest awhile. Perhaps I'll decide later if food is a good idea."

"If you do come to dinner, please look for me. I'll be the one asking for second helpings." He shook his head. "I'm sure my mother will be thrilled to meet you." Perhaps *intrigued* would have been a better word. For, while this young woman appeared to have money, she did not possess the social graces Mother so admired.

"If I'm able." She glanced back out toward the water.

"The first-class dining saloon is on D Deck," he said. "Between the second and third funnels. But I believe we're meeting in the reception room prior to dinner for appetizers. Say the word and I will save you a spot at the table."

"Perhaps." Her lashes took to fluttering in a most appealing way.

"That's enough for me. You will have the seat to my right."

"Hmm." She glanced his way for a second and then turned back to the water.

Just about the time he started to say something brilliant about the dinner menu, she reached into her little purse and retrieved her boarding pass.

"So sorry, but I really must find my room now." Her eyelashes fluttered as her gaze darted about.

"Yes, well, it's been nice meeting you, Jacquie." He reached for her hand, but she did not let him take it.

"And you as well." Turning on her heels, the vision of loveliness disappeared through the crowd.

Chapter Fourteen

Wednesday, April 10, 1912, Midafternoon
Aboard the Titanic

Tessa fought her way through the boisterous crowd on the Boat Deck, finally landing back at the stairway. From there, she some-how managed to find her way to B Deck. Her breath caught in her throat as she anticipated facing Iris for the first time. When she landed in front of B-54, a gentle rap on the door was all she could manage.

No one answered for a moment, and she wondered if perhaps she'd knocked on the wrong door. The very idea made her feel ill. Just about the time she turned away to ask for assistance from a steward, the door swung open. Iris met her with an undeniable glare.

"So. You made it."

"I—I did." Tessa swallowed hard and stepped inside the room.

Iris moved with deliberation across the drawing room. With her heart in her throat, Tessa followed behind her. She wanted to take in the beautiful room, to gaze at the exquisitely carved fur-nishings, but she couldn't seem to focus on anything but the angry young woman in front of her.

Iris stopped and turned to face her, arms crossed over her chest. "Let's come to an understanding right away, you and I, just so we're clear about where things stand."

"An understanding?" Tessa fussed with her hat, anxious to be rid of the cumbersome thing.

"Yes." Iris planted balled-up fists on her hips. "I've agreed to play along with this charade, but I will not go above and beyond the call of duty."

"I—I see."

Iris snatched the hat from Tessa's hands. "When we get to New York, you go your way, and I'll go mine. When we must be together on the ship I will do my best to play my role, but it won't be easy. I've never been asked to lie before, you see. I doubt I'm any good at it. Do you understand?"

"Well, I—"

"And another thing. Jacquie left the note for her grandmother on the desk. I don't plan to stay with the woman, so what you do with that note is up to you."

Before Tessa could respond, Iris tossed the hat onto the settee and stormed off into one of the adjoining bedrooms.

Tessa stood alone in the drawing room, unsure of what to do next. She found herself half terrified at Iris's cold reception and half thrilled by her opulent surroundings. Her gaze landed at once on the ornate wood-framed mirror above the elaborate mantel. She took in the red velvet wallpaper and the gilded sconces on the wall. Then her attention shifted to the desk with its letter holder and glass cruet with crystal drinking glasses.

Tessa walked over to the small desk and examined the craftsmanship then glanced at the settee. She could almost imagine herself seated on that settee, enjoying an afternoon cup of tea while waiting on a steward to deliver a tray of scones. A half giggle erupted as she thought about it. Her gaze traveled to the envelope on the desk, the one with the word *GRANDMOTHER* written on it.

Easing her way into the second bedroom, Tessa sighed as her gaze landed on the four-poster bed with its grandiose canopy. *Is this really to be mine?* The red brocade coverlet spoke of royalty, as did the plush velvet draperies on the nearby window. Rich green carpet covered the floor space beneath her feet, giving an invitation to kick off her shoes and bury her bare toes in it. Perhaps she could do that later.

Tessa gazed at the beautifully designed wallpaper in the deep wine color, and her breath caught in her throat. Truly, she had never witnessed such luxury. The vaulted ceiling gave the room the appearance of being overly large, and the delicately carved furnishings made her feel like a princess settling into her room at the palace.

The sound of someone knocking startled her to attention. She walked back out into the drawing room and opened the door leading to the hallway. A maid holding an armful of sheets and towels greeted her with a smile. "Beggin' yer pardon, miss." The maid offered a half curtsy. "I've come with extra linens. The young woman said you would need them."

"The young woman?" Tessa repeated her words.

Iris emerged from her bedroom. "I told her to bring them. You can put those down anywhere you like." She gestured to the maid with the wave of a hand as she disappeared into her room once again.

The maid gave her an odd look. Well, no doubt. Perhaps she was confused by Iris's unwillingness to help. Or maybe she wondered where Jacquie had gone. Regardless, she carried the linens into Tessa's bedroom, placed them on the dresser, and then offered a nod before leaving. With a sigh, Tessa perched on the settee, gazed out the window, and willed herself to keep from crying.

* * * * *

Iris flung herself onto her bed, refusing to give in to the temptation to cry. How she had landed on this godforsaken ship with a young woman who did not deserve to be here remained a mystery to her.

"Why?" She shook her fist at the ceiling, anger mounting. Why did the opportunity to travel to a new land have to come with strings attached?

To play the role of a servant came naturally. But to bow the knee to a person of a lower class than she? To pretend that Tessa Bowen was anything other than a pig farmer's daughter? The plan seemed ludicrous at best. How could Jacquie Abingdon expect such a thing after all she had done for her over the years?

Iris released a slow breath then dried her eyes and examined her reflection in the mirror. Her blond hair was a mess and her red-rimmed eyes puffy from crying. Off in the distance she heard Tessa moving around in the drawing room. Iris rose and made her way to the door, opening it with a flourish. "Are you leaving?"

"No. I thought I might take a little nap before dinner, but I have to get out of this corset first." Tessa's gaze shifted to the floor. "W–would you mind helping me? I can't reach the buttons at the back of this blouse."

Iris did her best not to groan aloud as she took a few steps in Tessa's direction. She mumbled a few choice words under her breath as she reached to unfasten the buttons. Had she been doing this for Miss Jacquie, she would have used greater care. Tessa was not Miss Jacquie, however, and never would be, in spite of the fancy dresses and rushed etiquette lessons.

The force at which Iris tugged at the little pearl buttons caused one of them to break off in her hand. She shoved it into her pocket and continued her task, not saying a word. When the time came to untie the laces on Tessa's corset, she did so with little care for the young woman's comfort.

"There you go, miss." She couldn't help the sarcasm that laced her words.

"I'm so grateful." Tessa turned to gaze at her with genuine compassion in her eyes. "I want you to know that. I really am grateful."

"Hmph." Iris flung the corset on the settee and turned back toward her bedroom door, ready to put an end to this charade before it even began.

* * * * *

With an hour and a half remaining before their arrival in Cherbourg, Nathan decided to have a look around the ship. The splendid weather called out to him, so he started by touring the Boat Deck in its entirety. As the *Titanic* headed out across calm seas, he found himself relaxing and enjoying the ride. So much so that after a few minutes of trying to make his way through the crowd, he finally gave up and settled into one of the wooden deck chairs.

A few feet away, a young man with a black camera took photographs of passengers. Nathan looked on as the man snagged shot after shot—of fellow passengers, the ship, even a bright-eyed little girl who danced across the Boat Deck.

"Nice camera you've got there," Nathan said as the fellow took the seat next to him. "A Kodak?"

"It is." The young man grinned as he passed the camera Nathan's way. "Are you interested in photography?"

"My father is. He's always looking at new ways to expand his insurance business and feels that photographs will aid in that quest. In fact, he has a Kodak just like this, which is why I recognized it." Nathan gave the camera a solid look and then passed it back. He extended his hand. "Nathan Patterson."

The man shoved the camera into his left hand and gave Nathan a firm handshake with the right. "Frank Browne. Nice to meet you." He paused and turned his attention to another little girl playing in the distance then snapped another photograph. Turning back to Nathan, he grinned. "I'm trying to get as many as I can because I won't be onboard as long as most. I'm disembarking in Queenstown."

"I see. Short journey, but sweet."

"Precisely. But I've got some excellent shots already. I've been to the gymnasium, the dining saloon, and even caught a rather candid shot of Captain Smith."

"He didn't mind?"

"Not a bit. He's quite an amiable fellow. Most of the passengers have been happy to oblige. They find my camera quite the novelty, I think."

"Perhaps one day cameras will be as common as pocket watches."

"Wouldn't that be something?" Mr. Browne chuckled. "In the meantime, I will do what I can to preserve the trip in film. I count it a privilege. I never dreamed I would travel on the *Titanic*, but a good friend made it possible by offering me the ticket from Southampton to Queenstown. I plan to enter the ministry, you see. Perhaps I will acquire stories to share with my parishioners."

"No doubt. Take good notes."

"I shall." The fellow paused to take another picture then looked Nathan's way. "Have you taken a look about the ship?"

"I plan to do that now." A gust of wind mussed Nathan's hair, and he did his best to tidy it with his fingers.

"Have a stop at the barbershop," Mr. Browne said. "You will find all sorts of souvenirs there—postcards, pennants, paperweights, and so on. Quite a few ways to spend your money."

"Sounds like a good idea." Nathan rose and began the journey to the first-class barbershop, the steady hum of *Titanic*'s engines whirring beneath his feet. He located the barbershop on C Deck.

Nathan paused to read the sign in the window: HOT LATHER AND SHAVE. Didn't sound like a bad idea. This morning's rushed exit from the hotel hadn't left much time to tend to his appearance. He stepped inside the small room, taking note of the bench on one side and the chairs on the others. His gaze traveled to the souvenirs, which were hanging from the ceiling above. Nathan smiled as he took in the penknives, banners, dolls, and ribbons with RMS *Titanic* embroidered on them.

"Shave, sir?" a fellow in a White Star Line uniform asked.

Nathan looked his way and smiled. "Don't mind if I do."

He took his place in the chair and listened in on the conversation around him. Most of the men spoke about *Titanic*'s near collision with the *New York*. Nathan tried to put the incident out of his mind, choosing instead to focus on the beautiful girl he had just met. Hopefully she would come to dinner. Either way, the seat to his right would be reserved for her. He closed his eyes and tried to imagine how the dinner conversation would go. Maybe she would talk about sheepdogs and bushes shaped like animals. No doubt Mother would be appalled. Nathan chuckled just thinking about it.

"I like to see you smiling." A familiar voice rang out, startling Nathan. He opened his eyes and gazed at James Carson with a niggling suspicion running through him. Why did this fellow keep turning up?

"Having a shave, son?" James drew near and placed his hand on Nathan's arm.

Please don't call me "son."

Nathan managed a quiet "Yes."

"I believe I'll join you." James took the seat next to his and lit into a conversation about his stateroom. On and on he went, soon talking about the weather, the length of time it would take to reach Cherbourg, and the smooth ride. Nathan tried to close his eyes and ears to it but could not. Something about the man's voice irritated him. Frustrated him, even.

After a few minutes, James fell silent. Nathan took advantage of the lapse in conversation to usher up a quick prayer. *Lord, forgive me. James is a kind man. He's done nothing to hurt me. Please help me to see him as You do.*

The next few moments were spent in pleasant conversation between the two. Freshly shaved and doused with minty lotion, Nathan eventually rose from his chair. James joined him, the two men now walking together toward their cabins.

After a moment, James paused and glanced Nathan's way. "You know, son, I've been thinking a lot about you lately."

"You have?"

"Yes." A smile turned up the edges of James's lips. "You've grown into a wonderful young man."

"Thank you, sir."

James's brow furrowed. "Yes, a man I'm very proud of, in fact. I do hope you will indulge me for a moment while I make an offer that, I pray, will hold some appeal."

"An offer?"

"Yes." James paused and gave him a warm smile. "You know that I have a growing steel mill. I need an overseer for my location in New York. I thought, perhaps, that I could talk you into the position."

Nathan's breath caught in his throat. "But you know I plan to work with my father when I return to New York. I felt sure you knew that."

"Ah." James shrugged and shifted his gaze to the floor. "Well, I did hear something along those lines. Just wishful thinking on my part, I suppose. I could really use you at the mill and would be happy to compensate you accordingly, of course."

"A nice offer, Mr. Carson," Nathan managed. "And I'm honored that you would think of me. But I'm very much looking forward to linking arms with my father. I'm sure you understand. Keeping it in the family and all that."

"Of course, son." James slung his arm over Nathan's shoulder. "Of course."

The two continued in light conversation until Nathan reached his stateroom. "Will we see you at dinner?"

"Of course. I plan to take full advantage of the menu." James rubbed his midsection and smiled. "Just one small disadvantage to sailing aboard *Titanic* that I see. I'll have to have my suits let out when I get home." He laughed and Nathan did his best to seem amused. Still, something about this whole exchange bothered him, more than he could say.

James headed off to his stateroom, and Nathan paused for a moment to think about the offer the older man had made. Though he found it flattering, it did seem odd that James would try to press him into a position at the steel mill. Indeed, everything about the man seemed odd these days.

After stepping inside his drawing room, Nathan found his mother seated at the desk, writing a note. She looked up with a smile. "Oh, there you are. I thought I might have to send the troops out to search for you."

"I've been on a sightseeing adventure."

"Ah." She paused and laid down the note card. "I will do that later, I suppose. I needed to get some rest."

"Are you feeling better?"

"Much." She smiled, and he could read the relief in her eyes. "Very much looking forward to dinner. I hope you don't mind, but James will be dining with us."

"Yes, he just told me. We took a walk together."

Mother's eyes brightened at this news. "Wonderful. So glad you agree."

Nathan paced the room and tried to work up the courage to broach a delicate subject. He finally turned to look at his mother's reflection in the mirror. "Can I ask a question?"

"Well, of course." She swiveled around to face him. "What is it?"

His stomach churned as the words were spoken. "Mother, did you ask James to give me a job?"

"Hmm?" She turned, her cheeks growing red. "What?"

"He offered me a job. Just now."

Mother's eyes sparkled. "Really? At his steel mill? Oh, I do hope you will take it, Nathan. He would be such a wonderful mentor for you, and the steel industry is growing, you know. Why, you could earn a fortune in no time."

"I plan to work with Father when we get back home. You know that. You both know that." He paused and shook his head, convinced that she had arranged the offer. "Mother, please tell me you did not put James up to that."

She paused. "I confess, we have discussed the issue on occasion, though I can assure you the offer was all his. James cares deeply for you, Nathan, and he sees something in you besides a desk job in a boring office." She rose and wrung her hands as she paced the room. "Would it really be so awful to take the position and forget the insurance business?"

"But why? Why would I do such a thing? All of my life, Father has been grooming me to work alongside him. He's proud of me. And I'm honored to join him."

Mother paled. "I understand, son. I do. But life has so much to offer. Why settle?"

"Settle?" He could hardly imagine her saying such a thing.

"Yes, son. When one settles, one regrets it, often for the rest of his—or her—life." She turned back around to face the window. Nathan couldn't help but notice the trembling in her hands as she reached for the note card. Something about all of this felt wrong, but he didn't know why. Whatever regrets she referred to were surely not his.

Perhaps, after a short nap, dinner would make all things right again. He hoped so, anyway. And with a certain young lady seated at his side, the conversation was sure to be delightful.

Chapter Fifteen

Wednesday, April 10, 1912, Midafternoon
Cabin B-54

From the moment she entered Cabin B-54, Tessa struggled with a headache. Less than an hour before the dinner bugle blew, she finally called for the steward, who brought headache powders courtesy of the ship's doctor.

When the nagging pain dulled, Tessa decided that food would probably help rather than hurt. Whether she wanted to do so or not, she should go to the first-class dining saloon. She couldn't imagine making a good impression on the people in first class but would give it a try. No doubt her dinner partners would find her efforts fascinating. At least one of them would.

A rush of warmth moved over her as she remembered the young man she'd met on the Boat Deck. Nathan Patterson. Yes, Nathan would likely find her entertaining, should she decide to take the seat next to his at dinner. Then again, she'd already given him plenty of fodder, hadn't she? Dropping to her knees and playing with a dog…in public? Talking about her brother, the gardener, who shaped bushes into animals?

Tessa squeezed her eyes shut and tried to block out the embarrassing memories. Oh well. Perhaps he wouldn't think less of her. Probably just thought she was new money.

I guess I am new money.

The giggle that followed lifted her spirits for a moment and put things in perspective.

The grinding of brakes could be felt below her feet, and minutes later *Titanic* slowed to a halt. Tessa walked to the window and peered outside, realizing they must have arrived at Cherbourg. Soon the bugler would signal the dinner hour. She didn't have much time to prepare for dinner.

Knowing that she could not dress alone, Tessa went in search of Iris. As much as she hated to admit it, Tessa really needed her suitemate—not just to tie her laces and button her blouses, but for company as well. Hopefully Iris would come around in time.

The other woman's icy reception did little to encourage Tessa's thoughts on the matter, but she managed to make small talk as she dressed. They started with the necessary undergarments and then moved to the irksome corset, which squeezed the life out of her. Afterward, Tessa chose a green satin gown, surely the finest of the lot. She thought about Jacquie's admonition to make a good first impression.

Without speaking a word, Iris fussed her way through the layers of tulle in the underskirt and managed to open the dress for Tessa to step inside. She slipped her arms into the capped sleeves and gazed at her reflection in the mirror as Iris did up the buttons in the back. The gown fitted to her body as if it had been made for her, the deep green color perfect for her eyes. The luscious skirt fanned out behind her, an ocean of satin and silk.

Her favorite part, however, was the delicate silk overlay that cascaded like a banner from her left shoulder down to the right side of her waistline. The iridescent fabric hung in shimmering softness, accentuating the beading at the squared neckline and then drawing the eye down to her waist, which appeared smaller than ever with the corset pinching the life out of her underneath it all. No one at dinner would be any the wiser, though some might wonder why she couldn't squeeze down a bite of food. How could she, with her stomach so pressed in? No wonder society girls were always so slim. They had no room for even the smallest morsel.

Tessa reached inside a little cloth bag on the dressing table and came out with a necklace, a lovely strand of emerald-encrusted silver rosettes. After securing it, she reached for the delicate ivory slippers, the ones with the eyelet design. She eased her way onto the chair in front of the dressing table and slipped the shoes onto her feet, relishing the way they made her feel.

"Will you be wearing the green hat or the burgundy?" Iris asked.

"Burgundy?" Tessa had never considered wearing a hat of a different color. Surely a green dress called for a green hat, right?

"You don't know anything about fashion, do you?" Iris rolled her eyes then lifted both hats at once, showing them to Tessa. "So, which will it be?"

"I will lean on your expertise," Tessa said after a moment's reflection. Surely Iris would see this as a gesture of kindness and support.

Iris placed the green hat on the settee and went to work, pinning the burgundy one onto Tessa's upswept hair. "You will draw the eye up and away from the neckline with this one. Speaking of the neckline, did you also want to wear the fox stole this evening, or do you prefer to save that for another night?"

Tessa shivered. "I can't even imagine wearing an animal draped about my neck." She thought of Maggie and felt the sting of tears. "Seems so...inhumane."

"Inhumane?" Iris let out an unladylike snort. "Left to his own devices, the cunning fox would surely eat you for lunch. So why not wear him to dinner instead?"

"Ah. Well, when you put it like that." Tessa watched as Iris reached for the odd-looking stole and slid it over her shoulders. She petted the little fox and decided to give him a name—Freddy. Perfect. He would keep her company and offer the perfect distraction in the dining saloon.

"There now." Iris stepped back and glanced at her. "As much as I hate to admit it, you look the part. Now all you have to do is act it. Think you can remember what you've been taught?"

"I—I hope so." She couldn't honestly say. "I plan to tell everyone that I have a sore throat. Hopefully they won't expect me to speak. Much, anyway."

"Yes, just keep your lips closed and all will be well." Iris's words were tinged with sarcasm, but Tessa did her best not to let them create offense. After all, Iris was right. The less she opened her mouth, the less opportunity to play the fool. Publicly, anyway. She gave herself a quick glance in the looking-glass, feeling once again like Alice, tumbling into Wonderland. Hopefully there would be no Mad Hatters at tonight's tea party. One could hope, anyway.

* * * * *

Wednesday, April 10, 1912, Early Evening
Outside the First-Class Dining Saloon

Twilight slipped off into the darkness of evening just as tenders ferried more passengers onboard *Titanic* in Cherbourg, off the coast of France. Nathan arrived at the reception room for appetizers just as the Astors came aboard with a woman that Mother called Margaret Brown.

"I've read about her in the papers," Mother whispered. "Not all of it good."

Nathan did his best not to gasp aloud as John Astor breezed by with his new wife. Likely Mother would be giddy at the idea that they were breathing the same air as John Astor, in spite of the latest rumors about the fellow's new wife so quickly replacing the old one. To Nathan's way of thinking, the fellow needed to be horsewhipped for treating his first wife in such contemptible fashion…but wife number two seemed content enough, strolling into the reception room on her new husband's arm with a peaceful expression on her face. Not that everyone there treated the woman as an equal. Many appeared to snub her.

Nathan offered them a polite nod and looked around, hoping to see the lovely young woman he'd met on the Boat Deck—Jacquie. If only he'd gotten her surname. Hopefully she would arrive in time for dinner.

To his right, James Carson chatted with Major Archibald W. Butt, a kindly gentleman who happened to be a close personal friend of the president. Mother seemed particularly thrilled by this news and did all she could to direct Nathan's attention to the man. Still, he couldn't stop searching the crowd for Jacquie.

"Oh my." Mother nudged him with her elbow as a well-heeled couple entered. "That's Benjamin Guggenheim." Mother leaned close to whisper, "And that lovely young thing on his arm is not his wife. I've met his wife, and she doesn't look a thing like this lady." Mother's voice lowered a bit more. "If one could call this woman a lady, I mean."

Thank goodness, a blast of the bugle signaled the evening meal and Nathan did not have to comment.

"That's our cue, I believe," Mother said.

They settled in at a fine table on the far side of the dining room and Nathan left the seat to his right empty, just as he'd promised, though Mother fussed a bit at having to sit on his left, as that put her out of hearing distance from the Astors at the next table. Only when Colonel John Weir, illustrious silver miner, asked to share their table did Mother perk up. Mr. Brayton, the fellow who had invited Nathan to join him for a game of cards, joined them as well, his bushy eyebrows quite the distraction.

A steward reached to unfold the napkin and placed it in Mother's lap. She took a sip of water from the crystal goblet and sighed. "This is all so beautiful."

"Did you see Mr. Ismay?" John Weir pointed to a fellow at a nearby table. "We owe the man a debt of gratitude. Without him, *Titanic* would not exist."

"After our close call with the *New York*, I wondered if she might meet an early demise," James said.

"Not likely." Mr. Weir chuckled. "As if a tiny thing like the *New York* could take down the mighty *Titanic*."

Nathan picked up his menu card and ran his finger over the White Star Line logo at the top, feeling the impressions made from the type. He glanced at the foods listed there and tried to make up his mind.

"What are you going to have, Nathan?" Mother asked.

"Hmm?" He glanced around, wondering why the elusive young woman had not yet appeared. "What?"

"What are you going to have for dinner?"

"Oh." He glanced again at the menu, turning up his nose at the ox tongue and thinking, instead, about the oysters. "I'm hungry enough for two dinners. And I think I'll order the Pineapple Royale for dessert."

"Sounds wonderful," Mother said. "I'm just thrilled at all that our fine ship has to offer, from the luxurious accommodations to the fine food."

"I daresay, *Titanic* is more than a luxury liner," James threw in. "She's almost as large as a small city—one set afloat."

"Yes, a city with all classes of people dwelling therein." Mother rolled her eyes then dabbed at her lips with her napkin. "I've seen more than my fair share of the lower set today, if you know what I mean."

"Mother." Nathan shot her a warning look, but she kept going.

She wrinkled her nose and placed her napkin back in her lap. "Well, I'm just not used to it, that's all. And I can't help but think this isn't good for them. You know how it is. Folks in the lower classes always want what they see in first class. That puts us at risk, which is disconcerting."

"I daresay the folks in second class are eating like kings tonight too. So I think our risk is minimal. Besides, first class is separated from the others." Nathan gripped his menu and silently prayed that the conversation would shift gears.

"Oh, do you see who's seated behind us?" Mother jabbed him with her elbow. "Isidor and Ida Straus."

"Straus?" Nathan glanced at the older couple then back at his menu. "Don't know them."

"Owners of Macy's Department Store." Mother rolled her eyes. "Honestly, if it's not the insurance business, you know nothing about it."

Nathan felt the sting of those words but did his best not to let it show. Oh, how he wanted to give his mother a piece of his mind, to tell her that the insurance business was far more important than she knew. But it wouldn't make any difference. He shifted his gaze back to the menu and tried to make up his mind about the various selections.

Nathan looked up just in time to see a vision of loveliness headed his way—the woman from the Boat Deck, dressed in an emerald-green dress straight off a fashion plate with a fox stole lopped cockeyed about her neck. If nothing else, the dress would please Mother. The woman in it? Well, that was yet to be determined.

* * * * *

Wednesday, April 10, 1912, Midafternoon
The First-Class Dining Saloon

Tessa made her way through the first-class lounge, inwardly ooh-ing and aahing at the elegant Versailles style. Garnering all the courage she could muster, she then took several tentative steps into the first-class dining saloon with its gold-plated fixtures and luxurious seating areas. She could scarcely get over the magnitude of the place—larger than any dining room she had ever seen. Her gaze traveled to the alcoves and then to the leaded windows. Truly, such finery did not exist in her world. Until now.

She made her way past the tables filled with chattering women and their plunging necklines, gaudy dresses, and pristine white gloves, her gaze traveling from table to table, person to person. Her gaze landed on the trio of young women who had behaved so flir-tatiously with Nathan just hours ago. One of the girls gave her an admiring look as she passed by, though Tessa realized the lovely green-satin gown had garnered the attention. Or maybe the woman was staring at the fox stole, which had slipped off to one side and dangled over her left shoulder as if ready to give chase.

C'mon now, Freddy. Tessa straightened the naughty fox and tried to focus. Just about the time she thought she might not find Nathan Patterson, she caught a glimpse of him seated at a table on the far side of the room with an elegant-looking woman to his left and several older men gathered round. She swallowed hard, whispered up a "Lord, help me!" prayer, and took a few steps in his direction.

He rose at once, his broad smile letting her know that her presence was most assuredly welcomed at the table.

"You came." He gave her a polite nod.

"I did." She felt her cheeks grow warm as she glanced his way.

He pulled out the empty chair to his right and she took a seat, her nerves in a frenzy as introductions were made all the way around. She found herself stuttering as she said, "I'm Jacquie Abingdon, of the London Abingdons," though she managed to get the words out. Nathan's mother looked duly impressed.

"My dear, is your father the steel magnate?"

Tessa didn't have any idea what the word *magnate* meant but nodded anyway and offered a brave, albeit forced, smile. She fussed with the fox stole, wanting to remove it, but she wasn't sure whether she should. Were the other ladies still wearing their wraps? No. She slipped Freddy off and slung him over the back of the chair. The waiter scooped low, snagged the little stole, and carted him off. To where, Tessa did not know. Or care, for that matter. The wait staff could use him for target practice and she wouldn't mind.

"Abingdon?" The fellow with the slicked-back hair glanced her way. "Why, I would know that name anywhere. Your father and I have done business together. I'm George Brayton, but I believe you used to call me Mr. B." At once Tessa's heart felt heavy enough to sink the ship.

"Don't you remember me?" The man glanced her way, a twinkle in his eyes.

Tessa's heart contorted as she gazed into the face of the older fellow. "I'm sorry, sir, but the incident seems to have slipped my memory." Her words came out shaky at best.

A hint of a smile turned up the edges of his lips, and his mustache twitched. "No doubt you've forgotten my face, as well. It has been some time since I visited with your father at Abingdon Manor. Six years, in fact."

"Ah." A wave of relief washed over her as she considered the lapse in time. Perhaps she could keep this charade afloat after all. If she played her cards right.

The man offered a kindly smile. "We've both changed, no doubt. I wore a beard back then, and you were just a slip of a girl, running through the hallways of the manor and generally underfoot."

"Well, then, little has changed." She managed a nervous chuckle.

"You are very much as I remember you." His eyes narrowed to slits. "Though the last time I saw you, you wore your hair in pigtails."

Tessa grinned. "Indeed."

A warm smile followed on his end. "The little caterpillar has transformed into a beautiful butterfly. Quite the lady, in fact." A tiny wink followed on his end.

The fellow's flattering words sent a shiver through her, though the part about looking like a lady brought an unexpected smile. She dabbed at her lips with her napkin. "Thank you, sir."

The man's gaze narrowed. "Only one thing perplexes me. I recall giving you a funny little name back then. I believe I called you *Little Blue Eyes*."

Tessa's stomach suddenly felt like lead. "O–oh? I don't recall."

"Yes. I remember it clearly." He took a sip from his water glass then put it back down on the table. "Such bright blue eyes on such a beautiful little girl. Only, now they appear green."

Tessa's gaze shifted to her water glass, which she picked up and drank from. Her trembling hand nearly gave away her nerves. *Calm, Tessa. Calm*. With what she hoped would look like a confident smile, Tessa put the glass down, gazed directly at the man, and batted her eyes. "My trick, sir, is to wear blue as often as possible. You can see for yourself that my eyes are neither blue nor green, but something of a mixture of the two. When I wear blue, well…" She dabbed at her lips once again in flirtatious fashion. "Let's just say that I know how to play the blue card when I need to. Tonight, as you can see, I went for the green."

"Indeed. You did." He quirked a brow. "And I find the green nearly as compelling as the blue."

"Perhaps." She brushed her hands across her skirt to dry her damp palms. "Though I can tell you that I tend toward the blue on most occasions. Perhaps when we are next together, you will see for yourself." Gracious, had she really said such a thing aloud?

The fellow looked more than a little interested. "Then I look forward to our next meeting very much."

Oh my. What have I done?

Tessa's White Star Line napkin tumbled to the floor. *Oh, posh.* The waiter leaned down with a flourish and snatched it up then offered her a smile. Would she ever get used to this?

In an attempt to calm herself, she took a couple of deep breaths.

Her gaze shifted from chair to chair as she took in the men first. The fellow across the table with the shiny bald head looked kind enough. So did the older fellow, the one with the shimmering white hair meticulously combed to one side. He had introduced himself as James Carson, a friend of Nathan's. Or perhaps a friend of Nathan's mother's. They appeared to be very chummy.

At last, she settled her gaze on Nathan's mother. The woman was a fine match for most of the other elegant ladies in the group, her nose equally as elevated and her hat a smidgen larger than fashion might dictate. Her brow furrowed as she took in Tessa's gown, but an admiring smile followed.

"My dear, is that a haute couture gown?"

Tessa felt a wave of panic sweep over her. *Haute couture?* Whatever did that mean?

"From Paris?" Nathan's mother added.

Ah. "No, it's not." Tessa reached for her napkin. "Though, I daresay my seamstress could easily find work in Paris. She's quite skilled and very fast, as well." Tessa tried to steady her breathing and willed her frantic heart to slow down.

Mrs. Patterson fussed with her gloves. "Well, it's lovely. And that shade of green is very nice on you."

"Thank you." Tessa cleared her throat, her hands fluttering to the neckline of her dress. "I do hope you will forgive me, but I'm struggling with a bit of a sore throat tonight. Please don't mind me if I listen in while the rest of you visit."

She turned her attention to the demitasse cup and saucer then fixed her gaze on the glass cruet and the silver ice bucket, which sat nearby. Glancing over the rows of silverware, she tried to remember everything Jacquie had taught her. Oh dear. Which fork did she start with, again? Ah yes, the one on the outside. She hoped.

The saltcellar she recognized, of course. And the toothpick holder. She couldn't make heads or tails out of some of the rest of it, though. Determined to stay focused, Tessa picked up the menu card and studied it, her heart in her throat. She recognized the words in English. Well, most of them. But the rest appeared to be in a different language. French, maybe? After examining the words written in English, she winced.

"Ox tongue?" She glanced up at Nathan, feeling a bit nauseated.

He shrugged. "It's never been a favorite."

She lifted the menu to read the rest but finally put it down, more confused than ever. How could she possibly eat oysters? Were they meant to be eaten?

Nathan caught her gaze and smiled. She knew that she should raise the menu and get back to the business of selecting her meal but found herself drawn to those twinkling eyes. Something in them rang of mischief. And caring. She could not deny that Nathan found her interesting. Not that she wanted to draw attention to herself, of course.

No, fading into the background was best.

She raised the menu and focused on her choices once again. She hardly knew how to pronounce these things, let alone eat them. A hint of a sigh rose up inside her, and she forced it down. The waiter appeared and shared his thoughts on the manager's special of the day. Tessa couldn't make sense out of what he said, but the way he described the foods made them sound delicious, in spite of their somewhat repulsive names.

"Have you decided, miss?" He held tight to his order tablet.

"Oh, I— No. Not yet." With the wave of a hand, she let him know that she wasn't quite ready. It would be easier to listen to the others first.

She listened closely as the others chose their foods. The man across from her ordered the Asparagus Salad with Champagne Saffron Vinaigrette. *Ah. So that's how you pronounce it.* To her right, a lady in a lovely red dress ordered the Vegetable Consommé. What in the world was *consommé*? Then another ordered oysters. Ick. Nathan lifted his gaze from the menu to ask for the beef. Mmm. Finally something she recognized. Sounded delicious.

None of the rest made much sense to her, so she mimicked everything Nathan had said, right down to the oyster appetizer. Then she fussed with her napkin and gazed at the wall decor.

"Oh, I hear the food onboard *Titanic* is to die for." Nathan's mother smiled. "No doubt we'll all put on weight on this journey."

"Not enough to sink the ship," Mr. Carson said, and he winked.

Mr. Weir leaned forward, placing his elbows on the table. Tessa knew that Jacquie would have been appalled by this but didn't say so.

"I read somewhere that *Titanic* needs seventy-five thousand pounds of meat to feed her passengers. Can you imagine? And something like forty tons of potatoes."

"Heavens." Mrs. Patterson's brows elevated. "If we're worried about the ship going down, let's toss the potatoes. I daresay my waistline can do without them." She giggled.

"There are forty thousand eggs aboard, as well," Mr. Weir said. "So don't think twice about asking for seconds at breakfast."

Tessa looked his way and he offered a wink, his somewhat bushy eyebrows elevating a bit beneath his wire-rimmed spectacles. She took in his overcoat with its stiff collar and tie. Perhaps he was as uncomfortable in that getup as she was in this ridiculous dress with its confining undergarments.

Mr. Brayton, a rather rotund fellow, took a sip from his crystal goblet then placed the glass on the table. "If the *Titanic* is sturdy enough to hold three thousand passengers, all our luggage, and thousands of pounds of cargo besides, I daresay she can handle any added weight around my midsection." He rubbed his extended belly and chuckled. A couple of the ladies snickered, and he went back to drinking.

Nathan looked a bit flabbergasted by the man's outburst. He shook his head and looked Tessa's way. "Miss Abingdon, what do you think of the journey thus far? Is it everything you imagined?"

Everyone at the table turned to face her. So much for disappearing into the background or feigning a sore throat. She steadied her breathing and reminded herself to use the proper manner of speech before she uttered a word, one the real Jacquie Abingdon would be proud of.

"I daresay the views are magnificent from my suite." She spoke with great care, enunciating every word. "And the room is all I imagined and more." She dabbed at her lips with the cloth napkin. "But, by far, the best part of the journey has been the people I've met along the way. I've already acquired new friends." She spoke of the dogs, of course. They had greeted her with enthusiasm, hadn't they?

"Indeed." Nathan quirked a brow. "New friends, indeed."

She felt her cheeks grow warm and drew her hand to her throat, hoping he would take the hint about her supposed sore throat. Why did this young man have such an effect on her? She couldn't be sure. Still, she'd better watch herself. No point in making herself vulnerable to anyone on this journey.

No, Tessa. Just get to the other side of the pond and start your life over. No thoughts of romance along the way.

Her gaze shifted back to his captivating eyes and she pressed down a grin. *No, Tessa. Do not entertain romantic notions, even for someone as handsome as Nathan Patterson.*

Chapter Sixteen

Wednesday Evening, April 10, 1912
The First-Class Dining Saloon

Nathan couldn't help but chuckle at the look on Jacquie's face when the waiter delivered the food. Her eyes widened as she took in the oxtail Mr. Weir had ordered. For a moment, she looked as if she might be ill. Just as quickly, she seemed to regain her composure. He had to give it to her—she recovered quickly from whatever moments of distress came her way. An admirable trait.

"They don't eat a lot of oxtail where you're from?" he asked.

Her usually rosy cheeks paled. "N–no."

"Same here. But I understand it's actually quite good."

"I'll never know." Jacquie shook her head with such force that he wondered how the feathers on her hat stayed in place. When the waiter delivered her plate of food, she gazed down at it as if she couldn't figure out what to do. She finally dove in, slowly at first and then picking up speed. Nathan noticed that she pushed the oysters aside. With a wink, he slipped them onto his plate. She mouthed a silent "Thank you" and kept eating.

Mother glanced Jacquie's way, her brows knitted together as she watched the young woman swallow her dinner in such a rushed fashion. No doubt she found her to be something less than proper. Not that Nathan minded. He found Jacquie easy on the eyes and easy to talk to. The rest of the group bored him to tears.

Mother and James chatted at length about their plans aboard ship, Mr. Weir went on and on about *Titanic*'s provisions, and Mr. Brayton couldn't seem to talk about anything except card playing and the like...until an unfamiliar woman entered the dining saloon and took her seat at the table behind them.

The rather somber-looking woman settled into her chair and fussed with the fur collar on her ornate velvet gown. She then unpinned her hat and set it aside, revealing a mass of disheveled dark curls.

Mother's eyes widened, and Nathan could practically read her excitement as she whispered, "Do you know who that is?"

He did not, of course, so he shook his head. Still, he kept his gaze on the woman as the waiter approached to take her fur collar.

"Edith Russell." Mother fussed with her necklace as if nervous. "She's a fashion writer."

"Oh, a fashion writer? Truly?" Jacquie swung around to give the woman a closer look. "My friend—er, lady's maid—will be thrilled with this bit of news. She's something of a fashion expert herself."

"Your lady's maid, a fashion expert?" Nathan's mother pursed her lips. "Unusual. Well, I daresay Edith is a story in and of herself. I heard one of the stewards talking about her just before the tenders arrived with passengers from Cherbourg. That's where she boarded, you see."

"Ah." Nathan tried to act interested but found it difficult. If not for the curiosity in Jacquie's eyes, he would tune out the rest of the conversation.

"Yes, I hear she's taken possession of a cabin on A Deck but has also acquired a second on E Deck to house her clothes." Mother leaned forward and whispered, "She's brought nineteen trunks aboard. Can you even imagine? All filled with clothes, no less."

"I read somewhere that she's got a successful buying-and-consulting service in France," Mr. Weir said. "Perhaps that has something to do with it." He reached for his water glass and took a sip then dabbed at his lips with the cloth napkin.

"Yes, and she's coming out with her own line for Lord & Taylor in New York." Mother squared her shoulders and gave the woman an admiring glance. "It's to be called *Elrose*."

"I sense a shopping spree in your future, my dear." James Carson reached over and patted Nathan's mother on the hand. "That should bring a smile to your face."

A cold chill settled over Nathan as he watched the exchange. He was unsure which bothered him more—James touching his mother's hand, or the fact that he had referred to her as "my dear."

"I can't wait to tell Iris," Jacquie said. "She will be so excited."

Nathan watched as his mother's eyes narrowed into slits. Mr. Brayton lit into another discussion about cards, and by the time they finished dessert, the older fellow had worked himself up into a lather about the idea. He rose and tossed his napkin on the table. "I don't know about the rest of you, but I plan to spend the night in a poker game once this grand meal is behind us. Any brave souls want to join me?" He took another swig from his glass.

"I don't believe so, sir." Nathan took a sip of his water and leaned back in the chair. "But thank you for the offer." He glanced Jacquie's way. "I had hoped to take a walk around the Boat Deck. I hear the moon is nice tonight."

"Sounds lovely." Her eyelashes fluttered in a soft, appealing way. Not like the giggly girls who had sashayed past him earlier in the day, but with more of an innocent air.

He offered a smile. "Perhaps you would consider joining me?"

"Don't be silly, Nathan," his mother said as she folded her napkin and placed it on the table next to her White Star Line coffee cup. "Miss Abingdon has already told you that she has a sore throat. The night air would only make things worse."

"Yes, you really must take care of yourself, Miss Abingdon." Mr. Brayton gave her a compassionate look. "I would never forgive myself if anything happened to you. Your father would have my head."

Jacquie paled. "I do suppose it makes more sense to go back to my room. I'm awfully tired."

"Can I walk you to your room?" Nathan asked, not quite ready for the evening to end.

"I suppose." She offered him a shy smile. "I'm on B Deck."

This started a new conversation about the various cabins, but Nathan wasn't interested in any of that. He simply wanted to offer his arm to this vision of loveliness.

And so he did. As she rose, he extended his arm in gentlemanly fashion and she took it then nodded to the group.

"Thank you for including me in your little dinner party. I apologize for not joining in the conversation more. Perhaps I will recover shortly." She gestured to her throat.

"I hope you feel better in the morning, my dear." Mr. Brayton nodded in her direction. "Until then, get some rest." He muttered something about the color of her eyes, but Nathan didn't hear all of it.

The waiter appeared with the fox stole, which she slipped into place. That done, she turned to gaze at the fashion editor seated at the table behind them. In doing so, she somehow got herself caught in the hem of the green satin skirt and nearly took a tumble.

"Oh my." Jacquie managed to get control of herself before

falling, and her cheeks flushed pink. A couple of the ladies at a nearby table whispered to one another, their words loud enough to be heard above the chatter in the dining room. Their critique of Jacquie's near-fall angered Nathan.

Apparently it upset the fashion designer too. Edith Russell gave Jacquie a warm smile and then offered her thoughts on the matter. "My only complaint about first class thus far is that it feels rather stiff and cold. No coziness to it at all."

"Indeed." Jacquie giggled then turned back to face Nathan, who gave her a nod. He offered her his arm again and she took it.

Across the table, Mother cleared her throat, and James Carson rose to help her with her chair. Nathan took advantage of the opportunity to usher Jacquie out of the room, away from the stares and whispers of those nearby.

Heads held high, they strolled out of the dining saloon. Unfortunately, Mr. Brayton followed close behind, still talking at length about the time he'd visited Jacquie's home in London. For whatever reason, this appeared to upset her. Nathan could feel her hand trembling.

The fellow leaned a bit too close to Jacquie, to Nathan's way of thinking. He could read the discomfort on her face and wondered if he should intervene in some way.

Nathan felt his temper rise up within him as he watched the exchange. This fellow had no business pressing his attentions on Jacquie in such a way. The need to protect her washed over him.

When Mr. Brayton turned off at the hallway, headed to the smoking room, Nathan gazed at Jacquie and did his best to think through his words before speaking them aloud.

"Jacquie, I hope you will forgive me if what I'm about to say is out of line."

"Out of line?" Her brow wrinkled. "How could anything you say be out of line? You're a perfect gentleman."

"Thank you." He allowed the compliment to sink in before continuing. "But I have some concerns and hope you will allow me to voice them."

"Please do."

"You are traveling alone, with no father or brother to watch over you." He spoke the words tentatively and almost wished he could take them back when tears sprang to her eyes. "I'm sorry. I don't mean to broach a sensitive subject. Rather, I had hoped to offer my services. If you have any need for—well, for help. For..." He hesitated, biting back the word *protection*.

"I see." Her gaze met his. "You want to be a big brother, of sorts?"

"Well—" He hadn't exactly thought of the word *brother*, but if it brought her some comfort, why not? "I suppose you could say that. I just want you to know that I'm here, should you need me. There are certain men about, men who have no concern for a young lady's welfare. If they see you on my arm, they will be less likely to bother you."

"Oh, I see." Her smile captivated him. "So you are offering me your arm, then."

Was that a look of interest in her eyes?

"I would like to be of service, yes," he responded.

"Might I remind you that I am not traveling alone, as you presume? My friend Iris is with me."

"Your lady's maid, you mean?"

"She is far more than that. We have been close"—Jacquie appeared to stumble over the word—"for some time now."

"Then I shall offer my services to Iris as well."

This garnered another smile from Jacquie, which settled the issue in his mind. He led the way beyond the reception area and toward the elevators. Once they arrived in front of the golden doors, he pressed the button and made small talk while waiting. When the doors opened, Jacquie glanced his way, her eyes wide.

"We–we're going to get inside this box?"

"Box?" Nathan raked his hands through his hair. "You mean the elevator?"

"Oh, yes." She drew her hand to her mouth as if embarrassed and then quickly pulled it away. "Elevator. Of course."

Several people flooded out, leaving it empty. He reached to hold the door open. "Well, sure we get inside. How else are we going to go to B Deck?"

"I presumed we would take the stairs, but if you insist..." Jacquie appeared to hesitate as she stepped onto the lift.

Nathan instructed the elevator attendant to stop at the B Deck then glanced her way. "If you're not feeling well, the stairs will tax you. For that reason, I thought the elevator might be best."

She gave his arm a little squeeze. "You are so kind to think of me."

"Of course."

Once inside, fellow passengers joined them, pressing in around them. After a few seconds Nathan could barely find Jacquie in the crowd. He did hear a gasp, followed by a giggle, as the elevator began to lift. Where had this girl been hiding? He couldn't quite figure her out. She wore the dress of a fine British young lady but talked about stealing apples and playing with sheepdogs, and she knew nothing of elevators? How could this be?

Perhaps she was, as Mother liked to call it, "new money." Far too new for any snobbery. Well, so be it. Aristocratic snobbery was far too highly rated, to his way of thinking. He preferred this sort of wide-eyed innocence. It looked nice on Jacquie.

In fact, everything looked nice on Jacquie. As she moved toward him, his gaze swept the length of her chestnut hair and then landed on her beautiful eyes, that greenish-blue mix she had spoken of. They twinkled with merriment as the elevator came to a stop and the doors opened. She stepped out of it, her wide-eyed wonder almost causing him to chuckle aloud. He didn't do so for fear of offending her. Still, she captivated him on every level.

Nathan's thoughts shifted to the young woman from the opera. Was she still onboard *Titanic*? Were those haunting blue eyes still singing their soulful refrain? Of course, she was off-limits. He knew that. Still, something about those eyes captivated him even now.

As he turned his gaze to Jacquie Abingdon's smiling face, all memories of the elusive woman in blue slipped away, like the evening breeze lifting his cares and sending them adrift across the mighty Atlantic. Why dream about heaven when one had already passed through the pearly gates?

* * * * *

Wednesday Evening, April 10, 1912
Cabin B-54

Iris ate a quiet dinner in her cabin and toyed with the idea of taking a walk around the Boat Deck. She longed to look up at the stars, to be swept away by their beauty, to feel the wind in her hair. And to think. Yes, with so many things on her mind, she needed time to come to grips with them. Though she tried to lay down her frustrations with both Jacquie and Tessa, she could not. Just about the time she thought she couldn't bear the idea of traveling across the Atlantic, feelings of excitement crept up. *Am I really going to America? Starting my life over?* Hope took root in her very soul.

Yes, a walk was definitely in order.

She reached for her jacket and draped it over her shoulders then opened the door leading to the hallway. She took a few tentative steps outside, unsure which way to go. Just as she rounded the corner, Tessa came into view. She walked with a handsome young man, about their same age, who gushed over her. At once, envy rose up inside of Iris. Of course a handsome fella like this would look at Tessa all dolled up in Jacquie's expensive gown and hat. What fella in his right mind wouldn't fancy a girl with money? She forced the feeling aside, determined to focus on anything but that.

As they passed by, Tessa glanced her way, and her eyes widened. "Iris?"

"I'm going for a walk, Miss Jacquie." Iris had to force the words but managed, in spite of the lump in her throat. "I do hope that's all right with you."

"Well, of course." Tessa pulled her arm from the young man's and took a couple of steps toward her, that crazy fox stole slipping around her neck in precarious fashion. "I don't like the idea of you going alone, though. Would you like me to come with you? I have so much to tell you. You're simply not going to believe who's just come onboard. A fashion editor. And she offered encouraging words just now when I tripped in the dining room."

This certainly piqued Iris's interest, but she tried not to let it show. Strolling the deck by herself would be preferable right now. "Thank you for the offer, but I would rather go alone. I need some fresh air." She felt the sting of tears in her eyes but willed them away. She would not cry again. Why bother?

The young man with Tessa gave her a nod. "You must be Iris."

"Yes."

He extended his hand. "Nathan Patterson. I've heard so many wonderful things about you. I can tell that you are a good friend to Jacquie."

"You have?" She stumbled over the words. "I mean, I am. We're very good friends. Indeed."

A few seconds later a little boy ran by, nearly knocking them down. The young man with Tessa chuckled as he put his hand up to caution the youngster. "Whoa there, fella."

"Sorry." The boy gave them a sheepish look then took off running again toward some unknown destination.

"Such a little charmer, that one," Tessa said as she followed the youngster with her gaze.

"Hardly." Iris cleared her throat and then fussed with her jacket. "And what is a child of that age doing up this late in the evening, anyway? He should be in bed by now."

"Speaking of which, it's high time you got some rest, as well," the young man said as he gave Tessa a compassionate look. "I'm so sorry you're not feeling well. I do hope tomorrow will be better."

Tessa's hand fluttered to her throat. "Oh, I'm sure it will be."

No doubt. Iris did her best not to roll her eyes.

The handsome stranger bid them both good night and headed off down the hall toward the staircase. Iris went that way too, turning back only long enough to assure Tessa that she could manage on her own.

Really, she had a lot to think about. Rich folks—even handsome ones, like the stranger on Tessa's arm tonight—were as crazy as loons at times. They cared more about their money and possessions than the lives of the people they came in contact with. Not that she cared to judge the young man. He seemed kind enough.

Besides, right now she had other things to think about—her future in New York, for instance. And if what Tessa had said was true, a certain fashion designer onboard might be just the connection Iris needed to begin her new career.

* * * * *

Wednesday, April 10, 1912
Willingham Hotel, Southampton, England

Jacquie settled into her room at the Willingham in Southampton. The simplistic style did not offer the luxury she was accustomed to, and it in no way compared to the room she might have been sleeping in tonight, had she stayed onboard the *Titanic*. Still, she found it to be clean and respectable. Best of all, it offered her the privacy she needed to sort things out in her mind. Tomorrow morning, Peter would come for a visit and they would put together a plan. Until then, she had a lot to think about.

After eating a late dinner, which the bellman was kind enough to deliver to her room, Jacquie settled into the bed. When she closed her eyes, she felt the gentle movement of the ship and almost thought herself still aboard the *Titanic*. She dreamed the most terrifying dream—caught onboard the ship, she found herself drifting from Peter. He stood at the dock, growing farther and farther away. Jacquie cried out, but the ship continued to pull her from the one she loved.

Desperate to get back to him, she stood at the railing of the ship and gave thought to jumping overboard. Perhaps she could swim back to shore and land safely in his arms.

The dream ended in a haze of tears and perspiration. Her eyes opened to the darkness of the room, and she steadied her breathing, realizing she had not traveled anywhere at all.

Still, she felt as if she'd somehow left her heart at sea, thousands of miles away from Peter and all she held dear. Terrified at the prospect of losing him, Jacquie pulled her knees to her chest and wept. The tears flowed with great force. In those moments, she grieved so many things—the loss of her home, her family. The guilt over putting Tessa—sweet, unselfish Tessa— on a ship bound for an unknown world. Agony over losing her good friend, Iris.

In that moment, as the emotions washed over her, Jacquie found herself calling out to the only One who could make sense of it. With her heart in her throat, she began to pray to the God of heaven, the only One who could heal her heart and make sense of the chaos she had created with this impulsive decision of hers. Surely He would see fit to forgive her and make all things right again.

Chapter Seventeen

Thursday Morning, April 11, 1912
Aboard the Titanic, *on the Boat Deck*

The morning of April 11 dawned cool and cloudy. After a leisurely breakfast in her cabin, Tessa decided to venture up to the Boat Deck for a walk. She managed to talk Iris into joining her, though a bit of arm wrestling had to take place first. Together they strolled the deck, Tessa attempting to make conversation with the young woman who seemed bent on staying cold and distant.

Beneath their feet, the steady hum of *Titanic's* engines brought a comforting whir. The ship breezed her way across the rolling waves, which seemed content to bow to her greatness. Off in the distance, hints of sunlight peeked through the clouds. Tessa found herself captivated by it all—the color of the water as it met the sky off on the horizon. The soothing lull of the ship as it pulled its way through the water. The crisp air over the Atlantic. All of it swirled together to create an exhilarating experience unlike anything she had ever dreamed.

Still, one thing perplexed her. Iris. When would the stubborn girl come around? Would the coldness never end?

Thank goodness, Iris finally spoke up, albeit about the attire of the other ladies on the Boat Deck. Over the next few minutes, she gave commentary on dozens of outfits as the ladies and teenaged girls strolled by with their parasols in hand. Many of the dresses Iris "simply adored," to quote her very words. Still others she found "exaggerated and ridiculous." Tessa found her comments intriguing. Clearly, Iris had made a study of fashion. She had quite an eye for it, in fact. And, to be honest, Tessa was just happy to hear Iris talking at all.

As they passed a woman with puffed sleeves, Iris rolled her eyes. "So painfully out of style," she whispered.

"Truly?"

"Yes. And see that woman with the gloves below her elbow? Hasn't she heard that modern women wear their gloves above the elbow now?"

Tessa did not respond but, instead, tugged at her gloves to make sure they covered her elbows.

"Look at this one." Iris nudged her as a crowd of older women headed their way, clustered together like baby chicks.

"Which one?" Tessa whispered.

"The lady in the hideous orange dress carrying the fuzzy little dog. See that feather hat? It's ridiculously large, and the color is completely wrong for the dress. She probably had to pack an extra trunk just to fit the hat onboard. No doubt her entire wardrobe is oversized."

"Perhaps she went to Paris on a shopping adventure. Last night at dinner, Nathan told me that his mother shopped while they were in Paris."

"Nathan. That's the fellow who walked you home? The handsome one?"

"Yes."

"You met for the first time yesterday?" Iris crossed her arms at her chest.

"Of course. We just boarded yesterday, after all."

Iris pursed her lips. "Hmm. Well, you two seemed quite cozy. I'm not sure I believe you're perfect strangers."

A flush of embarrassment washed over Tessa at once. "Iris! Take that back."

"I didn't mean anything by it. You just seemed...friendly."

"He's easy to talk to. And so is his mother. She's very fashionable. No doubt she thinks I'm dreadful. I had little to add to her conversation about clothes. I've never really kept up with such things. Most of my days were spent in a simple dress, one in constant need of washing thanks to my hours in the pig stall."

Iris rolled her eyes. "I get so tired of wearing a uniform. I dream of the day when I can wear whatever I like and be done with it forever."

"You can wear whatever you like on the ship. It doesn't make a bit of difference to me."

"It will to those who think you're Jacquie Abingdon. They will expect your lady's maid to be appropriately dressed. But when I get to America..." A dreamy-eyed expression came over her. "I plan to dress as I like and eat when I like and do as I like." She stopped walking and turned to Tessa. "You understand what I'm saying, don't you?"

"Not—not really."

"I'm trying to tell you that I have no intention of staying with you if or when you go to Jacquie's grandmother's house. Setting out on my own is all I've ever wanted. I have some money put away...." She paused. "Anyway, it's not much but it's certainly enough to get me started in a tenement house. And I don't care if I ever see you or Jacquie Abingdon again."

"I—I can't say I blame you there." Tessa sat on an empty deck chair, unsure of what else to say. "And, to be honest, I'm not sure what I will do once I arrive, either. Surely Jacquie's grandmother won't welcome me with open arms, letter or no letter. So I have to think of what to do should she boot me."

Iris pursed her lips. "I have dreams just like the rest of you. And I don't care if they seem unrealistic. They're mine. Truly, the only thing I own—my hopes. My dreams. And no one is going to steal them from me."

"I don't care to." Tessa felt her backbone stiffen. "Why would you say that?"

"Because you've been perfectly willing to steal another person's identity. You've done it with ease, no less." The smirk that followed punctuated Iris's harsh words.

"I didn't steal it. She placed it into my hands and gave me little choice in the matter. And if you think for one minute that this has been easy, you are wrong. It's not my fault. I'm here because..." Tessa started to mention her brother's name but thought better of it. She drew a deep breath, determined to calm this storm. "Iris, you can't go on being angry with me for the whole of the journey. We will both be miserable, and I cannot bear it."

"Miserable?" Iris let out an unladylike snort. "You, miserable? Dining in first class? Sleeping in a four-poster bed? Gazing at pictures with gilded frames in the first-class dining saloon?"

"Well, yes, but it's not all enjoyable. I've been miserable *especially* when I'm in places like the first-class dining saloon."

"Wearing a dress like that? One that would cost me two year's wages? You are miserable? Hardly."

"None of that can be helped," she argued. "I won't have a shilling's worth of fun if I know you're upset at me."

"A shilling's worth of fun? You should pay me ten shillings for having to listen to such nonsense. Would you lead me to believe that you are not enjoying every moment of this?" Iris's eyes shimmered with tears. "Truly? You've been handed the whole of the world on a silver platter and you're unable to enjoy it? I rather doubt that."

"A tarnished platter, perhaps. And if this is the world, then give me something else. For I assure you, I'm not enjoying myself. This is grueling."

A stirring behind her let Tessa know someone had joined them. She turned quickly to find Mrs. Patterson standing nearby. Tessa's heart leaped to her throat, and she prayed the woman had not overheard the conversation. From the look of concern in her eyes, she had certainly heard something. How much, Tessa could not be sure.

"Jacquie, we missed you at breakfast this morning."

"Ah, yes." Tessa managed to steady her breathing and willed her hands to stop shaking. "Well, we had breakfast in our suite this morning."

"I see." The older woman shifted her gaze to Iris, who didn't seem to notice. "Well, perhaps we will see you at dinner?"

"Of course." Tessa offered a weak smile.

"Fine. Oh, and dear…" Mrs. Patterson's words trailed off. "Would you like to join me for tea in the Café Parisien tomorrow at three? I would love to get to know you better."

Tessa's heart rate picked up. "That would be very nice. Thank you so much."

"Yes." Mrs. Patterson gave Iris another glance before looking Tessa's way again. "Well, have a lovely day, Jacquie. See you this evening."

Tessa offered a lame nod then turned back to Iris as Nathan's mother left them.

"Well." Iris crossed her arms at her chest. "I'm assuming that was Mama."

"Iris, lower your voice." Tessa spoke in a strained whisper.

"Why? She's long gone." Iris rolled her eyes. "And by the way, her hat was awful, so do not take any fashion advice from that woman, no matter how desperately you want to impress her."

"Who says I want to impress her?"

"She's Nathan's mother, right? Of course you want to impress her. Impress the mother, impress the son."

"Iris, you're making too much of this. Nathan is just a friend, and he's very easy to talk to. If I appear to enjoy myself with him, it has nothing to do with my current situation."

"It has everything to do with your current situation. Do you think for one minute he would look twice at you if he knew the truth?"

For a moment Tessa said nothing. Finally, through clenched teeth, she managed, "That is enough, Iris. You've overstepped your bounds."

"You mean I'm not playing my role to its maximum potential? Then I shall try harder to pretend to be beneath you, though all of society would dictate otherwise." With the snap of her wrists, Iris gave a bow and then took off walking ahead of her. Tessa hurried along on her heels, determined to make things right.

"Iris, please stop." Tessa sighed. "I can assure you, a young man like Nathan Patterson would never be interested in a girl like me, so this whole conversation is pointless. Why don't we talk about something we can agree on?"

"And that would be?" Iris narrowed her eyes to slits.

"That fashion designer. Edith Russell. I do wish you had been with me last night when she spoke to me. You would have loved what she was wearing. And I could tell from the expression on her face that she found the people in first class to be a total bore. *Cold*—I believe that was the word she used. And I have to agree. I would rather be rolling around in the mud with Countess than dining with hoity-toity women with noses so high they wouldn't drown if you tossed them overboard."

At this comment, Iris snickered. "And you're sure the woman you spoke to last night was Edith Russell?" she asked. "She also goes by Edith Rosenbaum."

"Quite sure. Mrs. Patterson said that she has taken on an extra cabin to house the nineteen trunks of clothes she's brought onboard."

"Oh, to be a mouse in that room!" The edges of Iris's lips curled up in a smile. "You have no idea how desperately I would love to meet Edith. Her new clothing line is all the rage. I've read about it in magazines. Her design style is perfectly in line with my taste. I would have to say Edith Russell *is* fashion itself."

Tessa paused to think through an idea percolating in her brain. "Perhaps I could ask Nathan to arrange a meeting."

"Really?" Iris's eyes sparkled with newfound excitement. "Do you really think that's a possibility?"

"Did someone call my name?"

She turned as Nathan's voice sounded behind her. Right away her nerves kicked in. "Well, hello there."

"Hello to you too." He waggled his finger in her direction. "You missed breakfast this morning."

"No, she had breakfast in her room," Iris quipped.

Nathan shrugged. "Ah. Well, we sat with a couple of fellas from Texas who just made a fortune in the oil business. Mother is not keen on folks with new money, so I sensed her displeasure from the start of the conversation to the finish. I could have used a diversion."

Iris paused and put her hands on her hips. "And my friend is your diversion?"

Tessa felt her cheeks grow warm. "Iris." She gave her a warning look. "He was just teasing."

Nathan appeared flustered. "I only meant to say that the conversation was awkward, at best. Could have used a bit of flavor, and Jacquie seems to add that." He gave Iris a curious look. "And I have no doubt you could have added to the conversation, as well."

"I am nothing if not conversational." Iris tipped her nose up a bit too high as she started walking once again.

They passed a woman in a large overly decorated hat. She carried a fluffy little dog in her arms. Tessa decided not to make a fool of herself over the pooch as she'd done that first day.

"So many animals on this ship." Iris rolled her eyes. "Always coming and going."

"Yes." With a nod, Nathan gestured at the pup's owner. "Nearly as many dogs as silk birds on hats."

"You understand what women like that are doing, don't you?" Iris said.

"Who?" Nathan asked.

Iris gestured to a group of women nearby, who were all wearing large hats. "Those preening birds. Our fine-feathered lady friends onboard. Have you guessed what they're doing?"

"Keeping the sunlight out of their eyes?" Tessa offered.

"No." Iris wrinkled her nose. "They're trying to preserve their youth. They feel that loading themselves up with feathers and silk birds will keep them young."

"Or help them take to flight." Nathan chuckled.

"*Titanic* is filled with people in every age group and every social status, that much is true," Tessa said.

They made their way along the crowded deck, in and among the various passengers, and Iris stopped with a gasp as an older couple walked by. "Oh my goodness."

"What's wrong?" Tessa asked. "Do you know them?"

"Know them?" Iris slapped herself on the forehead. "You don't know who Isidor and Ida Straus are? Why, they own Macy's Department Store in New York City. *Macy's*. Only the finest department store anywhere, loaded with a thousand things I would love to own. One day, of course."

Tessa gave the older couple another look. They appeared quite normal.

"If it makes you feel any better, I didn't recognize them either," Nathan said. "Saw them yesterday while strolling with my mother. She had a similar reaction, so I knew they must be important."

"Important?" Iris's eyes fluttered closed, and she mumbled something under her breath.

"If it makes you feel any better, I have been to Macy's." Nathan turned Iris's way. "I went last year at Christmastime. You should see their windows. Fully decked out with Christmas decorations of every kind. I'd never seen anything like it."

"Oh, the Macy's Christmas windows?" Iris gave him an admiring look. "You've seen them in person? I've only ever dreamed of such a thing."

"I have." He lit into a lighthearted conversation about the Christmas-themed windows, and before long, Iris was all smiles.

"Someday I'm going to own a fine home and shop for the things I need at Macy's. What a day that will be. I will host parties and show off my dress designs to the women who attend."

"I have no doubt they will see your talent and want to wear your dresses," Tessa said, meaning every word.

Iris gave her a look of appreciation. For the first time Tessa felt hope that her suitemate might very well get beyond being angry with her. Now, if she could just arrange a meeting with Edith Russell. Then she would win over Iris for life.

* * * * *

Nathan couldn't help but notice the awkward interactions between Jacquie and Iris. Something in the relationship did not ring true, but he could not put his finger on it. Determined not to overthink the problem, he offered Jacquie his arm. They led the way across the Boat Deck with Iris following closely behind. After a couple of minutes, Nathan paused and offered Iris his other arm. She took it but didn't seem terribly comfortable. Just as they reached the stairwell, a familiar man in a fashionable suit of clothes passed by. Nathan paused to greet him. "Good morning, Mr. Ismay."

The man nodded but did not stop.

"Do you know him?" Tessa gave the man a second glance.

Nathan nodded. "Bruce Ismay is the managing director of the White Star Line and one of the men responsible for this ship. I read a write-up in the paper about him. I'm not sure our American reporters have done him justice, to be quite frank. They seem to take aim at him at every available turn."

"Perhaps they're just jealous," Iris said. "Americans often think the Brits are snobbish when, in fact, they are simply more reserved."

Jacquie nodded as she glanced back at Ismay, who disappeared down the stairs. "I daresay he comes across as a man of great strength and character." The nod that followed on her end conveyed her assurance that the words she'd spoken were, in fact, true.

"All of this you can discern without knowing him at all?" Nathan chuckled. "He passed by in such a hurry. How could you tell?"

"I am a very good judge of character, and I feel he is a solid British gentleman, comfortable with his station and capable of leading others."

"Well, please pass your comments along to William Randolph Hearst," Nathan added, before enjoying a belly laugh.

"William Randolph Hearst?" Jacquie echoed the name and shrugged. "Who is that?"

Iris slapped herself on the forehead once more and looped her arm through Jacquie's. "Perhaps it would be best if you rested your throat, my friend."

Nathan bit back a laugh and turned his attention to an older man in a tweed coat approaching on the right. He nudged Jacquie and gestured to the fellow with a nod of his head. "Since you're such an excellent judge of character, tell me about this man."

"Hmm." Jacquie's nose wrinkled as the fellow settled his bowler atop his head, shifted his pipe to the other side of his mouth, and kept walking with his eyes straight ahead. She turned to face Nathan and gave a brusque nod. "He is a private investigator with Scotland Yard."

Nathan gave the man a closer look, trying to see the fellow through Jacquie's eyes. "He is?"

"No doubt. See how he draws his pipe to his lips? He's not really interested in smoking it. He's keeping a watchful eye on his surroundings."

Iris turned to look at the man. "Gracious. I would have guessed him to be a newspaperman, not a private investigator."

Nathan gave the fellow a closer look, noticing the way he paused to greet a cluster of beautiful young women nearby. "I daresay he's watching those ladies for a completely different reason."

"Perhaps." Jacquie wiggled her brows. "Or maybe that's just what he wants you to think. He's quite skilled at the art of distraction, you see."

"Well, I'm plenty distracted." Nathan quirked a brow. "Were I writing a mystery, *Titanic* would be the perfect place to set it. I would be the sleuth, out to solve the riddle."

"What riddle?" Jacquie asked.

"Oh, you know. The whodunit. The crime."

"Has there been a crime?" Iris stopped walking and crossed her arms over her chest. Nathan couldn't help but notice her sour look as she shifted her gaze to Jacquie. Very odd. Perhaps this would be a good time to change the direction of the conversation.

"Ah. Well, what of the young women?" Nathan gestured to the group of young beauties with their full skirts, the fashionable hairstyles, and curls fixed atop their heads. "What is their story?"

"They are fashion plates," Jacquie said. "Just stamped images. Not real at all. Caricatures, as it were, like so many of the women aboard this ship."

"Indeed?" This certainly caught his attention.

"Quite." Jacquie nodded and lowered her voice. "But the good detective knows this and is on to them. He's quite good at what he does, you see."

The fellow in the bowler leaned down and whispered in a young lady's ear, and the pretty blond giggled in response.

"Yes," Jacquie said with a chuckle. "He is *very* good at what he does."

Whether she knew it or not, Jacquie Abingdon was very good

at what she did too. Her charms captivated him and made him wish for a longer voyage at sea. Suddenly he longed for *Titanic* to slow her pace. If only this trip could be extended. Then, perhaps, he would have the time he needed to get to know this lovely young woman better.

Just as quickly, he thought of Father, and his heart swelled with pride. *Stay focused, Nathan. Soon you will be home, ready to begin the next chapter of your life.*

Oh, if only he could keep one foot aboard the deck of *Titanic* and another at home in New York. Then, life, as Nathan Patterson knew it, would be absolutely ideal.

Chapter Eighteen

Thursday Morning, April 11, 1912
Aboard the Titanic, *on the Boat Deck*

After walking along the Boat Deck with Jacquie and Iris for nearly a half hour, Nathan approached the railing and glanced out at the waters. He closed his eyes and allowed his body to feel the movement of the boat as she glided ever westward, the rush of waves lapping at her hull and creating a push-pull feeling. Odd, how the movement in both directions could make one feel as if they weren't going anywhere at all but rather swirling around in the same circular pool.

"Are you all right?" Jacquie asked, her sweet voice ringing out above the sound of the crashing waves below.

He opened his eyes and looked her way, noticing the concerned expression. "Oh, I'm fine. Just paying particular attention to the movement of the ship."

"Experiencing a bit of seasickness?" she asked.

"Not at all. Just keenly aware of the flow of the boat against water. Reminds me a bit of what it's like to play the violin."

"The violin?" This remark came from Iris, who sounded startled.

"Yes." He turned to face her, determined to win her over in spite of her sour ways. "*Titanic* is the bow and the water is the violin. One sails across the other, creating a steady rhythm and a soothing melody." He closed his eyes once again. "Do you feel it? It's really the friction of one moving against the other that creates the sound. Reminds me of life."

"Very intriguing," Jacquie said. "And lovely."

"Thank you." He opened his eyes once more.

To his right, Iris sighed. "Never would've thought to compare the ship to a violin. Not sure where you came up with that."

"I stopped playing years ago, but music is a part of me. Sometimes I think I hear it even when others don't."

"Clearly." Iris pursed her lips and looked at the water. "Because I, for one, don't hear a thing. Except the sound of the seagulls overhead, I mean. And the noise from the children playing just a few yards away."

"You cannot deny the sound of the water lapping against the boat," he argued. "It is most assuredly creating a melody. Haunting, really." Nathan had just opened his mouth to add something when the grinding of brakes caught his attention.

"Do you feel that?" Jacquie's eyes widened. "We're slowing down."

"We must be getting close to Queenstown," he said.

"I can't believe it. My first trip to Ireland." Jacquie gripped the railing and leaned over it so far, he thought she might fall. "You can't imagine how long I've wanted to visit. My father's people are from Dublin."

"Really?" This news startled him. "I thought that Abingdon was a British name."

"Oh, well, I—" She swallowed hard and pulled back from the railing. "Going back several generations, I mean." Her eyelashes took to fluttering. "And did I say Father? I meant Mother. Yes, my *mother's* people are from Ireland. Several generations removed."

Out of the corners of his eyes, Nathan caught a glimpse of Iris rolling her eyes. Why the young woman spent so much time in an irksome state confused him. She seemed to have some sort of issue with Jacquie, but why?

Perhaps he could turn this conversation around. "Mother and I visited Ireland a couple of years ago," he said. "There's something about that green countryside, those rolling hills, that reminds me of the countryside in central Pennsylvania where my grandparents live. But our most recent journeys took us to France. Have you been?"

"Oh, but of course." With the wave of a hand, Jacquie appeared to dismiss his question.

"Ah. Well, then, you know that nothing compares to Paris. The Eiffel Tower is amazing. Didn't you find it all rather remarkable?"

"Truly." She glanced his way and offered a tiny shrug. "I suppose."

"Tell me, which do you prefer—the Champs-Élysées or Versailles?" he asked. "Which is your favorite place to visit, I mean?"

"Oh." She paused and appeared to be thinking. "I've always been keen on spending time with the countess. That's by far my favorite thing to do whenever I have the opportunity." In spite of the cool breeze coming off the water, Jacquie's cheeks turned a rosy hue, and she fanned herself.

"Countess? Which one? The Countess of Rothes? She's onboard, you know."

"No." The edges of Jacquie's lips turned up in the cutest grin. "The one with the orneriest litter of babes you've ever met. What a rowdy bunch! I'm always cleaning up their messes." She clamped a hand over her mouth, and her face turned redder still.

He doubled over in laughter. "I wish I had your sense of humor, Jacquie. It's brilliant. I daresay you're as sharp as a tack. Very witty." A little wink followed. "For a girl."

Her smile faded at once. "For a girl?" She planted her hands on her hips and faced him head-on. For a minute he thought she might double up her fist and give him a pounding. "What is that supposed to mean?"

"Oh, I'm just teasing," he said. "I didn't mean to cause offense. But I hadn't heard that about any countess's family. You've intrigued me."

To his right, Iris grunted. "I thought we were talking about Ireland. What's all this mush about France? And countesses? I've never heard of either in Ireland."

"True." He nodded then turned his attention to the rocky cliffs in the distance for a moment. Just as quickly his gaze shifted back to Jacquie, who leaned forward, placing her elbows on the ship's railing in an unladylike fashion.

"It's beautiful." A tiny sigh escaped those lovely lips of hers as she gazed out onto the scene before them.

Nathan couldn't help but grin. Yes, *beautiful* was exactly the word he would have chosen too. Only he didn't happen to be looking at the green hills of Ireland. His gaze remained fixed on the prettiest girl on the *Titanic*, one with a razor-sharp wit to boot.

* * * * *

Iris watched the interaction between Nathan Patterson and Tessa with interest. No one could rightfully accuse Tessa of flirting. She did not possess the talent to flirt as so many polished society girls did. Still, she had a genuine way about her, a way of drawing a young man such as Nathan into her world. But she needed to watch herself. That line about her family hailing from Ireland almost gave them away. And what was the purpose of that comment about the countess? If Nathan found out that she referred to a sow named Countess from Gloucestershire County, the gig would be up in a hurry.

Gig. Pig.

For whatever reason, Iris started chuckling as she thought about the rhyme. For a moment, anyway. She watched as Nathan's gaze turned from the coastline to Tessa's peaceful face. He appeared to be mesmerized.

Another grinding of the brakes beneath their feet slowed the *Titanic* even more. Though they were still a great distance from shore, the huge vessel came to a complete stop.

"What's happening?" Tessa looked her way, wide-eyed.

"We are anchoring off Roche's Point. The dock at Queenstown isn't big enough to accommodate us. Tenders will arrive from the White Star Line jetty, bringing the final passengers onboard. And mail, as well, from what I understand."

Tessa still seemed alarmed. "I had hoped we could just get on with this journey. Head out to sea."

Nathan's expression shifted to one of concern. Leaning against the railing, he gave Iris a pensive look. "There's something I want to say, and it must be spoken before more passengers board the ship. I mentioned this in passing to Jacquie last night." His brow creased into a *V*. "But I need to share it with you, as well."

"Share what?" Iris fussed with the strings of her hat, which the wind had whipped into a little dance around her neckline.

"Many of the passengers are emigrants from eastern European countries. I heard some of the men talking about it last night. Countries like Syria and Croatia."

"Croatia." Iris echoed the word. She hadn't heard of that one.

The concern in his voice intensified. "Most of these folks

probably won't speak English or French. Most will be staying in third class, from what I've heard. I just want to make sure you ladies are properly chaperoned whenever you're around the men. Not to say that they are suspect because of where they're from or because of their social class. I don't mean that at all. I'm simply saying that the crowd is about to grow thicker, and the potential for mischief increases."

"But…chaperoned? Why?" This seemed a bit ridiculous to Iris's way of thinking.

"Because these people are total strangers." His brow furrowed, an indicator that he truly believed the ladies to be in harm's way.

"As are you." She planted her fists on her hips and stared him down.

His face paled, and he turned his gaze back to the shoreline as he muttered, "I understand, but my offer still stands. With so many people milling about, one could lose their purse."

Or their head. Iris fought the temptation to speak the words aloud. Really, she couldn't seem to control her tongue these days, though much of what she'd said over the past hour or so shamed her. If only she could get control of her emotions, then she wouldn't have to eat her words after the fact.

Her gaze turned to the approaching tenders. She read the name IRELAND on the first one and AMERICA on the second. Both were filled to capacity with passengers and sacks of mail.

Minutes later *Titanic* came alive with activity. Along with a bevy of new passengers, tenders brought several Irish locals with all sorts of merchandise, including the most delicate lace Iris had ever laid eyes on.

As the merchants spread their wares and called out for passengers to buy, buy, buy, she found herself wishing she hadn't thumbed her nose at Nathan's suggestion that he serve as chaperone. Perhaps having a strong male nearby would be an asset, particularly with so many rough-looking strangers about and calling to her at every turn. As folks pushed and prodded, she found herself feeling more anxious by the moment…until she laid eyes on the merchants with Irish lace in hand.

She watched as one merchant—an older woman with long gray hair—strung large pieces of Irish lace over her shoulders and walked the deck, calling out for people to have a look.

"Irish lace," Iris whispered. Oh, what she wouldn't give to have just a few inches of the delicate stuff. Seconds later she found herself standing in front of the woman, her gaze falling on a piece of Kenmare, her favorite. Her heart quickened as she took in the lovely pieces. How delicate. How lovely.

"You are fond of lace?" the woman asked. "I will give you a good price."

"Fond of it?" Her heart swelled with joy. "I adore it, especially the Kenmare lace. Have you ever seen anything so beautiful? I can imagine a nice dress with a bit of this lace on the collar and cuffs." She fingered a lovely stretch of it. "One day."

"Not one day," Tessa said as she stepped up next to Iris. "*This* day. You will have it today." She reached for her reticule and opened it to pull out some coins. Minutes later she pressed a full yard of the Kenmare into Iris's hands.

"A–are you sure, Tes—Miss Jacquie?" Iris found herself fumbling for words.

"Very sure. It's the least I can do." Tessa winked and reached over to give her a hug, at which point she whispered, "You're worth it, Iris. Worth this and much more."

"*Worth it.*"

Why the words pricked her heart, she could not say. Still, as Iris fixed her gaze on the Kenmare lace, she felt more valuable than she had in years.

* * * * *

Jacquie paced the lobby of the Willingham and waited, as she had for hours, for Peter to arrive. If he didn't show up by two o'clock, she would go into the dining room alone and have lunch. At least she wouldn't have to worry about Mother finding her here. Mother and Cousin Minerva were long gone to Paris by now.

She continued to pace the lobby, feeling the eyes of the bell-man on her. When he approached to ask if he could help her in any way, she simply shook her head and kept walking. Surely something had happened to delay Peter's arrival. Still, he should have sent a note to the clerk. Jacquie did her best to relax but found it difficult.

By 1:55, her heart had gravitated to her throat. By two o'clock, she knew she must face facts.

He's not coming. And I've made a complete fool of myself.

Chapter Nineteen

Friday Afternoon, April 12, 1912
Aboard the Titanic, *on the Boat Deck*

On Friday afternoon Tessa dressed in her prettiest pink gown to meet with Nathan's mother in the Café Parisien. She couldn't imagine what the woman might want to discuss. Perhaps she had discovered the truth—every awful bit of it.

The idea left Tessa in a dither. Would they bounce her off the ship if they discovered her secret? She did have a ticket, albeit in someone else's name. Would she have to betray Jacquie, should immigration officials figure out she wasn't who she pretended to be?

At ten minutes till two, Tessa gave herself a quick glance in the looking-glass and then ushered up a prayer—the first in a long while—for God's protection. She had no right to do so; she knew that. But still, one couldn't help but struggle with nerves on a day such as today.

She found Mrs. Patterson sipping a cup of tea at a table in the back of the café.

"Jacquie, my dear, you've come." The older woman gestured for her to sit, and she did. "Are you enjoying your journey?"

"I am. I'm getting a lot of rest, which is nice." Even as Tessa spoke the words, she thought about how leisurely this voyage had been in comparison to her days on the farm. At home, she scarcely had time to sit for a moment without Pa taking it out on her. Here, she could lounge about for hours on end, in seemingly endless days.

Unless it all came crashing down on her now. And from the look in Mrs. Patterson's eyes, something was about to come crashing down.

"Well, you look lovely, my dear, but I can tell something is troubling you."

"You can?"

"Yes, and that's why I've brought you here." Mrs. Patterson paused, and Tessa's heart now raced like Countess headed out of the farrowing crates.

The waiter, a handsome fellow with dark hair and a thick Italian accent, placed a tray of raspberry tarts on the table in front of them. Nathan's mother gazed at the sugary delicacies with longing, finally settling on the smallest one on the tray. She picked it up and took a nibble.

Still, Tessa could read the seriousness in the woman's narrowed eyes. Sooner or later she would get to the point of this meeting. When she did, would the ruse come to an end? Would Tessa have to bare her soul…and her sin?

"Jacquie, I simply must ask you something." The woman twisted her napkin around in her palms and then folded it and set it on the table.

"All right."

Mrs. Patterson poured Tessa a cup of tea and then glanced up at her. "Sweet girl, I know it's really none of my business, and I do hope you don't think I'm an old busybody, but I must know— why do you allow your lady's maid to speak to you in such a manner? It's no wonder you're so beaten down. She is taxing you, my dear."

Tessa fought to keep her composure as she pondered the older woman's words. "I'm sure I don't know what you mean."

"Indeed? I walked up on your conversation yesterday and was startled by the way she addressed you. No, *startled* is too soft a word. I found her tone and her words to be completely out of line for one in her station."

Mrs. Patterson gestured to the cup of tea, and Tessa reached for it, though her hand shook so violently that she nearly spilled it. She shifted her gaze to her lap and tried to think of something brilliant to say. Nothing came to mind, except "Oh, I see." So *that's* what this was about.

"If I had a girl such as that in my employ, she would be gone faster than this ship sailed out of Queenstown." Mrs. Patterson stirred a cube of sugar into her tea. "And I would certainly never think to allow her to travel with me in so fine a room as the one you're staying in. I would put her down in steerage to fend for herself. That would shake her up a bit, I daresay."

Tessa paused for a moment to think through a believable response. "Mrs. Patterson, I appreciate your concern. I really do. And I see your point, of course. Iris is…well, she's Iris. No doubt about it. But she has been in service with our family since I was in finishing school. Her mother started out as my mother's lady's maid."

Tessa swallowed hard as the lie was spoken. Though, it wasn't a total untruth, was it? Iris and Jacqueline had grown up together.

Offering a weak smile, she finally managed a shrug. "Perhaps we are too familiar?"

"I would say." Mrs. Patterson reached for her fan. As she spread it wide, the delicate lace caught the ripples of sunlight streaming through the café window. She waved it back and forth. "*Familiar* is exactly the word. Well, you must undo the familiarity at once."

"Undo it?"

"Certainly." Nathan's mother shook her fan in Tessa's direction. "Put her in her place at once, before this goes one step further. Don't allow her to speak to you as if her words carry weight. She's a lady's maid, for pity's sake. Her behavior was unacceptable."

"I see."

"I would encourage you to dispense with any informalities you've grown accustomed to at home. This is, after all, the *Titanic*. Social etiquette rules still apply. And if you want to hold your head up in the presence of people like the Astors and Edith Russell, you must adapt with every opportunity presented to you."

"I see."

Mrs. Patterson leaned over and gave her a gentle pat on the arm. "I do hope you will forgive me if I've overstepped my bounds, Jacquie. I do feel, in your mother's absence, of course, that I should offer such advice. Someone has to look out for you."

"I'm sure Mother would be very pleased to know that I am in such good hands." Tessa bit her lip to keep from saying more. If Mrs. Patterson had any idea how things were at home, she would realize that no one cared one whit about Tessa's well-being— not Mum, and certainly not Pa. And if Mum could see her daughter now, sitting like a peacock in a white wicker chair in the Café Parisien, she would probably hand her a broom and tell her to get busy cleaning the place.

Only Peter cared, and he was back in London now, carving bushes into animals and trying to figure out what to do with the real Jacquie Abingdon.

The real Jacquie Abingdon.

For whatever reason, the words caused a painful sigh to rise up inside of Tessa. Thank goodness Mrs. Patterson was none the wiser. No, she was far too busy going on about Iris to notice a thing. From there, Nathan's mother lit into a conversation about the Astors and then into a lengthy dissertation about Ida Strauss. Tessa couldn't make much sense out of any of it.

When the conversation shifted to the various authors onboard the ship, Tessa found herself wanting to doze off. Oh, if only she could pretend to be interested. But how—or why—would anyone care about books and such? It made no sense to her. And what did it matter if these writers penned mysteries or newspaper columns?

Finally Mrs. Patterson stopped talking and gave her a tender glance. "Jacquie, I can tell that you are weary. You look as if you might fall asleep at a moment's notice."

"I must confess, I am exhausted. Probably something to do with the lull of the ship." She bit back a yawn and forced a smile.

"Or perhaps because you laid awake all night fretting over the ugly things your lady's maid said to you yesterday." The woman leaned forward and pursed her lips. "I'm right, aren't I?"

"I did not sleep well last night." She had spent nearly an hour fretting over Iris's words but wouldn't say so now. Let Mrs. Patterson think what she wanted.

Tiny creases formed between the woman's brows. "Do as I say. Send her packing. Don't be bothered with her. Then you will sleep like a babe."

"No doubt I will." Still, she couldn't possibly send Iris packing. Where would she send her, anyway?

Mrs. Patterson rose with a dramatic sigh. "Well, I should be going, anyway. There's so much to do before dinner. I want to make a good impression on Edith Russell, you know."

"Ah." Tessa cared nothing for such things, but the mention of Edith's name did stir curiosity.

"Why I care what that woman thinks is beyond me. Have you heard the story of what she's done? She's been carrying around a little stuffed pig as if it's her baby. Strangest thing I've ever heard of."

As the word "pig" was spoken, Tessa's thoughts went to Countess at once. The sting of tears followed.

"Why a woman would attach herself to a pig is beyond me." Mrs. Patterson sighed. "Oh well. I must be on my way. I must freshen up my makeup and make sure the steward sent my new silk gown to be pressed before this evening's meal. Alas, a woman's work is never done."

"You are so right." Tessa rose, thinking the conversation had ended. Instead, Nathan's mother began to talk about the agonies of constrictive undergarments and the woes of hair styling.

In that moment, Tessa wondered what Mrs. Patterson would look like in the pig stall, chasing Countess hither, thither, and yon. The image made her smile. And then giggle.

"Well, I'm happy to see I've cheered you up." The older woman reached over to give her a warm embrace…so warm that Tessa found herself missing Mum. And Peter. And Countess.

In that moment, her emotions flip-flopped and the giggles ended, now replaced with sadness. She pictured herself running across the gardens at Abingdon Manor in search of her brother. Imagined him drawing near and wrapping her in his arms. Felt his gentle kiss on her brow. Listened to his brotherly teasing.

Determined not to cry, Tessa swallowed the lump in her throat, pressed back the sniffles that threatened to erupt, glanced over at Nathan's mother, and forced the happiest smile she could muster.

* * * * *

Friday Afternoon, April 12, 1912
Aboard the Titanic

Nathan spent the afternoon touring areas of the ship he had not yet seen and chatting with several workers onboard. Among his favorites was Herbert Pitman, Third Officer, who had been given the task of using celestial observations to chart *Titanic's* position. The jovial fellow spent nearly an hour sharing an enthusiastic conversation with Nathan.

Some time later, Nathan met up with the stoker he'd met the first day back in Southampton and had a short conversation with him.

"How are things down below?" he asked.

The fellow, black with soot, swiped at his eyes with the back of his hand. "Hot, sir. Just sticking me head out fer a bit of air. Me shift just ended. Need to catch a wink 'r two before headin' back." His brow arched and concern laced his words. "We've had a rough go of it, to be honest. We've had a fire smolderin' in the coal bunker off 'n' on from the moment we set sail."

"Oh?" This certainly piqued Nathan's interest. "Anything to worry about?"

"No, just one more headache when we're already battlin' so many others."

"Others?"

With a wave of the hand, the fellow mumbled something indistinguishable. "Oh, don't mind me," he said after a moment. "Just a bit put off by the lousy coal they've given us. Not what I would've chosen, for sure. But I suppose with the strike only just endin', we'll take what we can get, right?"

For whatever reason, the words "take what we can get" did not settle well with Nathan. He pressed them to the back of his mind, determined not to worry. Still, he managed to respond with "Right," and even offered a nod afterward.

After bidding the fellow a good day, Nathan continued his perusal of the ship in search of one room in particular. Finally he arrived at the stateroom he'd been searching for on A Deck. He knocked on the door and waited until someone answered.

A lady's maid opened the door, and he asked to speak to Miss Edith Russell.

"Is she expecting you?" the young woman asked.

"No." Still, he hoped she would see him, regardless.

"She is in E-19, doing inventory of some of the clothes in her new line. You will find her there, but don't expect her to be in a pleasant frame of mind. She's, well..." The lady's maid shifted her gaze. "She's had a rough go of it, of late."

"Ah. Well, I will approach with care."

And that's exactly what he did. Nathan took the elevator to E Deck and made his way to E-19, where he spoke with Miss Russell at length, finally convincing her to meet Iris in person. Doing so would endear Iris to both Jacquie and Nathan, or so he hoped. They would discuss the plan tonight at dinner, with Edith and Jacquie putting their heads together to come up with a plan.

He only prayed that Iris would forego her sullen ways when she finally met with Miss Russell in person. Hopefully Iris would say nothing about the little stuffed pig Miss Russell seemed so attached to. One could hope, anyway.

As he left the stateroom, Nathan's thoughts shifted, for

whatever reason, to James Carson's job offer. Something about it still felt odd. Contrived. Why it continued to nag at him, he could not say. Still, he would pay closer attention to the fellow to solve the riddle…if, indeed, there was a riddle to be solved.

In the meantime, he would head back to his cabin to dress for dinner. There, with Jacquie Abingdon seated beside him, all would be well.

* * * * *

Friday Evening, April 12, 1912
The Willingham Hotel, Southampton, England

A rap on the door aroused Jacquie from a light, tearful sleep. A dream, which had pierced her heart, faded away as she came fully awake.

Jacquie dried her eyes and glanced in the mirror, appalled at the reflection that stared back at her. The knocking continued, and she tried to gather her wits about her. Was it the bellman, perhaps? Worse yet, had her father located her? Figured out her scheme? She shivered, in part because the temperature in the room had dropped and in part because she found herself unnerved by the constant rapping.

She took a couple of tentative steps toward the door and leaned her ear against it as she called out, "Who's there?"

Only when she heard Peter's familiar voice did she reach for the handle to fling the door open.

Chapter Twenty

Saturday Morning, April 13, 1912
Aboard the Titanic

For whatever reason, Tessa found it very difficult to sleep on Friday night. She kept replaying Mrs. Patterson's words about Iris in her mind. Also, the excitement at dinner kept her thoughts tumbling. What a fascinating woman Edith Russell had turned out to be. And how kind of her to agree to meet with Iris. Tessa could hardly wait to hear what became of that.

When she rose earlier than usual on Saturday morning, Tessa found that a cold chill had gripped the air. Shivering, she reached for her robe. Or, rather, Jacquie's robe. For a moment she contemplated visiting the Turkish bath. Perhaps there she could shake off the icy feeling that now held her in its grip. Instead, she decided to take an early breakfast in the dining saloon.

She did her best to fasten her own corset strings without Iris, who slept soundly in the next room. Then she slipped on the simplest dress available, left her hair hanging in soft curls over her shoulders, and made the walk to the dining hall. As she landed on the Grand Stairway, the early morning rays peeked through the dome. She glanced up, mesmerized by the colors as the light hit the brass fixtures. For whatever reason, the dazzling rainbowlike display brought her hope. Strange. She'd been without it for so long, she scarcely recognized it now. Oh, if only this feeling would last!

When Tessa arrived in the dining hall, she found her usual table filled. Instead of taking a seat, she opted to take a caramel Danish from the buffet. Wrapping it in a napkin, she carried it out to the reception area and took a few bites. Moments later, still haunted by the conversation with Mrs. Patterson, Tessa wound her way through the hallway to the library. She tucked the Danish in her reticule and walked the perimeter of the library, wishing she knew more about books. Hadn't Nathan's mother gone on and on about the various authors onboard? Maybe Tessa should read one of their books.

From across the room she caught a glimpse of a young woman about her same age. The warm smile emanating from the girl put her at ease right away.

"Are you looking for something in particular?" The young woman rose. "Maybe I could help you. I've spent a lot of hours here since we set sail."

"I'm not exactly sure what I'm looking for," Tessa said. "I usually read fanciful novels. But maybe..." She tried to remember what Mrs. Patterson had said. "Maybe a mystery?"

"Ah. Mysteries." The woman's brows arched. "I love them... perhaps because life is such a mystery." She perused the shelves, finally landing on a book with a red cover. Tessa glanced down at it and read the title: THE DIAMOND MASTER.

"Yes, this will do."

"The library is quiet this time of morning," the young woman said. "Just have a seat anywhere you like. Oh, I suppose we should make introductions. It's so nice to meet you, Miss—"

"T—Jacquie Abingdon."

"Jacquie. Beautiful name. Very similar to my own. I'm Jessie, by the way. Jessie Leitch." A genuine smile followed from the young woman. She pointed to a little girl who sat at a nearby table reading a picture book. "And this is Annie, my little cousin."

"Nice to meet you. And Annie…" Tessa turned her attention to the child. "Good to meet you, as well."

As Tessa settled into a plush chair, she took a peek at Jessie. By the standards of many onboard, the woman probably appeared plain. Ordinary. The traveling dress might not be of the latest fashion, but it was clean and pressed, the deep burgundy still rich in color. And the hat would not impress Iris, to be sure. But Jessie's eyes sparkled with a vivaciousness that most did not possess. They emanated beauty of a different sort.

After a few moments of pretending to read the dull book, Tessa glanced up. She hated to break the silence in the room but decided to do so anyway. "Are you traveling alone?" she asked.

Jessie glanced up from her book. "No. We're traveling with my uncle, John Harper. Do you know him?"

"Know him?" Tessa shook her head. "No. Should I?" A shiver ran down her spine as she thought about the possibilities of someone finding out who she really was.

"He's a pastor in London. Quite well-known, so I thought perhaps you had heard of him."

"I'm sorry. I have not."

"Ah. Well, Annie here is his daughter. We're traveling to Chicago because my uncle has been asked to take the pulpit at Moody Church for several weeks." Jessie glanced toward the door. "We're expecting him at any moment. In fact, I felt sure he would be here by now. He spends many hours in the library studying for his sermons."

"I see." Tessa turned her attention back to her book. Or, rather, pretended to. She couldn't make heads or tails out of the story. She pulled her jacket a bit tighter, feeling a chill.

Jessie glanced her way and smiled. "I hear it's going to be even colder tomorrow."

"Yes." A ripple of concern washed over Tessa. "I've heard talk of icebergs."

With a wave of a hand, Jessie appeared to dismiss that idea. "I believe we're traveling south of the danger zone. That's my understanding, anyway. But don't fret. This is the *Titanic*. Uncle John says she could melt an iceberg with a glance."

Funny, how those words made Tessa think of Nathan. Hadn't one look at his handsome face melted her heart? She pressed back a giggle and tried to stay focused.

Jessie closed her book and shifted her position. "They call *Titanic* a floating palace, you know. It's Versailles and Buckingham all rolled into one."

"With even more interesting characters residing therein." Tessa giggled. "Have you ever seen such an assortment of people in one place? I feel as if all the world has converged on one ship. All of mankind is represented."

"Each in his own level, I daresay. The separation of classes frustrates me." Jessie's nose wrinkled. "That's why I'm enjoying my time in the library. The class distinctions aren't such an issue here. People in every class love a good book, and there are no walls to divide them between the pages." She offered a smile.

"True."

"Have you taken a look about the lower decks?" Jessie asked. "Quite a different world, I assure you."

Tessa shook her head. She had been born on a lower deck, so

to speak, but deception had elevated her to B Deck in a hurry. Not that she truly belonged here. No, she would likely be at home with those who danced and sang below. Her people, as it were.

"I met a fellow from Amsterdam this morning," Jessie said. "And some from Slovenia and the like. Honestly, they're all wonderful people, filled with dreams of a new life. God's people, all in one place, like a big family. I really must look at this adventure as a blessing. We weren't even supposed to be on this ship. We have the coal strike to thank for it."

"A happy problem, I daresay." Tessa offered her a warm smile.

A tall, stately fellow entered the room, interrupting their conversation. Tessa took one look at him and her breath caught in her throat. She recognized him as the man who had rescued her purse that first day as she had boarded the ship.

Tessa watched as Annie closed her picture book and rushed to his side, giving him a hug around the waist. "Papa!"

"Hello, my angel." He glanced Jessie's way and smiled. "Has my little doll been behaving herself?"

"For the most part." Jessie grinned then gestured to Tessa. "Uncle John, this is my new friend, Jacquie. Jacquie, this is my uncle, the Reverend John Harper."

Jessie rose and Tessa joined her, placing her book on the side table. She gazed into the kind eyes of the reverend and nodded. "I remember you, sir. You're the nice man who fetched my purse for me when I dropped it."

"Ah, yes." He flashed a welcoming smile. "As I recall, I bumped into you and knocked it out of your hand, and for that I do apologize. But I was happy to retrieve it for you, Miss…"

"Jacquie. I'm Jacquie Abingdon."

"Abingdon." His brow furrowed. "Have you ever attended Walworth Road Baptist Church in London?"

"I—I don't believe so, sir." Her heart fluttered to her throat.

"Strange. I felt sure I knew the name." His brow creased. "Then again, Abingdon is a popular name in London, is it not?"

"Yes. Indeed." A wave of relief washed over Tessa. "But all the more reason for me to thank you. You came to the rescue of a total stranger, and in the middle of a rather chaotic situation, I daresay."

"Uncle John is a good man to have around in a sticky spot," Jessie said and then chuckled. "At least that's what I always say."

"With so many pickpockets about, I wondered if I would ever see my reticule again."

"I'm not in the pickpocket business." Reverend Harper's care-free expression shifted to one of concern. "It's not pocketbooks I'm after, but hearts." He settled into a chair across from hers.

Tessa eased herself back into her seat. "Hearts?"

"Yes. If I snagged a reticule, the money inside would see me through a few days, perhaps, but not into eternity. I want to fetch hearts from people. Hearts for the kingdom, I mean."

"The kingdom?" She found herself more perplexed than ever. "You mean the British Empire?"

"No, my dear." A hearty chuckle followed on his end. "I daresay we have plenty of support for the British Empire already. This ship is all the proof we will ever need that the Empire is alive and well. But even she cannot assure the kind of peace and long-lasting security I'm referring to. I speak of the kingdom of heaven."

"Heaven?" At once Tessa's knees ached. She thought of her father. Thought of that rocky path. Remembered her rock prayers, how they had scarred both her knees and her soul.

In that moment, she felt as transparent as the glass surrounding the promenade deck. Did this man, this minister, realize the depth of her deception? Did he know she didn't belong on this ship?

From his calm, kindly expression, probably not. Still, she felt uncomfortable presenting herself to a minister as Jacquie Abingdon, particularly when he spoke of heaven. Likely she would never make it, if one could judge such things by behavior.

Reverend Harper rose and walked to a bookshelf then returned with a stack of books. "I do hope you girls will forgive me, but I've got to study."

"Of course, Uncle John." Jessie reached for her wrap. "Do you mind if we take a stroll on the deck?"

"Not at all. Just make sure Annie stays warm. It's chilly out there today."

"Of course." Jessie turned to face Tessa and extended a hand. "Would you like to join us for a turn around the deck?"

Overwhelmed at the young woman's generosity, Tessa nodded. "I would love that."

They made their way to the glass-enclosed promenade deck to avoid the cold. As they walked, Annie—who turned out to be quite playful and talkative now that they were outside the library—kept them entertained with her antics. She skipped along ahead of them, and Jessie kept a watchful eye on her.

Tessa enjoyed the peaceful conversation with Jessie more than she might have imagined. Though they were different in many respects, something about the young woman drew her in. Her kindness, perhaps. Her gentle way of leading the conversation back around to spiritual things.

Not that Tessa cared to discuss religion. No, thank you. After Pa's attempt to convert her to his cruel religiosity, she would rather steer clear of the subject. Still, as Jessie talked about God as if He were a friend, Tessa found herself curious. Intrigued.

At one point Jessie paused and gazed out over the waters, a serene expression on her face. "'In the beginning'"—she gestured to the ocean—"'God created the heaven and the earth.'" A lovely smile followed as the young woman closed her eyes.

There was something rather majestic about the tone of her voice. It captivated Tessa.

"'And the earth was without form, and void,'" Jessie continued, eyes still closed, "'and darkness was upon the face of the deep. And the Spirit of God moved upon the face of the waters.'" She punctuated each word with dramatic flair, adding just the right amount of volume.

"Goodness." Tessa shook her head as she recalled the woman's dissertation. "You sound like an actress on a stage."

Jessie chuckled and her eyes popped open. "More like a preacher behind a pulpit, but I come by it honestly, you see. I do spend a lot of time in church, after all. I did mention that my uncle's a pastor."

"Yes, but what did you mean by what you said?"

Jessie shrugged. "It's a favorite Scripture of mine. When I close my eyes, I can almost imagine the Almighty forming the seas by speaking them into existence. I picture His Spirit, that wonderful Comforter, over the waters. And it gives me hope."

"Hope?" There was that word again, the same word that had latched onto her as she gazed up at the ribbons of sunlight streaming through the glass dome above the Grand Staircase. Hope.

"Yes." The most peaceful expression settled on Jessie's face. "For as surely as the Spirit moved over the seas, as surely as He rose and fell with the tide, our loving Father is at work inside of me, bringing peace and comfort. I am His creation, after all, formed in His image." The young woman paused and gave Tessa a pensive look. "And so are you, Jacquie Abingdon. So are you."

"I—I am." She'd spent little time thinking of herself as a creation. Indeed, Tessa's only view of herself—other than the fictional life she'd imagined back in Countess's stall—was what had been spoken about her by her father.

"My father…" Tessa shook her head, unable to go on.

"What about him?" Jessie asked.

"He's…" She tried to get the words out, but they refused to come.

"When you want to share, I'm here." Jessie gazed at her with such intensity that Tessa wondered if she could see all the way to Gloucestershire County, all the way to the rocky path. "Until then, just rest in the comfort that your heavenly Father adores you. He does, you know."

This certainly contradicted everything Tessa had ever been taught. Obviously Jessie's God was considerably different than Pa's, to say the least. An adoring, loving Father? Bringing peace? Comfort? She could hardly fathom any of those things. Not with the picture Pa had painted in her head and ground into her knees. His God was cruel. Merciless. Intent on bringing pain when she failed.

Jessie slipped her arm through Tessa's and took a few steps down the corridor. She began to sing a little hymn as they walked, one that soothed Tessa's aching soul, if only for those few moments.

When they reached the starboard side of the ship, she caught a glimpse of Iris standing at the glass, looking out on the water. Tessa made introductions and her new friend graciously included Iris in the conversation, even asking her to join them for their walk. Iris seemed a bit hesitant to do so, but Jessie won her over with a lovely comment about her hairstyle.

Before long, the three ladies walked side by side with little Annie leading the way. The youngster hopscotched her way along, all giggles and smiles until she ran headlong into one of the passengers.

Nathan.

For whatever reason, Tessa found her cheeks growing warm when she realized he stood in front of them. A smile turned up the edges of her lips, and her heart flooded with joy. Jessie must have noticed, because she gave Tessa a "who do we have here?" look. Tessa introduced him at once, doing her best not to act smitten. Still, she could hardly deny the fact that feelings were growing, especially after witnessing the efforts Nathan had gone to with Edith Russell. Oh, Iris would be so thrilled when she found out!

"Am I interrupting anything?" Nathan asked.

"Not at all," Jessie said. "We're just having a little stroll around the deck."

Before long, Annie had convinced Nathan to join her in a game of hopscotch. Tessa watched, amused, as he hop-hop-hopped his way along. Only when he extended his hand and encouraged her to join them did she get nervous.

"Go ahead, Jacquie," Jessie said with a smile. "I'll stay and visit with Iris. You two play with Annie. I'm sure she's thrilled to have new friends."

"All right." Tessa could hardly believe it, but she found herself looking forward to skipping along the deck with the excited youngster. And having Nathan's hand in hers as she did? Well, that was just the icing on the cake.

* * * * *

Iris stood along the railing next to Jessie and watched the others in their game of hopscotch. She noticed Tessa's cheeks turning pink and couldn't help but smile when Annie's giggles filled the air.

Jessie leaned against the railing and chuckled. "Jacquie is a rare find, isn't she?"

"A rare find?"

"Yes. I've found her to be charming in every respect."

"Charming. Yes." Iris closed her mouth to keep from saying more.

"Have you worked for her for long?" Jessie turned her way, her soft brown eyes filled with kindness.

"No." At least she didn't have to lie. She'd only worked with Tessa for two weeks now. Well, two weeks and a handful of days at seas.

"There's a certain childlikeness about her that I find endearing," Jessie said. "She reminds me of a bird just nudged from the nest. I can almost picture her curled up at home on the sofa instead of traveling the Atlantic by herself." Jessie turned to Iris and took her hand. "Forgive me. She's *not* alone, is she? She's got you, and for that she is very grateful. I can tell by the way she looks at you that you are the best of friends."

"Yes. She's got me." Iris swallowed hard, realizing that she'd been anything but a friend to Tessa.

A broad smile followed from Jessie. "And what a blessed girl she is to have such a confidante. I've often thought that if I had someone about my age to share my joys and sorrows with, life would be much easier. You two must be very close."

"I…" She didn't know what to say, exactly.

"Do you have family, Iris?"

"My mother and father and enough brothers to form a ball team." She chuckled.

"Well, then, do take advantage of the time to get to know Jacquie as a sister. One can never have too many of those, especially with so many boys about." Jessie pointed to little Annie. "She's young, but Annie has become the kid sister I never had. And though her circumstances are difficult, we've made the best of it. I count it my joy—and honor—that the Lord has planted me in her life for such a time as this. I know you must feel the same about Jacquie, particularly since you're so close in age."

A coil of shame wound around Iris's heart as she thought about Jessie's words. In truth, she hadn't given Tessa a fair shake. The young woman did seem lost, just as Jessie had described. A bird out of the nest. Yes, that aptly described the situation. Iris's only plan, up to this point, had been to make the flight more difficult. Perhaps she should change course and offer a hand of friendship to Tessa. It would make the rest of the voyage more pleasant, after all.

Of course, it would require laying down her pride. Still, after Tessa's offering the other day—the lovely Irish lace—it might be time to toss her bitterness overboard. She would give it some thought, anyway.

Off in the distance, little Annie continued to play. The youngster's giggles soon filled the air, coupled with the sound of Nathan's laughter. Before long, Tessa joined in, and the threesome hopscotched down the corridor.

Jessie slipped her arm through Iris's as she watched them play. "I have the strongest sense we were all brought together for a reason. Do you feel it too?"

"I suppose." Iris shrugged, unsure of what to say. Still, she could not deny that something unusual now stirred her heart. The idea that a total stranger would take the time to speak so kindly to her brought a rush of warmth to her soul and made her want to be a better person, a person like the young woman whose arm was now happily looped through hers.

She continued to watch the others play until little Annie took a tumble and scraped her knee. Jessie drew near and kissed away the youngster's tears and then ushered her off to their cabin to tend to the wound. This left Iris alone with Nathan and Tessa.

She had just turned to head back to the cabin when Nathan called her name. Turning back, he pulled a slip of paper out of his pocket.

"Almost forgot to give you this."

"What is it?" She took the crumpled paper from his outstretched hand and tried to make sense of it. Just a combination of letters and numbers. E-19. Odd.

"It's a cabin number," Nathan said. "You're supposed to meet someone there at four o'clock today. Someone who's very anxious to meet you and hear your thoughts on the fashion industry."

She paused for a moment and tried to make sense of his words. "And who, might I ask, would that be?"

"Oh, no one special," Nathan said with a shrug. "Just one of our country's most notable fashion experts, Edith Louise Rosenbaum Russell. She wants to see your sketches, so take everything you have."

"I—I—I..." Iris would've said more, but the wave of dizziness that passed over her made it impossible. Had he really just said that Edith Russell wanted to speak to her? To look at her sketches?

She glanced down at the paper in her hand, clutched it to her heart, and took off running toward her cabin. Behind her, Tessa and Nathan cheered her on. Iris barely heard them as she ran ever forward toward her destination—the one she prayed would change her life forever.

Chapter Twenty-One

At four o'clock that afternoon, Iris stood in front of Edith Russell, barely able to speak. She finally managed a shaky "M–Miss Rosenbaum."

"Russell, my dear. Most people call me Edith Russell." The woman clutched a little stuffed pig in her left hand, never loosening her hold on it.

Iris bit back a nervous giggle at the name. "Miss Edith…er, Russell."

The woman extended her gloved right hand, still holding onto the pig with the left. "I hear you're quite the designer."

"I— You did?"

"Yes. Your friend Nathan came to see me yesterday. And then I spoke with your delightful friend Jacquie, as well. She sings your praises. Is it true that you had a hand in designing the dress she wore to dinner last night?"

"Well, I suggested the colors and the trim. And the fabric choice too, of course." A wave of heat washed over Iris as she let the flattery sink in.

"The dress was exquisite. And I adored the choice of hat. Perfect. No doubt you helped with that, as well."

Iris felt her cheeks grow hot as she nodded. "Oh, Miss Russell, it's only because of people like you that I'm interested in fashion at all. You can see how it is." She pointed to her simple dress. "I'm a lady's maid. In England, I stand no chance of becoming anything else, no matter how hard I work."

"But in America..." Edith quirked a brow.

"In America my chances to meet people in the industry are a bit higher."

"Dear girl." Edith reached for her hand. "Onboard *Titanic*, your chances are higher still. And with friends like Nathan and Jacquie, the possibilities have risen to greater heights. Clearly, we were destined to meet, you and I."

"Oh, I have no doubt about it." Had Providence arranged this meeting, or had it all happened by chance?

Edith put the little stuffed pig down on the settee and covered him with a lace-trimmed hankie, as one would tuck a child into bed at night. "People find me eccentric. Odd, even. They do not know the depth of my suffering over the past year since the tragic accident." The woman's eyes filled with tears. "You see, my dear, my fiancé, Ludwig, lost his life, and I, myself, am still recovering."

"I had heard as much, and I'm so terribly sorry."

"I'm sure you will understand what I mean when I say that I take comfort in my work. In that creative place, I am free from pain for a short while."

Understand? Iris felt exactly the same way. She could hardly get her words out fast enough as she attempted to explain. "I know what you mean. When I'm designing a gown—or a hat, even—my thoughts are solely focused on that, not on..." She paused and attempted to swallow the lump in her throat. "On the things I cannot change."

"Where are these designs of yours, dear? Anything you could show me?"

Iris's heart raced. "I've brought my sketches to show you." She opened her sketch pad and thumbed through the drawings, one after the other. Edith oohed and aahed in all the right places, pointing out both the things she liked and the things she didn't. Iris accepted the critique. Welcomed it, even. To have a woman like Miss Russell offer advice? Such a thing was priceless.

When they had looked through all of the sketches, Edith reached for the stuffed pig once more, cradling it in her arm like an infant. "We have much to discuss, you and I."

"We—we do?" Iris closed the sketchbook and tucked it under her arm.

"Yes, but a headache prevents me from doing so now. Would you meet me in the Verandah Cafe tomorrow evening for a late dinner? By then I will have put together a plan for your future with my new line. *Elrose* is to be featured at Lord & Taylor, you know."

"I—I know." Iris couldn't seem to manage anything else. "I would be honored, Miss Russell. Thank you."

"You are so welcome, Iris. And by the way, I love your name."

"Thank you." She felt her cheeks turn warm. "Mother named me after the flower. It wasn't until I reached my teens that I realized *Iris* means *rainbow*." She felt her lips curl up in a smile. "Suits me, since I love color so much."

"And all the more reason why we need to get you out of a lady's maid dress and into something that properly reflects your name." Edith smiled and placed a hand on her arm. "An iris is strong and beautiful, as well. And from everything your friend Jacquie told me at dinner last night, you epitomize both of those words."

"Jacquie told you that?"

"That and much more. She says you're the bravest, strongest girl she's met." Edith patted her on the arm. "She's very taken with you, Iris. You're lucky to have such a friend."

"Yes, I suppose I am." Iris took a couple of steps toward the door then turned back to give Miss Russell a smile. "I will see you tomorrow night in the Verandah Cafe."

"Until then, my dear." The woman's eyes narrowed and she held up her hand, so Iris paused. "Oh, just one more thing, if you please."

"Yes?"

Edith cradled her stuffed pig, winding his tail until a cheerful little melody sounded. "Promise me you won't let that Lady Duff Gordon get her hooks into you."

"Beg pardon?"

"Yes." Edith took a couple of steps in her direction. "She is onboard, and you know how she is."

"I—I don't, actually."

"Perhaps that's for the best. Just remember, your designs are much more in line with what I'm doing. Have you seen her latest?"

Iris nodded but chose her words carefully. "Yes, of course. The looser waists are a hit with the young women."

Edith visibly shuddered. "Well, yes, but slit skirts? And plunging necklines?" She shook her head. "We will not chase that cat down the back alley—do I make myself clear?"

"Y–yes."

"Good. Then we have an understanding." She cradled the little pig as it continued to pour out its little tune. "If there's one thing I've learned, it's that allies are a good deal more effective than friends. You and I will be allies in this business. And I promise you, Iris, you will look lovely wearing silks and satins. The light will shine off you as never before."

Iris nodded and stammered her thanks again before meekly leaving the suite. By the time she made it to the Grand Staircase, she just couldn't help herself. She hopped, skipped, and jumped her way all the way to B Deck. She could hardly wait to see Tessa and give her the news.

* * * * *

Jacquie walked the streets of Southampton completely alone, her heart in her throat. Yesterday's visit from Peter had left her reeling. She pushed back the tears, determined not to cry again. She'd spent most of the night wading through an ocean of tears, hadn't she?

His emotional words had left a sting unlike any she'd ever known. But the tears through which he spoke those words convinced her that he did, at least to some extent, care for her. Perhaps not in the way she had hoped, but at least he cared. And his offer to marry her—to grow into a relationship, as he called it— was, she supposed, generous. Still, how could she marry someone who didn't truly love her? To do so would be humiliating.

At once she thought of Roland Palmer, of how he would have settled for a one-sided relationship. Strange, when she thought about it. He might be willing to settle for such a thing, but she would not, though she had sacrificed everything she held dear to discover it. No, she could not force Peter into a marriage that he did not desire. True, his feelings might grow in time, but she would prefer they do so without being forced.

Jacquie pulled her jacket tighter to ward off the chill that enveloped her. It came from a place deep inside and held her locked in place. Frozen.

She could not go forward.

She could not go back.

Truly, she had no options. And when one had no options, what was the point in going on?

* * * * *

Late Saturday night, a cold chill fell over the *Titanic*. At that very same time, however, the icy chill that had hovered over B-54 thawed. Tessa found it quite ironic. From the moment Iris arrived back at the cabin after meeting with Edith Russell, all was forgiven. For the first time ever, the two girls could express themselves as friends. Real friends. And that's just what Tessa did as Iris helped her with her corset strings after dinner.

"I must admit, there are certain advantages to pretending to be someone I'm not." Tessa eased her way out of her undergarments and reached for her nightgown. "When I take on the role of Jacquie, I don't have to think about my father or of the poverty that held me captive from childhood. I can eat what I like, do as I like, and enjoy the admiration of people. Is it selfish to say I enjoy that?"

Iris shrugged. "Probably normal."

"I can see that having money would make one rather spoiled. That's certainly different from the way I was raised. Opposite of it, in fact."

"I'm afraid I haven't asked many questions about your life before you came to Abingdon Manor." Iris's nose wrinkled. "I— I should have."

"My life before…" Tessa felt the sting of tears but willed them away. "No young girl deserves such a life. My father…" She could not continue because the lump in her throat got in the way.

"He was unkind?" Iris asked.

"Unkind is too small a word. He was cruel. He *is* cruel." She shuddered, just thinking about it. Why did it take stepping away from the situation to see it for what it was?

Iris reached for a dressing gown and draped it over Tessa's shoulders. "If you want to talk about it…" She looped the sash around the gown and took a step back. "I know I haven't been the best friend, but I'm here if you need a shoulder."

"Thank you." Tessa paused to think it through. "Maybe tomorrow we can have a good long talk."

"That sounds good." Iris covered her mouth as she yawned. "Are you going to the church service tomorrow morning? I hear the captain is leading the one in the first-class dining saloon."

"I—I don't think so."

Tessa couldn't imagine it, in fact. Every time she thought about the Lord, her knees ached and her heart writhed within her. No, thank you. She would forego that ritual.

Still, as she gazed into Iris's peaceful face, as she contemplated all that had taken place over the past few days, she had to believe there was a God—somewhere, someplace—arranging all of this.

Just as quickly, guilt wriggled its way into her heart. If God did exist, He surely wouldn't care much for the fact that she'd spent the last several days lying about who she was. And Nathan. Sweet, kindhearted Nathan. He would surely run the opposite direction if he discovered she was a fraud.

Strange, she'd only known him a few days now, but the idea of disappointing him—or worse, losing him—brought an ache in her heart that she could not explain.

"Are you all right, Tessa?" Iris glanced her way, eyes filled with concern.

"Oh." Tessa took a seat on the edge of her bed and gestured for Iris to join her. "Just thinking." Should she share her heart with her new friend? Open up and talk about the things that troubled her?

"I have a lot to think about too." Iris settled into the spot next to Tessa and fluffed the pillow. "So many plans to make." She leaned back and sighed, a heavenly, happy sigh.

Tessa decided to forego any somber conversation and focus on her new friend to celebrate the day's news. Though she had seen snatches of Iris's sketches over the past few days, she asked to see them again. Tessa examined each one, completely in awe. How could anyone possibly possess so much talent?

She and Iris spent the next hour sharing stories, nibbling on chocolates, and talking about how exciting life would be once they reached New York. And as Tessa dozed off, all worries about losing Nathan floated away on the night winds.

* * * * *

As she drifted off to sleep, Iris thought about how much had changed in the few days they had been out to sea. First, the meeting with Edith. What an unexpected gift! And now, a friendship with Tessa. Could such a thing be possible? They were sisters, no less—the sort pressed together by life and circumstance, if not by blood. This sister she could empathize with on so many levels.

Similar upbringing, though it was becoming clearer with each passing day that Tessa had endured much at the hands of a cruel father. One need look no further than her knees to see the scars the man had caused. Iris had a feeling those scars ran far deeper than skin, however. Surely Tessa had endured much that she didn't speak of.

Iris thought back to her own upbringing. Though poor, Mother and Father had cared for her in the best way they knew how and had given her love in place of those material possessions they could not afford. Now that she saw Tessa's plight, Iris realized the depth of the gift her parents had offered.

Love, even in a home with little money, made one feel wealthy.

She thought of Jacquie and of the many years the spoiled girl had received everything she'd ever wanted and more. She pondered Mrs. Abingdon's disdain of her husband, the general stand-offishness that permeated every relationship in that family. Surely even money couldn't fill in the gap when one lacked true love.

Iris found herself praying as she drifted off to sleep—thanking God for His blessings and wishing the same on her new sister-friend. Oh, if only Tessa could know the kind of love she herself had experienced as a child. Then maybe nothing else would matter.

Chapter Twenty-Two

Sunday Morning, April 14, 1912
Aboard the Titanic

Early Sunday morning, Tessa got word that the lifeboat drill, scheduled for that morning, had been canceled so that passengers could attend Sunday service. This, she heard from Jessie Leitch, who greeted her on the Grand Staircase after breakfast.

"I would love to stay and chat," Jessie said, "but we're on our way to the service now. Captain Smith is officiating." Jessie's eyes lit up as she leaned against the railing of the staircase. "You should come with us. We can all sit together."

"I don't think so, but thank you for asking."

"Well, if you change your mind, please do join us. We're meeting in the dining hall for hymns and a message."

Minutes later, after strolling the enclosed promenade deck, Tessa found herself reconsidering. Perhaps she should go to the service and give it a try. She made her way back to the first-class dining saloon and stood outside the door. From inside, the sound of voices raised in song drew her forward. Still, she could not make herself go in.

Tessa leaned against the door as the music filled the air.

"Would you like to go inside, miss?" The steward reached for the handle to the ornate door, but she shook her head and took a couple of steps back.

"No. Thank you."

Even so, she couldn't quite tear herself away. As the voices rang out in harmonies that could only be described as heavenly, she found herself focused on the words.

> *O God, our help in ages past,*
> *Our hope for years to come,*
> *Our shelter from the stormy blast,*
> *And our eternal home.*

Something about the words "eternal home" pierced her very soul. She thought about her home back in Gloucestershire County and the pain she had endured at the hands of her father. Then her thoughts shifted to the home she would one day have in America, should Jacquie's grandmother be willing to take her in. That home didn't feel real yet. In fact, nothing felt real, did it? Surely this whole thing felt like shifting sand beneath her feet.

Grief washed over her afresh as she contemplated her role in this farce. How could she presume to ask the Almighty for help when she had so willingly joined in such a scheme to deceive so many? She pressed in to listen to the next part of the song, intrigued by the feelings welling up inside of her.

> *Under the shadow of Thy throne*
> *Still may we dwell secure;*
> *Sufficient is Thine arm alone,*
> *And our defense is sure.*

"What would that feel like?" she whispered.

"I beg your pardon, miss?" The steward gave her a curious look.

"I—I'm sorry." She looked away, afraid her misty eyes would give away her emotions.

Still, the very idea that she could feel secure caused joy like a warm blanket to wrap her in its cocoon. If she closed her eyes, she could almost picture God's arm—like the song said—wrapping around her. Would He truly defend her? Protect her? If so, why hadn't He done so those many times back on the rocky path?

Her heart ached as feelings of betrayal set in. They were quickly followed by tendrils of guilt that wrapped themselves around her heart and squeezed until she could scarcely breathe.

Who am I, to expect God to intervene on my behalf? A girl who pretends to be someone she's not?

Oh, but she hadn't always been such a girl, had she? No, only for the love of a brother had she agreed to play this role. Surely the Lord understood that sort of love.

The voices from inside the dining hall rang out again, a steady chorus.

> *Before the hills in order stood,*
> *Or earth received her frame,*
> *From everlasting Thou art God,*
> *To endless years the same.*

She couldn't make sense of those words. Before the earth received her frame? Before creation? God was there in the darkness of night?

"Yes, child. And I was there in your darkest hour, too."

Where those words came from, she could not be sure. They shook her to the core and brought the sting of tears to her eyes. Her heart affixed in her throat and she somehow missed the next few words of the song. All that remained were the words the Lord—had it really been the voice of the Lord?—had spoken to her soul.

No longer concerned with what anyone thought about her late arrival, she reached for the door handle. The steward stepped into action and pulled the door back, ushering her inside the room swelling with the angelic tune. She stepped into the back row, her gaze traveling the room until it fell on Jessie, who glanced up and smiled as she gestured for Tessa to join them. Tentative steps moved her toward them, and she took a seat beside Jessie, who continued to sing in an angelic voice.

> *O God, our help in ages past,*
> *Our hope for years to come,*
> *Be Thou our God while life shall last,*
> *And our eternal home.*

The song drew to an end, but the music inside Tessa's heart was just beginning, the melody clear and strong. She could hardly wait to see how it would end.

When the service drew to a close, Tessa lingered in her chair, unable to think past the words of the hymn the others had sung. Jessie remained too, though Reverend Harper and Annie went back to their cabin. The young woman slipped her arm around Tessa's shoulders, a gentle but kindly movement that caused a lump to rise in Tessa's throat. When the room emptied, Jessie finally spoke.

"Are you all right?"

"I—I have a lot on my mind," Tessa managed at last.

"I can see that." Jessie's warm smile brought comfort. "And I'm here if you want to talk."

"I know."

A couple of moments passed before Jessie leaned close and whispered, "Tell me about your father, Jacquie."

Trembling began immediately, and Tessa fought the urge to stand and run. Determined not to respond, she shook her head, her heart crawling up to her throat. "I can't."

Jessie seemed determined to persist. "I don't want to pry, but I have the strongest sense that the struggles you've had are wrapped up in him. You alluded to as much yesterday. Forgive me if I've overstepped my bounds, but my uncle has taught me to go straight to the source of the problem, and I cannot help but think that your father is the source. Am I right?"

Tessa released a lingering sigh and pondered her next words. Then, like a dam breaking, she told Jessie every horrible story— about the rocky path, about the weights, about the rock prayers. Careful to make sure that no one else was looking, she eased her skirt up to show the scabs and bruises on her knees, now mostly healed. Still, they ached as if the abuse had taken place yesterday, not weeks ago.

Jessie gasped as she took in the bruises. When Tessa lowered her skirts, the tears flowed—long, silent sobs, pulling up every bit of ugly emotion from inside of her and spilling it out like oil upon the sea.

When Tessa finally calmed, Jessie's eyes narrowed to slits. "You're telling me that your father forces you to repent for sins you've not committed?"

"Y–yes."

"And that he heaps guilt and condemnation on you though you don't deserve it?"

Tessa's throat constricted. "Yes, that's true."

"Oh, Jacquie!" Jessie's eyes pooled with tears. "You poor, sweet girl. What a skewed image you must have of the Lord. He isn't an ogre, ready to grind your knees into the rocks when you come to Him with a burden or even something you've done wrong. He loves you too much for that. The depth of His love for you exceeds that of the Atlantic beneath us. How I wish you knew that."

Tessa closed her eyes and pictured the water, the icy, deep waters of the Atlantic. If she tried all day, she could not swim to the bottom. How could God reach down out of heaven and love her with such depth?

"Jacquie, I can assure you, God won't take your sins, real or imagined, and hold them over your head. He wants you to come to Him, yes, and He will accept you with open arms when there truly are things on your heart that you need to repent of. You don't ever need to be afraid of Him."

Tessa opened her eyes and gazed at her new friend, taking note of the tears that trickled down her cheeks as well.

"Promise me this, my sweet friend." Jessie clutched her hand. "Promise you will spend some time praying about what I've shared. Picture God on His throne, His arms open wide, hoping you will run into them for a heavenly embrace."

This picture was almost too much for Tessa to bear. While she wanted to imagine such a lovely sight, when she squeezed her eyes shut, she only saw her father—drunk, angry, and ready to burden her with weighted bags and drive her knees into the broken rocks. They ached just thinking about it.

"How do you know if you can truly forgive?" she asked. "I don't know that I can release my father from the pain he has caused."

"Forgiveness is a choice. I stand as a testimony to the fact that forgiveness is a gift to the one who extends it, many times more so than to the one who receives. Does that make any sense?"

"I—I guess so."

"When you forgive someone, it's as if you're taking the key to the cell that's been holding them in bondage and you're placing it in the lock to release them." Jessie paused and slipped her arm around Tessa's shoulders again. "Release your father, Jacquie. I don't understand the extent of what he's done, but release him. In doing so, you will release yourself. Then take that key and toss it overboard. Lose it to the ocean's depth. That's what God does with our sin, after all. He casts it as far as the east is from the west."

At once Tessa saw herself standing on the dock at Southampton, ready to board the *Titanic* for the first time. New York, many miles to the west, seemed a distance too far to imagine. Now here she stood. Would the Lord really cast her sin—the bitterness, the anger, the deception—over a distance greater still? If so, she needed to experience this kind of forgiveness. Needed to learn how to extend it to her father.

"It will take time to heal," Jessie added. "But promise me you will ask God to show you how."

Tessa offered a slow nod, knowing such a thing would be difficult at best. Still, the idea of having a father—in heaven or on earth—offer her such an embrace seemed almost too good to be true.

Jessie gave her a playful nudge. "Here's what I'm going to pray. I'm going to pray that the Lord sends you a husband who will show you what a real father looks like, a man who will adore you and treat you kindly. One who will love your children as they deserve to be loved and who will never abuse his authority."

The idea sent Tessa's thoughts reeling. "W–why do you care so much about me?" she asked.

"I care because God cares. He sent me to you to share His message of love so that you would know what a treasure you are to Him." Jessie reached inside her reticule and came out with a lace-trimmed handkerchief, which she used to blot Tessa's eyes. "You are, you know? A treasure, I mean. More valuable to Him than any of the jewels you own." A light giggle followed as she pointed to the broach on Tessa's coat. "Though, I must say, that diamond broach is something to behold."

"Yes." Her hands covered it, shame settling over Tessa like a cloud. "It's lovely." *And worth more money than I could make in a dozen years.*

"*Lovely* is the right word. But I promise, you are lovelier still. And you're more valuable to the Lord than all the diamonds in the world."

"Valuable." The word made no sense.

"Yes, and think of this, Jacquie. It took thousands of years to refine those diamonds. Thousands. God can take a hard heart— harder than those diamonds—and polish them up and smooth them out in no time at all. If you let Him, I mean. It's a matter of being willing."

Willing.

Not a word Tessa spoke very often. She understood the idea of bending the knee because she had no other choice. But to bend the knee willingly? Out of love for a God she had, until now, deliberately stayed away from? She shivered.

"I'm sorry. I've kept you too long." Jessie smiled and patted her on the arm. "Please forgive me. I do go on at times."

"No, please don't apologize. I've enjoyed our conversation

immensely." Tessa felt peace well up inside of her, and she found herself reaching to give her new friend a hug. "You are a dear girl. Don't ever forget it."

"If there is anything dear in me, it comes from Above, trust me." Jessie laughed. "You don't know the rapscallion I was as a child."

"Hard to picture."

"Oh, I was. But God is gracious. Forgiving." She began to sing a haunting little song, something about God hiding her sin in the depths of the sea.

Hiding my sin?

A shiver ran through Tessa. She had much to hide, after all.

"I've decided that keeping things hidden is for the birds," Jessie said and then chuckled. "Let it all be out in the open—wide for all to see."

In that moment, Tessa knew what she must do. She had to relieve herself of the guilt of holding onto a lie. Of pretending to be someone she was not.

I'm not Jacquie Abingdon. I never will be.

She would start by telling Jessie. And then, as soon as an opportunity presented itself, she would tell Nathan too. Doing so would surely put an end to any possibility of romance, but she could not pretend one moment longer. To keep on pretending would put her at a far worse peril than the frigid waters of the Atlantic.

* * * * *

Through the glass in the dining room door, Nathan caught a glimpse of Jacquie, dressed in her Sunday finest and seated next to Jessie, the young woman they'd met only yesterday. Usually stoic, Jacquie now had tears streaming down her face. He had noticed her during service, of course, but hadn't felt led to approach her. Now he found himself relieved that her new friend had taken time to comfort her, though he longed with every fiber of his being to be the one to do so.

Still, the timing was not right. He could sense it in his gut. Feel it in his heart.

All night he had wrestled with his feelings for Jacquie. He longed to speak to her, to tell her about the emotions stirring within him. But something stopped him. He couldn't put his finger on it, but something didn't feel right, and her current emotional state only confirmed that.

Nathan's mother drew near and peered through the glass. "Everything all right in there?"

"I think so."

"She's a nice girl, but rather peculiar, I must say." Mother fussed with her gloves. "Doesn't seem to know her station."

"Her station?" Nathan released a sigh.

"Yes. She allows her lady's maid to speak to her as a commoner. Though, I must say, Edith Russell is smitten with her, and that has me intrigued. What a pair those two are. Very, very odd." She walked off, muttering to herself.

Nathan decided to take a walk to clear his head. He took the elevator to the Boat Deck and shivered when he stepped outside. The temperature had dipped. He pulled his coat tighter and walked to the railing on the starboard side of the ship, where he paused for a glimpse out at the Atlantic. Another shiver grabbed hold of him and held him in its grip.

To his right, a little girl's chatter in an unknown tongue caught his attention. He glanced over to look at the youngster. He recognized her as the same little girl he had seen on the deck that first day, the one with the dark curls who had danced her way into her father's arms.

Today was no different. The child's father swooped her up into his arms and held her close, then danced with her, a happy, jovial dance across the deck. The little girl's laughter rang out, and then she hugged her papa's neck. Her father responded by planting kisses in her hair and fussing over her in that strange, unfamiliar language. Nathan found it all captivating.

The little girl hopped out of her father's arms and grabbed his hands. Her daddy called out, "Manca!" which Nathan could only guess to be her name. The youngster's deep brown eyes sparkled with life and laughter, her giggles ringing through the air.

Something about the exchange touched Nathan's heart deeply. Though he couldn't bear the idea of saying good-bye to Jacquie, of seeing this journey come to an end, he longed to wrap his father in a tight bear hug and join him in the family's business. If only he could ask time to stand still for just a moment. Then perhaps he could straddle the Atlantic, one foot on deck and the other firmly planted on the shores of New York, where opportunities abounded.

* * * * *

Iris spent the afternoon working on her sketches, the ideas flowing as fast as the water from the indoor plumbing. How so many ideas could come at once remained a mystery, but she did not fight the process. Instead, she gave herself over to it, happy to wile away the hours doing the thing she loved most. Tonight she would meet with Edith Russell. Her future would be set.

Until then, she simply needed to finish what she'd started.

Chapter Twenty-Three

Sunday Night, April 14, 1912
Aboard the Titanic

When the sun went down on Sunday evening, the temperatures plummeted. In spite of this, several of *Titanic*'s passengers braved the cold night air out on the deck to witness a marvelous sunset with John Harper. Tessa stood next to Jessie, who commented on the brilliant colors as they faded from deep amber to a murky red-orange and then to a soft pink-blue. As the bits of light slipped off the horizon to the west, the good reverend slipped his arm over Jessie's shoulder and smiled. "Time for evening prayers and Bible reading."

Jessie nodded then turned to give Tessa a hug. "See you in the morning?"

"Yes, but I'm awfully tired. I hope to sleep in." So many wonderful things had happened today. And now that Jessie knew her secret—knew she was really Tessa, not Jacquie—she felt sure she could sleep like a baby.

The reverend offered her a gracious smile then gestured to the now-darkened skies. "It will be beautiful in the morning."

"Oh, I've no doubt."

Tessa decided that a cup of hot chocolate was in order. She headed inside to the Café Parisien, where she sipped on the warm, creamy liquid, finally feeling the evening's chill lift. Lost in her thoughts about the blissful day, over an hour went by. Though sleepy, she decided one more stroll around the Boat Deck was in order before retiring to her room.

Tessa wrapped her scarf a bit tighter around her neck and headed off. Halfway down the Boat Deck, she paused to gaze over the railing and caught a glimpse of slushy mounds of ice in the water below. They billowed like little white clouds, fluffy and harmless, bits of white cotton on a sea of water as black as night. The little mounds captivated her, held her spellbound for some time.

Until the shivering began in earnest. Perhaps she should go back inside now, back to the warmth of her cabin. Yes, she would wait up for Iris so that she could hear the details of her meeting with Miss Russell.

Tessa pressed her gloved hands into the pockets of her coat and took a few rapid steps toward the stairwell. The man she recognized as Mr. Bruce Ismay approached, dressed in a deep blue suit but no overcoat, in spite of the cold nip in the air. He leaned against the railing and glanced her way. "Is your journey going well? Are you comfortable?"

"Oh, very, sir." Tessa nodded and smiled. "Thank you so much for asking."

"My pleasure." He tipped his hat before she headed off toward the stairs.

Just before she reached the steps, Tessa heard a familiar voice ring out from behind her. "I thought I just might find you here."

She turned to see Nathan, and her heart sailed to her throat. Though she had hoped to put off talking with him until tomorrow, here he stood, with a smile as broad as the Atlantic on his face.

"Happy to see me?" he asked as he took a few steps in her direction.

"Yes." She swallowed hard, realizing the moment had come for revealing her secret. "I've been wondering about you. Did you have a good day?"

"Very relaxing. And this evening has been nice. I went to the hymn-sing in the second-class dining saloon."

"And how was that?"

"Nice." He began to hum an unfamiliar song and before long took to singing, "'For those in peril on the sea.'"

"I gave some thought to going to one of the concerts in the reception room but decided against it. It's been an exhausting day."

"You've been on my mind all day." He drew near and extended his hand. She tentatively slipped her fingers through his, loving the comfort they brought. "Are you all right?"

"All right?"

"Yes. I don't mean to pry, but I saw you with Jessie earlier. You were crying. I just wanted to check on you."

Their hands still clasped, he led the way to the side, where they joined two other couples in gazing out over the railing at the sky above. She glanced up, taking in the brilliant twinkling of stars, which dotted the night with electrifying beauty.

"I'm fine." Of course, this feeling would probably slip away once she told him the truth. Tessa swallowed the lump in her throat and continued to gaze upward.

Nathan gave her fingers a gentle squeeze and then glanced up at the sky. "I've seen the stars a thousand times, but never like this," he said. "I only wish I had a telescope. Then I could really see them in their full splendor."

"I prefer to see them from a distance," Tessa said. Then she sighed. "The whole thing reminds me of a painting I once saw. It's as if the canopy of clouds rolled back and left an inky-black velvet sky covered in sparkling diamonds." She giggled, feeling a little giddy as the words rolled off her tongue. "Do you find that silly?"

"Not exactly how I might've described it, mind you, but I do find it beautiful."

"Oh, it is beautiful, isn't it? Strange, how the sky never looked this perfect from the farm."

"The farm?"

Her heart quickened, and she fought to think clearly. How could she repair this slip of the tongue? Perhaps she didn't need to. Maybe she should just open up and tell him the truth. She would start by sharing about her home. "Well, I...yes. Our family owns a farm. It's a lovely place." *Lovely* might be a stretch, but emotion welled up inside her as she thought about the home she now missed with a passion.

He nodded. "I've always wanted to live in the country. It's hard to see the stars in New York. But in the country, I would imagine you can practically reach out and grab them."

"It's true." She nodded. "Sometimes I go out to the pasture at night and look up at the stars. They look like candles, lighting the sky."

A lovely conversation ensued as they walked together, hand in hand. After some time, a delicious silence grew up between them. They paused and gazed upward once again.

"It's a shame the moon isn't out tonight."

"Would have been lovely." She sighed. "I've always wondered what holds it in place."

"The Lord. With just a word, He keeps all of creation exactly where He wants it to be."

"Like a puppeteer? With a string?" she asked.

"No. Like an artist, with a paintbrush in hand."

As Tessa clutched the railing, the wind ran its graceful fingers through her upswept hair and loosened it into fine ribbons around her face. The smell of saltwater lingered in the air, and she breathed it in. She could almost envision the Lord snatching her sins and tossing them into the roiling waves below.

Perfect peace settled over her. She longed to wrap it like a blanket around her. But first, she must relieve herself of the guilt by confessing her shame to Nathan. She would tell him all... and he would help her sort out what could be done about it.

As she opened her mouth to speak, a cry came from the look-out's nest above.

"What's going on up there?" Nathan glanced up. The sound of a bell ringing three times pierced the air, followed by heated dialogue from above.

"I don't know." She squinted to have a better look but could not make out the figures.

Seconds later, the ship jolted, and she tumbled toward Nathan. He caught her in his arms—a delicious problem—but the strangest sound took her by surprise.

A hideous scraping noise, long and grinding, from well below the railing. A tremor from beneath the deck shook her ever so slightly, and in that same moment, shards of ice sprayed the deck. Several fell around them, and she leaped to her right to avoid being hit.

"W–what was that?" Tessa asked.

"I'm not sure." He leaned over the railing alongside several others who appeared just as perplexed as they. Behind them, a mammoth piece of ice hovered over the ship, as if daring them to gaze upon it.

"Nathan, did we...?" She shook her head, unable to finish the question.

At once voices began to overlap, as people nearby tried to make sense of what had happened.

"Just a bump, I daresay," an older fellow said with the wave of a hand.

"Yes, nothing to fear, folks," one of the crew members called out. "A little berg won't get in *Titanic*'s way. She'll show it who's who and what's what." A round of laughter followed from all. A couple of the men picked up the shards of ice and tossed them to and fro like balls.

"Who's on first, fellas?" one of the men called out and then laughed.

Tessa relaxed and allowed Nathan to slip his arms around her once again. Off in the distance, Mr. and Mrs. Astor strolled by, hand in hand. They paused to speak to another man but seemed content with the explanation that *Titanic* was in no danger from the little scrape with the pesky berg.

"What were you about to say?" Nathan pushed a loose hair out of her eyes.

Her heart quickened. "I wanted to tell you something that's been troubling me, Nathan. But I think you'd better sit down." Tessa gestured to a deck chair, and he sank into it as she took the spot next to him, ready to unveil her sin once and for all.

* * * * *

Nathan listened in silence as Jacquie shared her story. Only, she wasn't really Jacquie, was she? Still, nothing about this made sense. Surely she teased him with this far-fetched tale about her so-called pretense. Yes, Jacquie had quite the imagination and used it even now to draw him in.

On the other hand, the concern in her eyes conveyed such pain, such emotion…

He trembled, half from the cold and half from the realization that she'd played him for a fool over the past few days.

"You're not making this up?" he asked after she finished her lengthy explanation. He gazed at her tear-streaked face under a starlit sky and prayed she would laugh. Tell him she'd made it all up as some sort of a game. Instead, she shook her head, tears now falling in rapid succession.

"No, Nathan. I–I'm not. Every word I've just spoken is true. And I'm so awfully sorry that I—"

She stopped mid-sentence as several crewmen rushed by.

In that moment, a half-dozen things happened at once. Bruce Ismay lit into a heated conversation with one of the crewmen. Several other men appeared from below, and the words "taking on water" rang out. Nathan shook his head, looking back and forth between the men and Jacquie—Tessa—to make sense of it all. Only when he heard the words "Prepare to evacuate!" did the whole thing begin to feel like a horrible nightmare.

* * * * *

Monday Morning, April 15, 1912, 12:05 a.m.
Aboard the Titanic

Iris sat across the table from Edith Russell in the Verandah Cafe and attempted to focus. All around them, their fellow passengers spoke in animated voices, many speculating about the strange scraping sound they'd heard earlier and the odd tremor they now felt. Then, as the ship slowed, as the brakes sounded and everything drew still, she realized they must be in some sort of trouble.

Still, she couldn't seem to focus on anything right now except the conversation she'd just had with Edith. Hours of blissful chatter about fashion had led to the job offer of a lifetime, one she could still scarcely believe. What a perfect way to end her evening.

Or had she imagined it all, along with the quiver of fear that now ran through her as the anxiety in the eyes of surrounding passengers increased? Was the whole thing a murky dream?

"What do you suppose we've missed?" Edith rose and walked to the window. She turned back to Iris, her brow wrinkled. "Do you think we're really in danger?"

"This is the *Titanic*. She's the ocean's queen." Iris tried to steady her voice. She looked around the restaurant, taking comfort in the fact that so many remained at their tables. "Besides, they would let us know if something serious had happened." Closing her sketch pad, she rose from her seat. "Don't you think?"

"One would think. But why else would they have stopped? Doesn't make any sense."

Just about the time she felt sure the others were overreacting, a wild-eyed young woman rushed into the room and spoke urgently. "They want us on deck. We need to hurry." As her words rang out, Iris's breath caught in her throat.

A steward appeared behind the woman; his brow was knitted in obvious concern. "Everyone into your life jackets and then to the lifeboats!"

Iris looked about, noticing that a handful of passengers stayed in their seats, some sipping drinks, others eating.

"It's just a precaution," an older fellow muttered. "Really, nothing to worry about."

"Haven't they heard? This ship is unsinkable!" the woman across from him said and then laughed.

Edith looked at Iris, her eyes wide, then took several fast steps away from the table and out of the room, muttering something about her pet pig.

Iris shook her head, wondering what sort of woman this new boss of hers might be. Not that she had time to think about it. With the crowd now pressing in around her, Iris felt herself being nudged along. What else could she do but head to the lifeboats?

* * * * *

Monday Morning, April 15, 1912
Just Past Midnight, Southampton, England

Jacquie curled herself into a fetal position in the hotel bed, her heart as heavy as a stone. In a hazy, dreamlike state, she wondered if perhaps the last few days had been merely a horrible nightmare. Would she awaken in her own bed at Abingdon Manor and chuckle at how real it had all seemed, or would the sun rise over Southampton, casting its light on her sin for all to see?

Overcome, she beat her fist into the pillow and tried to pray. Her prayers bounced off the ceiling and slapped her in the face. Surely even God Himself had forsaken her.

She needed answers.

She needed a plan.

Moments later, her thoughts swirling, she sat up in the bed and released a slow, agonizing breath. Only one thing made sense.

With no one to turn to, she would have to go away—away from London, away from Southampton—away from England.

Tomorrow.

Tomorrow she would go to the White Star Line and purchase a ticket to leave everyone and everything she knew.

Where she would go, she could not say.

Did not care.

She would go somewhere. Anywhere.

Anywhere but here.

Chapter Twenty-Four

Monday Morning, April 15, 1912, 12:10 a.m.
Aboard the Titanic

Nathan watched as the lifeboats were swung out and lowered from A Deck, where he now stood, frozen in place, both by the cold and the terror that gripped him.

Stay calm, Nathan. Stay calm.

The words "Women and children only!" rang out across the chaos, and he looked on as wide-eyed, terrified passengers in their cork-filled life jackets were marshaled into haphazard lines. A few pushed their way to the front, but for the most part, the women seemed too frighten to board the lifeboats, which dangled precariously over the side of the ship. Many argued with the seamen, insisting they were safer onboard *Titanic*. Nathan could see their point, certainly, but he knew they were better off following the captain's orders.

He turned to seek out Tessa but could not find her. She must have slipped away through the crowd. He ushered up a frantic prayer for God to keep her safe then turned his attentions back to an elderly woman who needed assistance. When the woman saw the boat swinging to and fro, she cried out, terrified. Another younger woman took her arm and, with a lighthearted voice, assured her that this was all just a silly precaution. Then she began to rave about the glassy sea and the twinkling stars above.

"It's just a slight mishap, I'm sure," the girl said as she helped the woman into the lifeboat. "We must look at this as an adventure. Something we can tell our children and grandchildren about."

At this point the older woman lit into a conversation about her grandchildren. Minutes later, she was all smiles as she settled into her seat in the lifeboat.

Nathan continued to work alongside several others, convincing the ladies to heed instructions. In the back of his mind, he wondered about Mother. Had she made it safely into a lifeboat? And Jacquie. Er, Tessa. Where was she?

He did his best to still his racing heart every time he thought about her, about everything she had just shared. How could everything change in the blink of an eye?

He forced his attention back to his work. The first boat met its quota of passengers and was lowered with great care onto the murky blackness of the Atlantic, and the process began again with the second lifeboat. And the third. By the time they had loaded a half dozen or so boats, *Titanic* began to list. Nathan only noticed it in passing at first, but with each ten or fifteen minutes, the angle intensified.

He watched as a family of five attempted to board a lifeboat. The father was turned away and his oldest son, as well. The boy looked to be about twelve or thirteen.

"My boy!" His mother let out an ear-piercing shriek, and the seaman finally conceded to let the young man into the lifeboat, though he relayed instructions to everyone within hearing distance that no more should do so.

Finally convinced that he was no longer needed, Nathan ran to the other side of the boat, where passengers were being loaded in a similar fashion, though many lifeboats on this side were not limited to women and children only. He watched as Mr. Ismay helped several women board a boat.

In the crowd he caught a glimpse of his mother, and Nathan's heart leaped for joy. "Mother!"

"Nathan!" She ran his way and propelled herself into his arms, the cork-filled life jacket swallowing her frame. "I thought I wasn't going to be able to find you."

"I wanted to go back to the room but couldn't get away. We have to get you on a lifeboat. Quickly."

"I can't get on without you." She clutched his hand. "Promise me you won't leave me alone on one of those boats. I'll be terrified. You know I can't swim."

"Please don't worry. The ship is built to withstand a bit of water, and I'm sure they've already got the problem under control. The lifeboats are surely just a precaution. And you've got your life belt. No need to worry. Climb on in."

"But I can't go alone. You know me better than that. I'll be too frightened."

"You must. I've got to stay here and help. They're calling for people to go to the cabins and wake people up."

Mother placed her hands on her hips. "Well, if you won't go with me, James must."

"I doubt they'll let him on, Mother. It's women and children only."

She pointed at the lifeboat being lowered beside them, which was filled with a vast array of men and women. "No, see? Men too. I'm going to find James. He was in the smoking room."

She took off running in the opposite direction, disappearing from view seconds later. Nathan wanted to run after her but realized it would be pointless, with this crowd. Besides, as he made his way through the maze of passengers, the face of the one he'd been searching for came into view.

He saw her from a distance, helping children into a lifeboat. Working with great care, she helped those who could not help themselves. But he would make sure she got into one of the lifeboats too.

She.

Whoever "she" was.

Right now, her name didn't matter. Tessa. Jacquie. Who cared? All that mattered was getting the woman he loved to safety.

* * * * *

Monday Morning, April 15, 1912, 12:27 a.m.
Aboard the Titanic

Violent shaking held Tessa in its grip as she worked alongside others loading the lifeboats. How many times had she heard fathers cry out to their children, "Go on, now! Be brave. Daddy will be along in the next boat."

She knew it wasn't true, of course. There weren't enough lifeboats for everyone. Not even close. Oh, but how her heart ached with every family torn apart! How she fought to hold back the tears as terrified children clambered into shaky lifeboats.

Just about the time she'd decided to run to the Verandah Cafe to look for Iris, she saw Nathan's face through the crowd. He raced through the mob of people and swept her into his arms, pressing kisses into her hair. In that moment, everything she had worried about faded away.

"We've got to get you into this boat." He gestured to Lifeboat Eleven.

Tessa shook her head. "No, I have to find Iris." The trembling in her arms and legs made walking nearly impossible, but she knew she must try. For Iris's sake, she must try.

"Tessa, please. I beg of you. Get in."

She had just opened her mouth to argue the point when Jessie and little Annie drew near. Tears dribbled down the youngster's cheeks, but Jessie looked unshaken.

"Jessie!" Tessa wrapped her arms around her friend. "Oh, thank God you're all right."

"Miss Jacquie!" Annie hurled herself into Tessa's arms. "Oh, Miss Jacquie, Papa is still on the ship. He won't come."

"Uncle John told me to keep the faith," Jessie said, her shoulders squared. "He said we are to get into a lifeboat and do as we are instructed." She grabbed Tessa's hand. "You must come with us."

Tessa looked back at the crowd, suddenly feeling woozy. The mob grew larger by the moment, people now crying out and shoving one another. In that moment, the decision was made. She could join them, but not before saying good-bye to Nathan. She reached out for him, and he drew her into an embrace then planted kisses in her hair.

"It's going to be fine," he whispered, his breath warm against her ear. "But I'll feel better if you're on the lifeboat."

"Promise you'll get on one too?" The words came out with a visible tremor.

He squelched her concerns with a gentle kiss, one that almost made her forget the situation taking place around them. Almost. Then, with the crowd pressing in, she felt herself slipping from his arms.

"God will take care of us." She felt the assurance of the words as they were spoken.

"He will."

With Nathan's help, the ladies boarded Lifeboat Eleven and settled into their seats. The boat rocked back and forth, hitting the side of the ship. Annie's gut-wrenching cries ripped the night.

"Miss Jacquie, it's so c–cold." The youngster's teeth chattered, and Tessa pulled her into a tight grip. Her head ached, in part from the trembling and in part from the chaos of people crying out around them. Seconds later, Jessie joined them and they huddled together, barely looking up as others entered.

A woman dressed in a fabulous mink coat made her way into the boat, beginning to instruct the others and generally play the role of captain of their little lifeboat. Behind her came Edith Russell, holding what appeared to be a baby in a blanket. She took her seat and fussed over the blanket, cooing and coddling, as if to comfort the little babe.

As they huddled together to ward off the cold, Tessa found herself gripped with fear.

Where is Iris? Is she all right?

Tessa squeezed Jessie's hand and gazed into her friend's eyes, feelings of delirium settling in. Surely this was all a dream. A terrifying dream from which they would awaken in the morning. Yes, in the morning she would stand onboard *Titanic*'s Boat Deck, drinking in the sunshine and anticipating their arrival in New York.

In that moment, she thought about the letter Jacquie had written to her grandmother. The one on the desk in the suite.

"Oh, no!"

"What is it?" Jessie asked, her voice laced with compassion.

"I—I left something in the room."

"No bother." Jessie gave her hand a squeeze. "We will be back in our rooms in no time. You can fetch whatever it is then."

Tessa did her best to calm down. Really, what did it matter now? She would trade a thousand letters just to see Iris again. She would forego all of this—her new life in America, the opportunity to begin again—just for one more conversation with her friend.

Tessa steadied her breathing, but the trembling in her arms and legs could not be squelched. Bitter cold racked her extremities, and she rubbed her arms in an attempt to calm herself.

"Jessie, do you still believe what you said this morning on the ship?" she managed at last. "About God being a merciful Father?"

"I—I do." Tears streamed down Jessie's cheeks.

"Then pray, Jessie. Pray for Iris. Pray that He will bring her to us."

* * * * *

April 15, 1912, 12:33 a.m.
Aboard the Titanic

Iris rushed to her room to find her life jacket and fetch the yard of Kenmare lace, which she tucked into her sketch pad. Glancing down at the desk, she happened to notice the letter addressed to Jacquie's grandmother. Tessa would need this. Iris snatched it and pressed it into the inner pocket of her jacket. She then fussed with the strings on her life jacket, finally getting them fastened. Afterward, she made her way through the throng of people in the Grand Staircase toward A Deck.

Never had she seen so many people pressed together in one place. Somehow she found herself on the starboard side of A Deck moments later. Perhaps the mob had pressed her there. When she saw Nathan at the ship's edge, she could hold back the tears no longer.

"Iris!" He called out to her and waved.

She ran that direction, and he gave instruction for the lifeboat to pause in midair. "I—I can't make it from here."

"You must. They can fit you onboard, Iris. Go. Now."

She released a puff of air, tucked her sketch pad under her arm, and somehow managed to grab hold of the edge of the life-boat, which now hung suspended several stories above the vast expanse of water below.

As she scrambled over the edge of the icy-cold boat, Iris lost her grip on the sketchbook. It slipped out of her hand, and she cried out. For a moment, it appeared to float through the air, as if defying gravity. Then, quickly, the errant pages slid over the edge of the lifeboat and fell down, down, down into the waters below. She let out a shriek, her heart broken.

Gone!

Gone were her dreams, her plans.

Gone was the hope that she could make something of her life, be something—someone—more than she had been.

All gone. Buried in the depths of the sea.

With the cries of those ringing out around her, no one could hear her wails, surely. Reaching over the edge, she gazed down, nausea setting in as she realized how far down the water was.

"Don't!" A woman in a mink stole pulled her back. "You'll tip the boat and we'll land upside down!"

"But…" She gazed into the murky darkness of the water as the sketches, her precious sketches, disappeared from view. Her heart sank with them.

Iris heard someone call her name and glanced across the lifeboat, seeing Tessa. Suddenly the sketch pad meant nothing. She flew to her friend's arms, tears flowing as their lifeboat was lowered to the sea.

* * * * *

April 15, 1912, 12:44 a.m.
Aboard the Titanic

Nathan looked on as Iris landed inside the lifeboat, and then he gave the "all clear" signal for the boat to be lowered. He felt his heart sink as the women disappeared from view. Still, others needed him.

Off in the distance, a rocket fired into the sky, its colors lighting the night and bringing a surge of hope. Surely another ship would see. Would come. Several minutes later another rocket shot off, and then another. With each colorful blast, his hopes rose.

Nathan continued to work alongside the other men loading the boats until he heard someone call his name. Looking across the crowd, he saw James Carson, dressed in full tuxedo with every hair in place.

"Son!"

The word did not carry its usual sting until James followed it with a question.

"Where is your mother?"

Nathan shook his head, his thoughts tumbling. "She went to look for you. I tried to get her into a lifeboat, but she wouldn't go alone, and I can't go. It's women and children only."

James's eyes reflected his concern. "I will go to your cabin to find her."

"No." Nathan squared his shoulders. "I will go myself. Please stay here and take over for me, James." He turned, half ashamed at the bitter outburst and half proud of himself for standing up for what was right. He would fetch Mother himself and situate her in a lifeboat. What would happen after that, he could not say.

As he took his first steps away from the crowd, James grabbed his arm.

"Nathan, listen. Please."

"I don't have time right now, James. Surely you can see that." He glanced back but continued to walk, the older man now following on his heels.

"I know, but this is important. We might not have another opportunity, and there's something I must get off my chest regarding your mother."

Nathan stopped and put a hand up. "Please, James, don't." He didn't want to hear any of his mother's indiscretions in his last minutes of life. "Whatever happened is over and forgotten. All that matters is this moment, and in this moment I have to get Mother safely onboard a lifeboat."

"I'm not talking about the past, son. What I have to tell you affects our future." James's eyes filled with tears as the ship jolted, the deck now dangerously tilted. "I must tell you this before you go."

"What is it, James?" Truly, this fellow was wearing his patience. Nathan grabbed hold of the railing, his gaze landing on a familiar little girl several yards away. Manca. The girl who'd danced with her father on the deck. Nathan watched as an impatient seaman tried to force the tiny child across a ladder, a makeshift route to the hoisted lifeboat, which hung at a precarious angle. The little girl clung to her father's leg, unwilling to budge. Not that he blamed her. To climb aboard that ladder would be impossible for an adult, let alone a child.

"I have always loved you like a son, Nathan." James reached out and pulled him into an uncomfortable embrace. "Though I could never acknowledge you as my own."

Nathan's gaze shifted back to the man, his heart in his throat as he wriggled away. "Acknowledge me? What are you talking about?"

James shook his head, his cheeks now wet. From the spray of water splashing over the deck, maybe, or were those tears? "Listen to me, Nathan. All that I have in this world is wrapped up in my company, and it's worth a pretty penny. All of it, I have left to you. All of it."

Nathan shook his head, his thoughts reeling. Surely the tilt of the ship had done something to James Carson's reasoning. Off in the distance, the little girl's cries split the night. Her father lifted her and handed her to the seaman, who flung her onto the ladder where she clung, screaming.

"Do you understand what I'm saying, son?" James reached for his hand. "Everything I have is yours."

"But why?"

As the ship jolted once again, James doubled over and grabbed the railing. He rose, eyes brimming. "Because you are my boy, and I love you. I always have, even when I couldn't acknowledge it."

Confusion swept over Nathan. Before he could spend another moment thinking about what James had said, however, his gaze shifted back to Manca, who gripped the ladder and cried now louder than ever. The little girl's father called out to her in a language unfamiliar, obviously trying to get her to work her way across the ladder to the lifeboat. The terrified youngster would not budge. She hovered, several stories high, over the water.

Nathan turned away from James and took tentative steps toward Manca, gripping the railing the whole way. He glanced back at James one last time, torn. If what James had said was true...

But it couldn't be.

It couldn't.

Manca's cries pierced his heart, and Nathan glanced back to see the child's father attempting to help her across the ladder. The youngster slipped and nearly fell as she tried to grab onto her father. She refused to let go, now putting both of their lives in danger.

"Help her, son," James called out from a distance away. "I will find your mother."

No doubt he would. Anger rose like a fire inside of Nathan's belly as he made his way toward the little girl. *One thing at a time.* Deal with the issue in front of him, and then make sure Mother made it onto a lifeboat.

Off in the distance, Manca held her father in a death grip, her shrieks echoing across the starlit sky. Nathan slipped onto the ladder behind them and took hold of the little girl, leaving her father free to ease his way off the ladder and back onto *Titanic*'s deck.

"Manca?" Nathan tried to steady his voice as he held the child with one arm and the ladder with the other. He pointed to the lifeboat on the far end of the ladder. "Manca, you must get into the boat. Hurry."

With tears streaming, she shook her head, and a string of words escaped in a language unfamiliar. From the deck of the *Titanic*, the child's father pleaded with her.

The youngster looked at him, eyes wide. There she clung, unable—or unwilling—to move an inch.

The world tilted as *Titanic*'s bow lowered. Nathan lost his grip on the child, who slipped from his arms, but he caught her in midair. She let out a piercing scream as he pulled her back onto the ladder. Fear now held the youngster frozen in place. Fear and icy coldness, which gripped him with such violence that he could not stop shaking.

As the ladder swayed, Nathan swept the child into his arms and eased his way toward the lifeboat. From inside the boat, two of the ladies rose and extended their arms, willing the youngster to make the jump. She refused. Nathan lifted her over the railing and dropped her inside, which caused the boat to rock.

The moment he let her go the lifeboat pitched wildly. The icy cold air caused Nathan's fingers to go numb, and he lost his grip on the ladder. The world began to spin as he fell down, down, down into the blackness of the night.

Chapter Twenty-Five

April 15, 1912, 12:51 a.m.
The Atlantic

Shivering. Pain. Stabbing. Deafening cries.

In. Out. In. Out.

"No!" Nathan cried out as the icy-cold water pierced his skin, a thousand needles driving themselves in at once.

He gave himself over to the darkness that now enveloped him as everything faded into a haze. "Lord, not my will, but Yours be done." The words of Jesus washed over him afresh as the pain held him frozen.

Just as quickly, James Carson's words played over in his mind, taunting him: *"Do you understand what I'm saying, son? Everything I have is yours."*

"Oh, God!" The cry went up as the reality of the man's words sank in. "Merciful God!"

"You are my boy, and I love you. I always have!"

A cry rang out. A woman's voice, angelic and strong. Nathan forced his eyes open, straining as an unfamiliar face came into view. He tried to focus as he took in the image of the woman leaning over the edge of a half-empty lifeboat.

Moments later, strong arms reached down to grab hold of

him, and he felt himself lifted—miraculously lifted—from a watery grave to a chance at new life.

* * * * *

April 15, 1912, 1:30 a.m.
Lifeboat Eleven

Seated inside Lifeboat Eleven, Tessa fought to keep her thoughts straight. In spite of the bitter cold, she felt feverish. The trembling in her extremities grew worse as time passed, and she felt herself moving in and out of consciousness, her thoughts more twisted than ever. Shivers racked her to the bone, and she wondered if maybe she had died.

In her delirious state, Tessa saw herself a young girl—maybe six—running across the farm, chasing Peter's elusive shadow. Older and more nimble, he raced along, his boyish laughter filling the air.

"Wait for me, Peter!" she cried out, kicking up her heels. "Don't leave me."

Through the blurry haze he turned and offered her a smile, but then his face—his beautiful face—grew fuzzy. He continued to run far, far away. Before long, the shadow disappeared, as did he. All that remained was his voice, that precious, soothing voice.

"Tessa? Tessa, are you all right?"

She paused to catch her breath and leaned over as a stitch in her side caused her to double over in pain. "Please! Don't. Leave. Me. Please. Stay with me, Peter."

"Tessa? Oh, Tessa, wake up!"

The dream grew fuzzier still, and her head felt hot. Just as quickly, she shivered, gripped by icy tentacles that stung her legs and arms.

"Peter, please!" With pigtails flying in the breeze, she ran across the meadow, beyond Countess's stall and away from the house. Chasing his shadow.

Shadows.

Shadows.

Murky, gray shadows.

"She's in shock."

Tessa heard the voice but could not respond. With her head swimming and her thoughts so muddled, how could she?

Why is it so cold?

"If I should die before I wake..." Tessa whispered the words as she knelt down in front of her father. Pa took hold of her shoulders and pressed her knees into the rocky path. Gravelly bits tore holes into her flesh, causing intense pain.

"If I should die before I wake..."

"Repent, girl." Pa's drunken breath made her stomach sick. "Ask the Lord to forgive you for your wickedness."

"Oh, God!" She tumbled to and fro, rocking back and forth, back and forth. Her stomach revolted and she could not hold its contents.

"If I should die before I wake..."

She emptied her stomach then leaned back in a haze, her thoughts in a whirl.

"The letter!" she cried out. "How will Jacquie's grandmother know me without the letter? I will have no place to go!"

"Tessa!" Someone shook her with such force that she almost came out swinging. "Tessa! Please."

Tessa tried to force her eyes open but only managed a second's glance. In that moment, she took in vast miles of darkness. And then—Iris's face. Slowly, the faces of the others came into view. Annie. Jessie. Edith Russell. In that moment, every image of Peter faded away.

* * * * *

April 15, 1912, 1:58 a.m.
Lifeboat Eleven

Iris held Tessa close but could not stop the tears from flowing. She had never known such fear. Or such cold. The trembling gripped her until she could scarcely move.

"Tessa!" Iris held her close and fought to warm them both.

Just an hour ago, she had mourned the loss of her sketchbook, that silly, meaningless thing. Now she feared for the life of her friend.

"Oh, God. Please, God!" she cried out to the heavens, begging for mercy.

From across the lifeboat an unfamiliar woman approached. Her movement, though cautious, caused the boat to rock. The woman came and knelt in front of Tessa. She reached out her hand to feel her forehead then glanced at Iris. "I'm a doctor, dear. Alice Leader." She pulled off her scarf and wrapped it around Tessa's neck. "We must keep her warm. She's feverish. I daresay she's also in shock. I feel sure it will pass once we're rescued."

"Rescued." Iris spoke the word aloud, as if to convince herself.

Rescued. Yes, Lord.

Iris tightened her grip on Tessa and nodded. She would not be moved, no matter how long they had to sit in this boat waiting on someone—anyone—to help.

Alice returned to her seat, and Iris's gaze shifted up to *Titanic*, that mighty queen floating so close that she could practically reach out and touch her. Still, what a strange and frightening angle the ship now held. Very odd.

"She's taken on too much water." Jessie's voice sounded from beside Iris. "She will go down."

"We must row out before she does." The able seaman in charge of their boat spoke with calm assurance.

"We should stay here!" another woman called out. "My husband is on that ship."

"We cannot," another argued. "To do so now would be certain death to us all. We will be caught in the surge as the ship goes down."

The words settled into Iris's heart with the weight of a ship's anchor. The cries of the people left onboard the ship did little to squelch her fears. Even from here she could hear the women crying out, could see the men as they threw themselves onto the collapsible lifeboats. Many were dragged back across the deck, their screams piercing the night.

From up above, a woman's scream sounded, followed by a man's voice: "Women and children first? I'll show you!"

In that moment, a small bundle flew through the air toward the boat next to theirs. She watched from a distance as one of the women caught it and the cries of a babe sounded from inside the blanket.

"Merciful God in heaven!" a woman's voice cried out from the other boat. "It's a baby!" The child's wails were nothing in comparison to the cries coming from his young mother onboard the ship above.

Iris shuddered and closed her eyes.

She heard the sound of little Annie's voice. The child spoke with an obvious tremor. "J–Jessie, where is P–Papa? Is he still on the ship?"

"I don't know, sweet girl." Jessie's voice sounded calm and strong. "Maybe he's on one of the other lifeboats. We can pray about that, all right?"

"All right, Jessie." Annie sighed.

At that moment, a sweet strain caught Iris's ear as a familiar melody filled the night air. From onboard *Titanic*, the sound of violins filled the night. Iris strained to make out the song but could not.

"Oh, Jessie, listen! It's Papa's favorite song. If we sing it, maybe he will come to us." Annie's voice took on a pleading tone. "Sing, Jessie. Sing!"

Jessie's soothing voice rang out, the familiar hymn cradling Iris as she continued to hold Tessa in her arms.

> *Nearer, my God, to Thee, nearer to Thee!*
> *E'en though it be a cross that raiseth me;*
> *Still all my song shall be nearer, my God, to Thee,*
> *Nearer my God to Thee, nearer to Thee.*

Iris glanced down as Tessa's eyes fluttered open briefly. She pulled her friend closer and rubbed her arms to keep her warm as the lifeboat moved farther and farther away from the ailing ship.

Jessie continued to sing, and before long the lady doctor joined in. Little Annie's voice offered the sweetest melody of all, pure and angelic as she lifted her song heavenward.

> *There let the way appear steps unto heav'n;*
> *All that Thou sendest me in mercy giv'n;*

Angels to beckon me nearer, my God, to Thee,
Nearer my God to Thee, nearer to Thee.

Iris glanced up at *Titanic*, her heart in her throat as the bow pressed down into the water and the stern lifted high. Deafening cries pierced the night, and still Jessie sang on.

* * * * *

Tessa moved in and out of consciousness. In the foggy, feverish haze, she heard cries. Screams. She felt the movement of the lifeboat. And then, voices raised in song. She thought perhaps the angels had come to sing over her. They *were* singing, weren't they? Yes, what a lovely melody. Familiar. Sweet. The words, haunting and holy, pierced her soul, ushering her into God's presence, a place she had never before visited.

Or if on joyful wing, cleaving the sky,
Sun, moon, and stars forgot, upwards I fly,
Still all my song shall be, nearer, my God, to Thee.
Nearer, my God, to Thee.
Nearer to Thee.

In spite of the fog that clouded her mind, Tessa somehow managed to open her eyes. Off in the distance, *Titanic* rose in brilliant splendor out of the sea, a tall, regal woman perched for greatness. Her twinkling lights flickered and then faded in a ripple, leaving only darkness.

Then, with the cries of her people raised in ghastly chorus, *Titanic*—beautiful, graceful *Titanic*—slipped off into the Atlantic, her song forever fading in the vast waters below.

* * * * *

Early Monday Morning, April 15, 1912
Southampton, England

Jacquie awoke with a start, the vivid dream still fresh in her mind. She felt herself gasping for air. Sitting up in the bed, she tried to calm her nerves, but they refused to be stilled. After a few slow, calculated breaths, she finally willed herself to stop shaking. Still, the nightmare replayed itself in her imagination.

She walked along the deck of *Titanic* and paused to stare down into the waters below. A sudden jolt of the ship sent her overboard, and she flew through the air like a bird in flight. Beneath her, the water beckoned, a ceremonial baptism for her sins. Her deception. Icy water swept over her like a shroud, drowning her guilt and shame.

The scene faded as Jacquie came awake. She shivered and pulled the blankets over her shoulders as the truth surfaced— the blessed, wonderful truth.

It was only a dream.

Yes, thank God, it was only a dream.

Chapter Twenty-Six

A heavy fog held Tessa in its grip. She pressed her way out of it on several occasions, the cold night air forcing her to think twice about whether or not she had died.

Hell isn't supposed to be cold, is it?

And yet, she could not deny the icy bitterness that held her tight in its grip. She gave herself over to it, convinced she must not turn back toward shore. What would be the point in going backward, after all?

After what felt like countless hours, someone nearby let out a cry, one that startled her back to consciousness momentarily.

"A ship!"

Tessa tried to lift her head, but the heaviness remained. She squinted to see, and lights from across the water came into view. She saw it all through a haze, a blur. Tessa thought she heard Iris's voice raised in a prayer of thanksgiving but could not be sure. Then, just as quickly, she felt sure Jessie sang over her, a hymn pure and sweet.

Yes, she had surely died. But heaven—if one could call this heaven—was a far cry short of perfection.

* * * * *

Iris let out a cry as a ship came into view. The tears flowed with such abandon that she couldn't see past them. To her right, little Annie awoke with a start and cried out again for her father. Jessie soothed her and then gripped Iris's hand.

"Tell me I'm not seeing things. That's really a ship, isn't it?"

"It is." Iris nodded, her heart in her throat. "Oh, it is!"

As the ship pulled near, the cacophony of voices from the other lifeboats joined into one horrible song. Wails for the dead. Cries of relief for the living. Shouts and triumphant cheers for the impending rescue. All of it merged together in Iris's mind. Through it all, the violent cold held her frozen in place, unable to move. Would she ever thaw?

"Iris, look." Jessie pointed off to the east, where the early morning skies peeked open, the tiniest bit of light shining through. "Dawn."

Iris closed her eyes, refusing to look. Instead, she turned her attention to the ship, finally able to read the name on the side.

"She's the *Carpathia*!" the seaman's voice rang out. "Come to save us!"

His shouts awakened the little baby in the other boat, and the little one's cries merged with Annie's, who wept aloud for her father. Still, with *Carpathia* looming before them on their right and the sun peeking through on the left, the time had come to dry their eyes.

With the growing sunlight, Iris could finally see. Truly see. The gray skies gave way to an eventual flood of light, and the morning sun shimmered over the icy waters.

"Oh, Jessie!" Iris looked around, stunned to find that they

were surrounded on every side by icebergs, brilliantly white and as solid as stone. Huge mounds of ice, many taller than she. Others, as tall as a building. They glistened under morning's light, a shimmering spectacle.

Their seaman began to row toward the mighty ship, slipping around the icy mounds. When they reached the ship's edge, a little sling-like contraption was lowered, and Iris looked at Jessie.

"You go up with Annie first. I need to tend to Tessa."

Jessie reluctantly agreed. The lifeboat's seaman did all he could to help, and within minutes Iris found her feet safely planted on the deck of *Carpathia*. All around her people rushed to help, many offering hot cups of coffee, others coming to their aid with warm blankets and clothes.

She took a steaming mug of coffee from a young steward about her age and then turned her attention to Tessa, who was lifted onto a chair and covered with a blanket. Iris offered her a few sips, but she could not seem to drink it. Her eyes fluttered open for a moment and she glanced at Iris as if to ask, "Where are we?" before drifting off to sleep again. Anguish merged with relief, and Iris collapsed into the chair next to Tessa, where she wept until she drained herself dry.

* * * * *

Every bone in Nathan's body cried out in pain as he boarded the *Carpathia*. His head still ached from the fall he'd taken hours prior, and his shoulder, wrenched when he'd hit the water, caused unbearable pain. Still, he was alive.

Alive.

And though he longed for sleep, he could not think of himself right now. He must find Mother. And Tessa. Winding his way through the hundreds upon hundreds of people—many still in wet clothes—he searched for familiar faces. Some of these poor people were dressed only in their nightclothes or wrappers. Others wore even less, particularly the children. Oh, how he longed to stop and offer assistance, but what could he do? Thank goodness for the good people aboard *Carpathia*, who worked feverishly to provide what they could to meet the vast needs.

His heart lurched when he saw a woman in a dress like one of Mother's, but she had red hair. On he went, searching through the mob for a sign of someone he loved. Just when he thought the chances had dwindled, he caught a glimpse of Jessie Leitch and her little niece, Annie. They stood in tattered dresses, their hair matted and dirty. But they were very much alive and appeared to be searching through the crowd, as well.

Nathan rushed their way, pressing his way beyond the mass of people. "Jessie!"

She looked his way, her tearstained face awash with pain. "Nathan! Oh, Nathan, I'm so glad to see you. Have you seen my uncle John? We've searched everywhere for him."

Nathan felt his heart drop. He hated to give her this news but had no choice. He reached out to put his hand on Jessie's arm and spoke in a strained whisper so that Annie would not hear. "There was a fellow in our lifeboat. He told a story of a preacher who prayed for him even as he faced death in the water."

"Uncle John?" Tears rolled down Jessie's cheek.

"From his description, yes. He said that your uncle took off his life belt and gave it away."

"No!" Jessie gasped.

"Yes." Nathan's heart warmed as he remembered the story the

fellow had told. "He said, 'Don't worry about me. I'm not going down, I'm going up.'"

"Sounds like Uncle John," she whispered through the tears.

Nathan nodded. "According to this fellow, your uncle jumped into the water as the ship began to sink and then went from man to man, preaching the gospel till the end."

"Really?" Tears ran in rivulets down Jessie's cheeks.

"Yes. Apparently many prayed with him, so I've no doubt he has carried them off to heaven with him. I'm sure they are enjoying a worship service even now." He trembled just thinking about it.

"Papa's in heaven?" Little Annie's voice sounded, and Nathan realized she had overheard.

He knelt to her level. "Yes, sweet girl. He's in heaven now, celebrating with the angels." When the youngster began to cry, Nathan consoled her with a hug. "Your papa was a brave man, Annie," he whispered in her ear. "A man you can be proud of. One of the fellows in my lifeboat was saved because of your daddy."

As he spoke the word "daddy," Nathan could not help but think about James Carson and their final conversation, and he began to tremble with the memory. Those few words from James had changed everything.

Annie began to cry, and within minutes an older woman approached with a blanket and hot tea, which she offered to the youngster.

Nathan turned to Jessie. "Where are the others? Tessa? Iris?"

"Let me take you to them." She gripped his arm. "But Nathan, Tessa is…"

"What?"

"She's not well. The doctor said she's in shock, but I believe she's very ill as well. She has a fever. We're very concerned about her."

Fear gripped Nathan's heart. He had nearly lost her once, to the mighty Atlantic. He would not lose her again. Not if he had anything to do with it.

* * * * *

Through the haze, Tessa felt angels wrap her in their arms. All around her she heard the cries of those in need. So strange, how the sunlight rippled off the water in the distance so beautifully. Mesmerizing, even. And those lovely bits of ice! How they twinkled under the early morning sunlight, happy beacons of hope.

Before she could give them another thought, Tessa found herself lifted and carried to a new place—a warm place, one with a nice, soft bed and soothing voices of people all around her.

Still in a dreamlike state, she settled back against the softness and allowed herself to sip the warm liquid that a host of compassionate angels pressed to her lips. She would have to remember to thank them later.

Would there be a later?

Her eyes fluttered closed and she saw her brother's face, his handsome, loving face, and she wept for joy. When she opened her eyes again, he disappeared from view. Now she cried in earnest.

And then, through the fog, a familiar voice came, one that caused her heart to leap for joy.

"Tessa!"

Nathan's face came into view. In that moment, she knew she must have died. He must surely be an angel, come to usher her into God's presence. If so, she would go willingly, never looking back. For to spend eternity with Nathan would be to spend it fully loved.

* * * * *

Monday Morning, Just after Dawn, April 15, 1912
Southampton, England

Jacquie was awakened just after dawn by the sound of weeping in a nearby room. Moments later, she heard a stirring in the street below, followed by the sound of voices raised in high-pitched screams.

She rose in a hurry and glanced out of her hotel window onto the scene below, mesmerized by the sudden flurry of activity near the dock. Her pulse quickened as she pondered what might have happened. She dressed quickly and made her way out of the room and down the stairs to the lobby below.

One glance at the desk clerk's face was all it took to convince her that something horrible had happened. And the sobs from a woman in a nearby chair only added to her confusion. Jacquie rushed to the counter to speak with the clerk, who appeared dazed and pale.

"What is it? Why are they crying?"

For a moment he didn't answer, but his wide eyes shared his grief. "It's *Titanic*, miss."

"*Titanic*?" Jacquie's heart sailed to her throat. "What about *Titanic*?"

The fellow shook his head, his eyes growing misty. "She's gone down in the middle of the Atlantic. Most everyone onboard is feared dead."

Jacquie felt the room begin to spin. She cried out, "No!"

The clerk's eyes misted over. "I'm so sorry. But I'm afraid it's true."

Outside, people rushed by, many crying out in anguish, others shouting to be heard. None of this made sense. Surely she would go back to her room, doze off, then awaken again to learn that she had dreamed all of this. One final look in the desk clerk's eyes convinced her otherwise.

"We've been asked to hold steady for a few hours," he said. "Later today, or perhaps tomorrow, the White Star Line will post a list of survivors. Or maybe a list of the dead. I'm not sure which."

"So there are survivors?"

"Yes. But no one knows how many. More dead than alive, I'm afraid."

The words "more dead than alive" shook Jacquie to the core.

"I will send word to your room if I hear anything. How would that be?"

She could only nod in response. No words would come.

Jacquie fought back tears as she ran down the hallway and up the stairs to her room. Once there, she prayed as never before. She would go on praying, too, until news came of the young women she had placed aboard the *Titanic*. In the meantime, she would beg the Almighty for forgiveness…and plead for mercy.

Chapter Twenty-Seven

Monday, April 15, 1912, Noon
White Star Line Offices, Southampton, England

After several hours of fretful prayer, Jacquie could wait no longer. Just before the noon hour she made the decision to go to the White Star offices. She ran as fast as her feet could carry her, fighting her way through a mob of people. Tears flowed with such force that she had to stop to catch her breath several times along the way. Surrounded by a large crowd of people, she could barely see which way to go. All of them moved en masse toward the offices, their cries mingled with shouts and rushed conversations.

Along the way, she tried to collect her thoughts. She also attempted a prayer, but the words "God, please!" were truly all she could manage. After that, bile rose to her throat and she felt sick.

Getting close to the White Star Line offices was impossible in this crowd. She pressed her way through as best she could, but there was no list to be found. Not yet, anyway. The tears dried up and then just as quickly started again. She thought about Tessa. Poor, sweet Tessa. Then her thoughts shifted to Iris, and she remembered the young woman's dreams to become a fashion designer. To think that those dreams might have been cut short ripped Jacquie's heart out.

All around her, the newsboys called out to would-be patrons, offering sensational headlines about *Titanic*'s demise. Jacquie bought a copy of the *London Herald* and read every word, her heart aching and her throat tight as she took in each line. Still, she found no real answers there. Until *Carpathia* docked in New York, there would be no solid answers for anyone. How would she survive until then?

Survive.

Tessa.

Iris.

Oh, God!

By midafternoon, the crowd could only be described as frenzied. Jacquie backed away as several people took to quarreling. She understood their emotional outbursts, of course, but now feared for her safety, as well. These feelings were all mixed up with the shroud of guilt that wrapped her in its embrace. If the worst had really happened to Tessa and Iris...

No, she wouldn't let herself think like that. All would be well.

At two o'clock, a fellow in a White Star uniform made his way through the crowd, urging people to remain calm. How could they? She leaned against the wall of a nearby building and waited, silent prayers rushing heavenward at lightning speed. When she opened her eyes, she saw a familiar face in the crowd. For a moment she thought it a mirage. Just as quickly, she realized it was not.

"Peter!"

She ran his direction and flung herself into his arms, tears flowing. He held her close and ran his trembling fingers through her hair, his nearness bringing the only comfort of the day.

"Jacquie. Have they posted the list yet?"

She shook her head.

He grabbed her hand and they made their way through the crowd to a quieter spot. Peter sat on the edge of the street, buried his face in his hands, and wept with abandon. "I put Tessa on that ship to save her life. Now I've sent her to her grave."

"Y–you don't know that." The words caught in Jacquie's throat. "We haven't seen the list of survivors."

"I pray she's on it." He used the back of his hand to swipe at his eyes. "If not, I will never forgive myself. I'll be to blame—"

"No." Jacquie sat next to him and grabbed his hand. "I'm the one at fault here. Don't you see? I'm the one who set the original plan in motion. You had your reasons for wanting her to go, but I had mine, and my voice was the persuasive one. If we've anyone to blame, it's me."

Peter looked her way and raked his fingers through his messy hair. "We were both at fault. And we are both to blame. And I pray to God she is alive. Otherwise—" He blanched. "I don't know what I will do."

Jacquie flung her arms around Peter's neck and held him close, allowing him to grieve. When he finally calmed, she continued to hold him tight.

Until she saw, out of the corners of her eyes, another familiar face.

"Mother!"

Jacquie rose, hiked her skirts, and ran straight into her mother's arms.

* * * * *

Monday, April 15, 1912
Aboard the Carpathia

Iris worked onboard the ship alongside Edith and the Countess of Rothes. The women became friends in a short period of time. Together, the trio did what they could to ease the burdens of all who remained, particularly the children, who desperately needed food, clothing, and hugs.

Iris's heart was touched by a duo of little French boys who had been dropped, nearly naked, into one of the lifeboats just before *Titanic* met her awful fate. No one seemed to know where they had come from or where they were headed. New York? Elsewhere? With no parents to be found, she could not say.

They enlisted the help of a woman named Margaret Hays, who was fluent in French. She spoke with great tenderness to the boys, who looked to be about two and four. The little curly-headed waifs did not seem to have a care in the world. In fact, they rather enjoyed playing with Miss Hays's Pom pup, which offered the perfect distraction.

Of course, there were hundreds of others with similar stories. Mothers without babies. Babies without fathers. Sisters without brothers. All around Iris, people grieved their losses. She did her best not to weep in front of the others, though she felt emotion welling up inside of her many times over. Pressing it down was the only thing that made sense, especially with so many others needing her help. She must keep going, no matter how she felt on the inside.

"I've heard that many haven't given up hope," the countess said as she dished up bowls of soup for the survivors. "Some are saying that another ship has surely come to fetch the rest of the survivors."

"Do you think that's possible?" Iris asked.

Edith shook her head. "No, my dear, I do not. If there had been another ship, don't you think the captain of *Carpathia* would have informed us by now?"

"But someone has to go after those poor souls," the countess said, still filling bowls with soup. "Surely."

The conversation continued, and before long several others nearby had joined in. A couple of them took to arguing about it, emotions higher than ever. Iris decided to escape the bedlam for a few minutes. She turned to Edith, determined to move on.

"I really must go and check on Tessa. Do you mind?"

"Of course not." Edith gave her a compassionate look. "How is she this morning?"

"From what I've heard, she's still feverish, but the ship's doctor says that she will recover. They have turned the second-class dining room into a hospital to care for the injured. She is still there, along with dozens of others." Iris shuddered, remembering some of the injuries she had seen in that room. So much pain. If only she could do more to ease it.

"Everyone onboard has been so kind," the countess said as she handed a bowl of soup to a woman with two little ones. "Giving up their rooms, providing clothes… And did you hear that Margaret Brown has started a campaign to raise funds for the survivors?"

"No." Edith looked intrigued by this. "Already?"

"Yes." The countess nodded.

Edith squared her shoulders. "Well, I must find her so that I can contribute. It's the least I can do. The very least."

Iris wondered at Edith's generosity. After all, the entire *Elrose* line had gone down on the *Titanic*. All nineteen trunks, filled with lovely clothes and other items she had gathered in Europe.

But Edith bore it well. In fact, many of the survivors appeared to be of sturdy stock, more concerned about the needs of others than their own woes. There were a pitiful few who could not cease their mourning, but Iris's heart bled for them, particularly the young mothers who could not locate children or husbands. Whatever she could do to be of service, she would do. Truly, helping others was the only thing to take her mind off of what had happened.

She made her way to the hospital, where she visited with Tessa and then assisted the doctor as he offered food and drinks to his many patients. She tried not to cry aloud at the sight of those who were wounded but found it difficult to hold her emotions in check, particularly where the children were concerned. Many of the older ones were simply overcome with grief and emotion, but the children tugged at her heartstrings in a different way. Their cries made her want to run from the room, to escape the pain.

As the hours wore on, Iris found herself working alongside a young man about her same age, a *Carpathia* steward named William Kenney, who hailed from New York. The amiable fellow found any number of things to keep her busy and always managed to lift her spirits whenever she would get down. He served as the perfect distraction, his lighthearted approach to work admirable.

Now, if only she could somehow get word back to England, to Jacquie. Then perhaps she could draw a breath without feeling sick inside. Until then, she would just keep moving. One foot in front of the other.

Just keep going, Iris.

Just keep going.

* * * * *

Tessa spent most of the day in fitful sleep, waking only occasionally. When she came fully awake in the midafternoon, the prior hours felt like a terrible dream of some sort. A blur.

She listened to Nathan's tearful explanation of what had happened but could not make sense of it. If the *Titanic* had gone down, why did she not remember it? In the blink of an eye, she had gone from standing on the Boat Deck to lying in a bed aboard the *Carpathia,* her head swimming. People on every side cried out, many in pain, others overwhelmed with grief for missing loved ones. Tessa's heart broke as she tried to put the pieces of the puzzle together, but none of this seemed real.

Her questions were many, but the primary one, no one seemed able to answer. "Why, Lord? Why have You spared me when so many others are gone?"

With her thoughts in a whirl, she laid the question to rest until she could think more clearly.

* * * * *

Nathan left the ship's makeshift hospital after visiting with Tessa, anxious to be of service to the others. Now that Tessa rested comfortably, he felt safe in leaving her to tend to those in need. When he reached the Boat Deck, he saw little Annie playing with a group of children.

Jessie sat nearby in a deck chair, looking on. In spite of her losses, the young woman appeared peaceful as always. Nathan took a few steps in her direction and realized she was humming a familiar melody. A hymn.

She stopped singing and looked up as he drew near. "Nathan." Jessie offered him a warm smile and gestured for him to sit beside her. "Have you been down to the hospital to see Tessa?"

"Yes. She is much better."

"Praise the Lord." Jessie reached over and put her hand on his arm. "I'm so glad. She really cares for you. I've known that from the beginning."

"Really?" This certainly got his attention.

"Of course. Her feelings for you are genuine, Nathan. And so is her heart. She truly longs to live her life in a way that brings honor to God, and I can't help but think that life will include you." A smile turned up the edges of Jessie's lips.

Nathan's heart flooded with joy at this proclamation. "Thank you. I would love nothing more."

They grew silent for a moment. Jessie glanced out at the sea, then back at him, tenderness in her expression. "Nathan, I've been afraid to ask, but—is there any word of your mother?"

"No." Nathan shook his head, a lump rising in his throat. "I am afraid that she…" He couldn't say the words. They would not come.

"I'm so sorry, Nathan." Jessie's eyes brimmed with tears. "My heart goes out to you."

Nathan swallowed hard and closed his eyes to keep from showing too much emotion. In that moment, the entire scene with James Carson played itself out in his memory. He saw himself standing aboard *Titanic*. Heard James call him "son." Agonized over the words that were spoken after, words that challenged everything he had ever known—or thought—to be true.

Just as quickly, Nathan forced the images away. He opened his eyes, looked at Jessie, and sighed. "What do you do when you find that everything you once thought was real is not?" he asked. "When everything you counted as true turns out to be false?"

"Then you trust in the One who is the epitome of truth." She brushed away the lone tear that trickled down her cheek. "He alone has the answers."

For a moment, Nathan didn't say anything. Finally, he worked up the courage. "When I think of Mother, my heart is twisted up in knots. I loved her, perhaps more than anyone else. But I saw her flaws as just that. She never hid them from me."

"There is much to be said for a person who does not pretend to be something—or someone—they are not."

"True." He paused to think through Jessie's words. "My heart is heavy at her loss, but those feelings are all twisted up with anger at her for not telling me the truth. She let me believe..." He bit back the words, unsure how much to share.

"It's all right, Nathan." Jessie nodded. "You can tell me."

And so he did. He shared everything he had learned from James Carson and every emotion that had held him captive since. As he spoke, Jessie remained silent, just listening.

"Mother let me believe that my life, my lineage, was something other than what it truly is." Nathan rose and paced the deck, finally looking her way. "Not that I would trade places or situations. You have no idea how grateful I am to have the relationship with my father. He has been a rock in my life, a solid foundation."

"Do you suppose he knows?"

"My gut says he does. And if that's the case, then he has accepted me as his son all along, knowing the truth."

Jessie rose and took a few steps in his direction. "He has exemplified Christlikeness then. He sounds like a wonderful man, one to emulate."

Nathan felt the sting of tears but willed them not to come. "I've never known such love and acceptance. But how do we begin again if we are not truly father and son?"

"You *are* father and son in every way that matters. No doubt he will need you more than ever now." She gazed into his eyes with such intensity that he felt his heart quicken. "Go to him, Nathan. Walk with him through the grief of losing your mother."

"He truly loved her, in spite of all of her flaws. And in spite of…" Nathan's words drifted away on the wind. He raked his fingers through his hair. "I don't know how he did it, but he loved her in spite of not only her indiscretions but her ongoing fascination with James Carson."

As he spoke the name of his real father, Nathan felt the breath go out of him. In that moment, all the bitterness he'd felt toward the man faded away, replaced with a strange sense of pity and loss.

"A man can forgive a great many things if the love of God is resident inside of him." Jessie's lashes grew damp. "This, I learned from Uncle John."

Nathan realized those words were meant for him. With the Lord's help, he would forgive his mother. And James.

"Go home, Nathan," Jessie said. "Give of your time to your father so that you can both heal. Then prepare yourself for a wonderful life ahead. God has spared you, and you must live a life worthy of the calling. We all must."

"The calling." He paused and then shrugged, gazing off to the sea. "What has He called me to do?"

"To love others." Jessie gestured to the crowd of people surrounding them. "And that's exactly what I know you will do."

From across the deck, Nathan heard the sound of laughter as the children played. He glanced over to see a little girl.

Manca.

His heart quickened and he took a few steps closer to get a better look. Yes, the same little girl—a bit more disheveled, perhaps, but with the same happy smile. She danced and played, this time with Annie.

From across the deck, Manca's father appeared and took her by the hand. As always, he danced with her, spinning her around the deck of the *Carpathia* as if nothing had happened, as if they had their whole lives ahead of them—hopeful, joyous lives, unencumbered by tragedy.

At just the right moment, the little girl noticed Nathan and offered a shy smile. He took several steps in her direction, knowing that the language barrier would prevent him from speaking his heart. Still, he could say all he needed to with a warm embrace.

With joy overflowing, he swept the youngster into his arms.

Chapter Twenty-Eight

Wednesday, April 17, 1912
White Star Line Offices, Southampton, England

Jacquie remained at the hotel in Southampton for the next two days with her mother at her side. Their conversations shifted in and out from sheer relief to angry accusations and shouts. The fact that Mother would even still talk to her, after all she had done, was a miracle in itself. She would forever thank God for the opportunity to begin again.

Together, they braved the call to Father, who wept with open abandon upon hearing that she had not actually boarded the *Titanic*. This, of course, was followed by the grim news that she had sent Tessa and Iris in her place. Father's silence upon hearing this had been deafening. There would be much to sort out once Jacquie arrived back at Abingdon Manor, but at least her parents wanted her back. For that, she was truly grateful.

In the wee hours of the night, as she lay awake praying for Tessa and Iris, Jacquie found herself knotted up on the inside. If only she could go back in time just a week or two. She would change everything. Especially now, knowing that Peter did not care as deeply for her as he had once implied.

Peter.

Her heart still twisted within her as she thought about him, but those emotions were now intrinsically tied to Tessa and Iris. She prayed harder than ever that God would see fit to spare them, in part so that Peter could go on with his life, free from guilt.

On the afternoon of the seventeenth, the desk clerk sent word to Jacquie's room that a survivor list had been posted at the White Star Line offices. With her chest tight, Jacquie and her mother made the journey on foot alongside dozens of others and waited in line until they were at the front.

Only when she put her finger on Tessa's name did she feel life might be worth living again. And when she found Iris's name listed below it, Jacquie finally found herself free to breathe once more. She flung herself into her mother's arms and wept, relief washing over her like the morning tide. Life had offered her a chance to begin again. This time she would get it right.

* * * * *

Wednesday, April 17, 1912
Carpathia's *Dining Room*

Iris worked to the point of exhaustion. The evening before the *Carpathia* was set to arrive in New York Harbor, she could hardly keep her eyes open. And yet she must. There were decisions to be made. Where to live, specifically. Going to Jacquie's grandmother's home no longer made sense. In light of the tragedy, she should figure out a new plan. Edith had offered to take her in, and that idea held some appeal. Still, settling apart from Tessa just felt wrong. No, until Tessa recovered—fully recovered—she would not leave her side.

Iris found herself leaning on her new friend William more and more as the hours went by, listening to his advice and gleaning from the information he shared about New York.

"Things are going to be chaotic when we arrive," he said as they settled into chairs in the dining hall. "I've heard that all sorts of people are standing by, ready to be of help. The Red Cross is there, along with other relief societies."

"Where will all these people go?" Iris asked, gesturing to the roomful of passengers. "What about the poor mothers who have lost their husbands? They have no source of income. No way to survive. They can't afford to pay rent."

"The captain told us that the Municipal Lodging House has opened its doors. They have room for seven hundred. They will be providing food and shelter to any survivors in need."

Iris felt some sense of relief at this news. Still, with so many grieving around her, any small sense of relief felt like a betrayal.

"There's no way to know how many families are affected," William said. "But we must be prepared for a huge crowd when we reach the dock. Ambulances. Reporters. Family members. It's going to be more overwhelming than we know." He flashed a concerned glance her way. "I need to know that you are all right. Will you promise to stay in touch?"

"I—I will."

"Thank you. I want you to feel free to call on me, should the need arise."

She nodded, overwhelmed by his generosity and kind nature. Truly, if even a fraction of the people in New York were as kind as William Kenney, she would get along just fine.

* * * * *

Thursday, April 18, 1912
Nearing New York

On the morning of the eighteenth, Nathan managed to send a wire to his father. Sharing the news about Mother was the hardest thing he had ever done. It took every ounce of strength to get the words out. Nathan couldn't even imagine what his father must be going through. Soon. Soon they would be together and could grieve alongside one another.

While onboard, Nathan knew he must remain focused on what he could do to help. He worked tirelessly alongside Margaret Brown to help raise funds and to care for the sick. Many of the wounded would require surgery when they arrived in New York. Others wandered the ship in a daze, as if in a dream. Still others— mostly the children—went back to life as normal, as if nothing had happened. Oh, if only he could do the same.

Tessa, his precious Tessa, continued to improve. With her fever gone, she could finally take a bit of nourishment. Once he got her home, he would tend to her every need until she was fully recovered.

Home.

What a blissful word. Once he reached his home, he could think more clearly. Put these awful memories behind him.

Of course, not all of it had been bad. He thought back to all the wonderful moments onboard *Titanic*—those wonderful moments, gazing over the railing, basking in God's presence. Meeting new friends like Tessa. And John Harper, that wonderful, godly man who had shared God's love until the very end.

For the first time in over a week, Nathan found himself thinking about that elusive girl in blue—the one he had seen first at the opera and then again onboard *Titanic* that first day. Had she survived? There had been no sign of her on the *Carpathia*. Surely only the worst could be assumed. She seemed a phantom now, only an illusion. Perhaps she had never existed at all.

Right now he needed to focus on the people in front of him, the ones who truly did exist: Tessa. Iris. Jessie. Annie. They were his to care for, and he would do so with all the love and compassion the Lord had placed inside of him.

* * * * *

For days, Tessa had rested in the makeshift hospital while those around her tended to the needs of others, but on the afternoon of the eighteenth, she rose, washed her face, and did what she could to be of service to those less fortunate.

Nathan still hovered over her, of course. In fact, she couldn't convince him to let her do much on her own. His caring nature and obvious love for her brought feelings of warmth and security like she had never known before.

Yes, she had known such feelings. Peter had cared for her well-being, had he not? Enough to send her off to a new life. She must get word to him as quickly as possible, must let him know that she was alive and well. No doubt he was sick with worry. As soon as they got settled in New York, she would do so.

As they drew near to the harbor in New York, her heart raced. Tessa joined Nathan, Iris, and William on the upper deck, looking on as the ship reached the shore. Jessie stood nearby, keeping a watchful eye on Annie, who played with little Manca. Tessa gasped as the Statue of Liberty came into view.

"Oh, Nathan! She's—she's beautiful."

"Strong and triumphant," he said. "Just like you."

Tessa nodded, feeling that same sense of strength rise up within her. She continued to look out across the landscape, taking in the tall buildings, the shoreline, and finally, the harbor. When they arrived, the *Carpathia* sailed past her own Cunard pier, making her way to drop off *Titanic*'s lifeboats at the White Star Line pier.

Tessa's breath caught in her throat as she watched the lifeboats being lowered. Though she had repressed the memories of that terrible night, they resurfaced in a moment as she saw the boats coming down. Her eyes filled with tears, and she leaned into Nathan to keep from showing her emotion publicly.

He held her close, speaking soothing words over her. She felt his tender kiss on her brow and glanced his way, now trembling. In that moment, his lips met hers for a kiss so sweet that she thought her heart might take flight. There, in the arms of the man she loved, Tessa felt security like she had never known before. She held him close, determined to never let go.

When *Carpathia* returned to her own pier, excitement welled up inside of her. Even from a great distance she could see the crowd, could hear their cries as the ship approached.

"Have you ever seen anything like it?" She pointed to a line of limousines that ran all the way down the avenue and beyond what could be seen from their vantage point.

William gestured to the vehicles. "Captain says that Mrs. Vanderbilt spent the day telephoning friends, asking them for use of their automobiles," he said. "Many of our passengers will need transportation."

"Well, God bless Mrs. Vanderbilt." Iris offered a smile then looped her arm through William's.

"I also heard that the Pennsylvania Railroad has sent representatives to the pier," William said. "There will be a special train of nine cars to carry passengers to Philadelphia or points west of there. For free, I mean. No cost."

Tessa could hardly believe their generosity. "People really are kind at times like these."

If she hadn't believed it before, she certainly did by the time they left the ship. From the minute Tessa's feet touched down on solid ground, she was surrounded on all sides by well-wishers offering their help. She tried to respond as best she could but found it difficult to speak.

Through the crowd, a man in an expensive suit pressed his way through, sprinting toward Nathan. Only when he flung his arms around him and called out the word "Son!" did Tessa realize who he was.

In that moment, she thought about her own father and wondered what he was doing. *How* he was doing. She pictured Mum's face and felt a strange sense of longing. Interesting, how the pain of the past could fade in such a way, replaced with hopeful feelings about the future.

With Nathan's hand in hers, she faced his father, her emotions welling. After a brief introduction, the older man pulled her into their embrace. After a warm hug he offered her a tearful smile, followed by words so sweet they would've made the angels sing: "Let's go home."

Turning to slip her arm through Nathan's, she prepared to do just that.

Chapter Twenty-Nine

May 11, 1912
Abingdon Manor, Richmond, England

Jacquie spent the better part of the next three weeks holed up in her room, ashamed to face her parents or Roland, who stopped by the house on more than one occasion to visit with Father. Cook graciously brought her meals to her room, but Jacquie only picked at them, her appetite far from its usual state. Many times over she made her apologies to Mother, who told her it would be best to forget the incident and put it in the past.

Still, she could not. The ache of losing Peter remained, though not with the same severity. Now, whenever she thought of him, she just felt foolish. Of course, these feelings were all mixed up with the guilt that plagued her when Father sent him packing. She prayed he would find another job and secretly celebrated the news that the chief groundskeeper at Richmond Park had hired him on.

Still, there was the issue of Roland. Avoiding him hadn't been easy, and she could do so no longer. By the time the third Saturday in May arrived, she had no choice. Father and Roland were to appear at a public event today to share the news of their merger, and Jacquie was to go along. To save face, according to Father.

To save her soul was more like it. For, while she did share some of Mama's concerns that people would talk, she cared far more about doing the right thing. And doing the right thing meant offering apologies to Roland.

With her heart drifting to her toes, she descended the stairs. Her gaze landed on him. He was as tall and stately as ever, as he stood in the foyer talking to Mother. A low chuckle sounded as Father slapped him on the back.

As she landed on the bottom step, Roland glanced her way. His eyes clouded over a bit as he took her in. "Jacquie." She half expected a terse look, but he extended a hand graciously. Then again, he had always been a perfect gentleman.

"Roland." She took his proffered hand and allowed him to lead her into the foyer.

"Cook will serve lunch in a half hour," Father said. "After that, we will be on our way." He looked back and forth between Jacquie and Roland. "If you two don't mind, I need to take care of a pressing business matter that demands my attention."

"And I promised to telephone Minerva. She's probably wondering why I haven't done so already." Mother scurried from the room.

Jacquie did her best to calm her nerves, but the trembling hands gave her away. Left alone in the room with Roland, she had no choice but to do the obvious. She took a few steps into the parlor and eased her way down onto a settee. He sat opposite her, making light chatter about the weather.

She put a hand up to stop him. "Roland."

"Yes." He grew silent, and an undeniable awkwardness settled over the room.

"I—" Her eyes filled with tears. "I have something I must say to you." She closed her eyes for a moment and tried to formulate the right words. Truly, this man deserved far more than an apology. She had betrayed him in the worst possible way. The fact that he was willing to sit in a room with her and treat her civilly said much of his character.

"I must ask for your forgiveness," she said at last.

He reached for her hand, his eyes brimming with unshed emotion. "Jacquie—"

"I do not deserve it. I know that. But until I receive it, I won't be able to rest my head on the pillow at night and sleep in peace. I promise you, this has nothing to do with what people will say or even what my parents wish. This is my heartfelt plea to ask for forgiveness, though I know in my heart that I do not deserve it." The sting of tears followed, and she swiped at her eyes with the back of her hand in a most unladylike fashion.

Roland stood and paced the room, finally coming to a stop in front of her. "Jacquie." Just one word, but he spoke it with such kindness that it gave her hope. "I cannot pretend that your leaving didn't wound me, and all the more when I heard the particulars." He paused and his gaze shifted to the ground. "I understand what it feels like to care for someone with that kind of passion."

"You do?"

"Yes." His gaze met hers. "I understand it because that's how I feel about you. It's how I've felt about you from the moment I first ventured through the door here at Abingdon Manor all those months ago. Don't you see?"

Jacquie leaned forward and put her head in her hands as shame washed over her afresh. "Oh, Roland."

"I also know what it's like to be loved and not reciprocate those feelings. My parents nudged me into a relationship with a young woman back in New York that I did not care for. Pretense was all I could offer. I withheld my heart because it did not belong to her."

Jacquie sighed. Perhaps he really did understand, then.

"I thought I could convince myself to love her, but I could not." He dropped into the chair across from her once again. "So, I do understand your dilemma. Truly. I don't hold it against you for not reciprocating my feelings." A flicker of pain settled in his eyes. "I had hoped for more, of course. I believe we all hope for real love, even when it seems elusive at best."

She struggled to come up with something comforting, but no words came.

He gazed at her with great empathy. "You have asked me to forgive you."

"Y–yes."

"How could I withhold forgiveness from you when the Lord has so graciously offered it to me, time and time again?"

She felt the tears as they dampened her lashes but didn't bother brushing them away. Instead, she spoke with all the sincerity she could muster. "Roland, you're truly one of the best men I've ever known. I do hope you know that. You deserve someone who can give you her heart in its entirety. Right now mine is…" The only word that came to mind was *splintered*, but she dared not voice it.

"Say no more, Jacquie. We will put this behind us and move forward as friends." He leaned forward and rested his elbows on his knees as he gazed at her. "If you will have me as a friend, I mean. Right now, I could use one."

"Me too." She reached into her pocket and pulled out his beautiful ring. "But I must offer this back to you."

He shook his head. "Do me a favor. Put it away. Keep it safe. Maybe one day you will wear it—as a thing of beauty, I mean. Not as a token of anything other than that." He gazed at her with such tenderness that she felt shame wash over her afresh. "It would bring a certain degree of comfort to know that I'd added a bit of extra sparkle to your eyes with that little gift."

"You are too kind."

"I'm not." He shook his head. "I'm just a man who trusts that the Lord has his future in the palm of His hand."

"The Lord…" When she spoke the word, a lump filled Jacquie's throat. She shook her head, tears now dribbling down her cheek. If God had her future in the palm of His hand, she had much to be concerned about, for surely the Almighty found her to be the most despicable of people right now. She shivered then whispered, "What an image that is."

"I can trust Him, Jacquie. You can too." Roland paused and seemed to disappear into his thoughts for a moment. "Perhaps that's why the news of losing you to another man didn't carry the sort of sting one might expect. I have to believe that the Lord was not taken by surprise by any of this. And I daresay He's big enough to contend with both my will and my heart, heavy as the latter may be."

"You are a good man, Roland Palmer." Jacquie stood and offered him her hand.

He rose and took it in his own then kissed the back of it with great tenderness. "I am not. But I serve a great God. He gives me the capacity to be a better man with each passing day." Roland sought out her gaze. "If you will take a few steps toward friendship, I would be grateful."

"Of course. We are the best of friends, truly, for you have offered me something that only a friend could—forgiveness." Her heart overflowed with gratitude as she thought about his generosity.

The clock chimed the hour, and Jacquie realized Roland still held her hand in his own. She gave it a squeeze then offered him her arm. "Are you hungry?"

"Starved." He quirked a brow. "I was so nervous about this afternoon's event that I couldn't eat a thing for breakfast."

"I haven't eaten much of late, either," she countered, "but feel like I could manage a feast this afternoon."

"Well, you're in luck. Your mother tells me that the cook misunderstood her instructions and thought the event was here. She has prepared enough food for everyone in the county."

Jacquie couldn't help but laugh as she and Roland made their way toward the dining room together.

* * * * *

The weeks passed at an alarming pace. Nathan did his best to put the past behind him but found himself overwhelmed with memories of the *Titanic*.

Memories of Mother.

Memories of…James Carson.

Strange, how grief could be all mixed up with feelings of anger and betrayal. Stranger still that Father—the only father he had ever known—played such an integral role in Nathan's healing, offering himself as both counselor and friend. And while he spoke the truth, revealing tales that Nathan had not cared to hear, one thing remained clear: Father was a man of grace and mercy.

Never was this more apparent than on a Saturday evening in May when he called Nathan to his study. Father's eyes brimmed with tears as he spoke. "I thought you should know that I'm planning a memorial service for your mother."

"How can you do that?" Nathan rose and walked to the

window then gazed out at the garden. He turned back to his father. "How can you forgive her, after all she did to you?"

His father rose and took several steps in his direction. "That's a question I've had to ask myself many times over the years. There's really only one answer, because there's only one truth, and that's an eternal one. Men will fail us. Given ample opportunity, they will wound, betray, and neglect us. Many will say they have no choice in the matter, that they acted not of their own volition. In the end, humans are just that—human. They tend toward selfishness."

Nathan bit back a caustic response.

Father's expression softened. "There is a truth, however, that stands the test of time. No ship can penetrate it, no iceberg rise up against it. Nothing anyone builds or claims ownership to, short of the Almighty. It is the truth of God's love for us—love that crashes through even the coldest, most frigid heart."

He stood in front of Nathan and put his hand on his shoulder. "Son, we can't repair what has happened in the past, but we can ask God to melt our hearts as surely as those icebergs in the North Atlantic will melt in the summertime. When the thaw comes, the risk for damage is lessened. Do you understand what I'm saying?"

"Yes, Father."

Father offered a smile. "Don't let your heart be hardened, my boy. Remember, in this world we will have trials and tribulation…"

Tribulation. A word he knew quite well.

"But we can take heart"—Father's eyes filled with tears as he pointed heavenward—"because our Savior has overcome the world."

Nathan had much to overcome, to be sure. Much to forgive. But already he felt springtime coming. His heart, hardened by forces unseen, was melting. He could feel the gentle hands of the

One who had spoken it to life, massaging, warming, urging him to breathe again. Live again.

The man standing before him offered the finest example of that. Nathan would live every day of his life following in his father's footsteps.

* * * * *

Tessa peered through the open door leading to the study, her eyes filling with tears as father and son stood in a tight embrace.

In the few weeks she had known Mr. Patterson, one undeniable conclusion had been drawn: not all fathers were like hers. Some, like this wonderful man, lived to serve and care for others. Lived to extend grace and forgiveness even when it made no sense.

And now, as she looked on through the open doorway, Tessa found herself more vulnerable than she had been since that fateful day aboard *Titanic* when Jessie had encouraged her to take her bitterness and toss it into the Atlantic. Watching a father—a real father—express his love in such an open way nearly pulled her heart from her chest.

Mr. Patterson looked her way, and a smile lit his face. He opened wide his arms and gestured for Tessa to join them in their embrace. She drew close, the smell of peppermint filling the space between them as he spoke words of love over her. Her thoughts traveled back to Jessie's heartfelt words that fateful day aboard *Titanic*: *"Rest in the comfort that your heavenly Father adores you. He does, you know."*

Here, in Mr. Patterson's loving, fatherly embrace, she truly believed it was so.

Epilogue

May 30, 1912
Abingdon Manor, Richmond, England

Dear Tessa:

I should have written this letter weeks ago, but every time I tried to do so, the words would not come. I struggle to get them out even now. How can I ever begin to make right what I've done? I cannot go back and undo the past. Oh, how I wish I could! But neither can I move forward until I am relieved of this awful guilt.

When we first met, I couldn't see past myself. My vision is less clouded now, and I cannot deny the obvious: my selfish actions put you in peril and nearly cost you your life. Every time I think about what you went through on Titanic, I feel sick inside. I should have been the one in that lifeboat, not you. I should have been the one facing death.

A thousand times I have thanked God for sparing your life, and Iris's too. A thousand times I have begged Him to forgive me for the role I played. Only recently have I begun to think He might be willing to do so. Though I don't deserve it, I ask—no, I beg—you to forgive me, as well. Perhaps that way I can move forward into whatever life has to offer without the weight of guilt pressing me down.

On a happier note, I received a letter from Grandmother, telling me of your visit. It warms my heart to know that you have taken the time to get to know her. She had nothing but kind things to say about you and about your young man. From what she shared, Nathan is both handsome and kind. Grandmother has always been the sort to play matchmaker, and she feels sure you two are a perfect match. If this is the case—and I pray it is—then I will have the consolation of knowing that you met him aboard the ship. I suppose it's true what Roland says—that God can bring good out of bad. Then again, Roland always manages to see the good in everything and everyone…even me.

I haven't been to America since I was a little girl, but I would love to visit you, should you decide to stay on in New York. Grandmother says that you seem content. That brings such peace to my heart. She also said that you are a beautiful, refined young lady, with "impeccable manners and exquisite taste in hats." I couldn't help but chuckle when I read the line about hats, though I suspect Iris has played a role in that. You once told me that feathers belonged on peacocks, not on hats. Do you still feel that way? I rather envision you wearing a feather-plumed hat and loving it.

Truly, I envision you as a young woman of great strength and character and will be proud to call you friend, should you allow me that privilege. I look forward to hearing from you, and I offer you all my best wishes for happiness.

Sincerely,
Jacquie Abingdon

* * * * *

June 10, 1912
New York

Dear Jacquie,

How wonderful to hear from you. Many times I have thought about you and wondered how you were doing, so your letter brought the answers I needed and made me feel close to you once again. I am delighted to hear that you are back home with your family and pray they can wrap you in their arms of love.

Speaking of family, I have heard from Peter. He seems happy in his new position at Richmond Park, but I sensed the sadness in his words when he spoke of you. His regrets are many. No doubt he has already shared them with you. I pray you can let go of whatever pain he has caused and find joy in the days to come.

You asked about Nathan, and I am pleased to share our news. He has asked me to be his wife, and I have happily agreed. The ceremony will take place in his father's home in early August. Oh, how I wish you could come. Iris will stand up for me, and I feel sure she would love to share that honor with you. Of course, she has insisted upon designing my dress. I pretended to balk at first but truly wouldn't have it any other way.

I think you would be very proud of her, Jacquie. New York has opened up a whole new world of opportunities, and she is enjoying every moment. She has made a new friend in William, a young steward who works aboard the Carpathia. William is very interested in helping those less fortunate and has encouraged Iris and me to join him. You can't imagine how many events we have all attended and how many families we have helped. Together, we are all learning to let go of the past and to get on with the business of living.

As I read your letter, particularly the part about the weight of guilt, I thought about my life in England. I remembered that rocky path where I spent so many hours weighted down with guilt I was never meant to carry. I know the burden you are carrying right now, in part because I have borne it so many times myself. I also know that letting go of that burden is possible if you ask the Lord to help you.

Please allow me to ease your mind. You asked for my forgiveness and I wholeheartedly extend it, though we both know that I carry my own responsibility in the matter. No one forced me to board Titanic. I went of my own choosing. As a result of that decision, I witnessed unspeakable horrors. And yet, for whatever reason, my life was spared.

Many times I have asked the Lord why He chose to let me live when so many around me perished. I may never know. Nathan says that we must live our lives in a manner worthy of the grace God has bestowed. As you can tell, Nathan is quite the philosopher. No doubt he and Roland would get along nicely!

Am I sorry I came to America? Not at all! Am I sorry that I chose to board Titanic to make the journey? The only answer I can give is this: I'm not sure I chose Titanic. In so many ways, I believe she chose me. And should she ask me to climb aboard one last time to sail from one shore to the next, I would not hesitate to do so. For on her decks, I laid down one life…and found another. In some small way, I have you to thank for that.

All my love,
Tessa

STAND TO YOUR POST
by Bennett Scott (1912)

When the mighty ship *Titanic*

Started from Southampton Bay

There were cheers

And fond good-byes too

As she proudly steamed away

But soon alas disaster came

And filled our hearts with woe

Although in sorrow now we weep

We yet are proud to know

Every man at his post

As the big ship went down

To save precious lives

There we find them

They died like heroes true

Now something we must do

For the wives and the little ones

They left behind them

About the Author

 Award-winning author Janice Thompson, who also writes under the name Janice Hanna, has published nearly eighty books for the Christian market, crossing genre lines to write cozy mysteries, historicals, romances, nonfiction books, devotionals, children's books, and more.

Janice formerly served as vice president of the Christian Authors Network (christianauthorsnetwork.com) and was named the 2008 Mentor of the Year by the American Christian Fiction Writers organization. She is passionate about her faith and does all she can to share the joy of the Lord with others, which is why she particularly enjoys writing.

Janice lives in Spring, Texas, where she leads a rich life with her family, a host of writing friends, and two mischievous dachshunds. She does her best to keep the Lord at the center of it all. www.janicehannathompson.com

AMERICAN TAPESTRIES™

Each novel in the American Tapestries™ series sets a heart-stirring love story against the backdrop of an epic moment in American history. Whether they settled her first colonies, fought in her battles, built her cities, or forged paths to new territories, a diverse tapestry of men and women shaped this great nation into a Land of Opportunity. Then, as now, the search for romance was part of the American dream. Summerside Press invites lovers of historical romance stories to fall in love with this line, and with America, all over again.

NOW AVAILABLE

Queen of the Waves
by Janice Thompson
A novel of the *Titanic*
ISBN: 978-1-60936-686-5

Where the Trail Ends
by Melanie Dobson
A novel of the Oregon Trail
ISBN: 978-1-60936-685-8

COMING SOON

Always Remembered
by Janelle Mowery
A novel of the Alamo
ISBN: 978-1-60936-747-3

A Lady's Choice
by Sandra Robbins
A novel of women's suffrage
ISBN: 978-1-60936-748-0